GIRLS
FROM DA HOOD 3

GIRLS FROM DA HOOD 3

KaShamba Williams
Mark Anthony
MadameK

www.urbanbooks.net

Urban Books
10 Brennan Place
Deer Park, NY 11729

ISBN-13: 978-1-893196-83-4
ISBN-10: 1-893196-83-6

First Printing April 2007
Printed in the United States of America

10 9 8 7 6 5 4 3 2

Submit Wholesale Orders to:
Kensington Publishing Corp.
C/O Penguin Group (USA) Inc.
Attention: Order Processing
405 Murray Hill Parkway
East Rutherford, NJ 07073-2316
Phone: 1-800-526-0275
Fax: 1-800-227-9604

BROOKLYN'S FINEST

By
KaShamba Williams

Brooklyn's Finest to the Rescue

Fire and Marcy ran through Jackson Memorial Hospital on 12th Avenue in downtown Miami frantically trying to find their mother, Adrianne.

"What room is she in, Fire?" Marcy asked, not concerned with the embarrassing looks she received from the onlookers because of her gold knee-high go-go boots and her leather tipsy skirt that exposed her bare ass. The matching gold leather bikini bra just barely covered her nipples. And the way she was running around in the hospital, one was about to flop out at any given moment.

"I don't know, Marcy. Would you stop asking me fuckin' questions! I'm tryin'a find out just like you. You should've stayed your ass in the house last night and you wouldn't have to worry about people looking at you like that." Fire was upset but even more distressed that Marcy wasn't home when she got the news.

"It wouldn't matter any other time how I'm dressed.

And this ain't the first time you seen me dressed like this. I don't give a fuck about anybody else!"

Both of them were stressing because they had no clue what happened to their mother. One thing they did know for sure. She was a lover of that boy—heroin. They'd just learned that she had a near-death experience and was rushed to Jackson Memorial.

"I wonder what kinda shit Mommy got involved in this time? This shit is getting real old. I'm tired of seeing her like this. I'm moving back home soon and I swear this time when I go back to Brooklyn, I'm staying. Mommy needs to just leave that shit alone. I can't take this." Fire's feet moved quickly, and her head moved just as fast, turning from side to side, trying to get assistance.

The girls were originally from New York, Brooklyn to be exact. They grew up in Marcus Garvey Projects, but when their mother got into a squabble with her sister Metta over Metta's man Dorsey, Adrianne decided it was time for a change. Not just for her, but for her daughters as well. They were coming of age, developing into young ladies.

Marcy was always the closest, but the one who followed behind the path of her sister Metta. Adrianne realized early that Marcy was a sucker for a man just like Metta was.

Fire on the other hand was much like her sister Jaletta. She was wild and carefree and always scheming on a man to get money. That's what scared Adrianne the most because Jaletta was murdered and raped behind a drug dealer. In her mind Adrianne believed that relocating to Miami, Florida with her man Warren would give them a fresh start. However, she was wrong as wrong could be. The Miami heat nightlife took its toll on all of them, sucking each one of them in.

"This is not the time to complain, Fire. What's done is done. Excuse me, ma'am." Marcy gripped onto the ledge of the nurse's unit desk in an effort to get help. "Adrianne Evans, what room is she in?"

The young African-American LPN named Shanice glanced up at Marcy and immediately recognized her as being one of the many dancers at The Golden Club that tricked for cash. Shanice smoothed her hair down and took her pleasant time keying in Adrianne's name to find out what room she was in. She hated female strippers because she couldn't keep her man Tricky away from them.

"WELL?" Marcy's eyes were damn near popping out of their sockets.

Shanice began to read the notes off the screen, and Marcy leaned over more to read them along with her.

"Ma'am, you can't do that. This information is confidential and only privy to hospital staff. I'm going to ask that you back away, please." Shanice kept it very professional. She wasn't about to lose her cool over this home-wrecking female she considered a tramp.

"This is some bullshit. Lemme see that shit! What room is she in? I'm gonna turn this unit out if I you don't tell me, bitch!"

While Marcy was going through the motions with Shanice, Fire had managed to obtain the information from a unit manager opposite of them. "Let's go, Marcy," she said. "She's not even on this end. I know where she is. Stop wasting time on that bitch and let's go."

Shanice breathed tightly through her nose as other nurses were finally standing behind her with their hands folded listening to them.

Fire pulled Marcy from the wing, down the corridor to the Intensive Care Unit. Soon as they approached, they read the instructions posted on the entrance door about the visiting hours.

"I don't give a fuck what time visiting hours are. They gonna let us in this muthafucka." Marcy applied pressure to the door handle, and they went in to face a life-changing experience.

Before It Happened . . .

The sweltering Miami heat crawled beneath Adrianne's bed sheet, torturing her boney frame. Restless, she kicked off the sweat-soaked sheet.

I never had to deal with heat this damn bad in New York. I should've stayed my ass in Brooklyn.

It was five forty-seven in the morning and Adrianne hadn't slept a wink all night. But in truth, it wasn't the heat that kept her up tossing and turning. It was her heroin addiction shaking her to the core, screaming in her ears and driving her crazy. She needed a dose badly.

Adrianne had become a dedicated heroin abuser six years earlier, shortly after moving from New York to Miami with her man Warren, the man who introduced her. She uprooted her young daughters and followed him to Miami, but quickly learned her dreams for their future weren't her man's dreams. He had other plans. Plans that didn't include her or her daughters. He took everything from her, when he left them high and dry in his hometown, except his heroin addiction.

Adrianne's once curvaceous body was reduced to a bag of bones. Her cute face and dimpled cheeks became sunken skeletal remains. Her long, full curly hair began to fall out in clumps from lack of maintenance, and her golden-brown complexion became ashen and pockmarked. Sadly, Adrianne looked a mess to everyone except to herself. She was too caught up in her addiction to recognize her significant changes, and her appearance was no longer on her list of concerns.

As she tossed and turned, Adrianne thought she heard a noise outside her window. It sounded like a car pulling up in front of the small home they were renting. She ran to the window wishing, hoping and praying it was her daughters returning home from the strip club. Unfortunately, it wasn't. The car with the loud music was pulling up at the house across the street.

"Damn!" Adrianne yelled, gripping her head in pain. As she lay back in bed, she wondered, *Where the hell is Fire and Marcy?*

From the outside looking in, people would assume Adrianne was a loving and concerned parent wondering where her nineteen- and twenty-one-year-old daughters were. In truth, she was only concerned about their whereabouts, because she needed to purchase some junk (heroin) to feed the dope monkey on her back. She knew about her daughters shaking their asses and sleeping with men for money, but she didn't give a fuck unless she wasn't getting a cut of the money. As long as they kept the bills paid and kept her sickness fed, it was all good. At the moment, because her monkey hadn't been fed all night, she was furious.

Finally, as Adrianne was slipping in and out of sleep,

she was snatched from her irritated state by the sounds of Fire and Marcy entering the house. Sometimes just the two of them could be louder than an entire party. This particular morning she was patiently waiting to hear their sounds. In fact, their voices sounded like music to her ears.

"Bitch, you must be drunk. That nigga was gorilla-black kind of ugly, and you know that nigga is ug-ly!" Fire's voice echoed through the small two-bedroom house.

"I'm drunk, but that doesn't change the fact that he was cute because he was, and it ain't the liquor talking." Marcy was just as loud, her words slurred.

Adrianne leaped out of bed and almost tripped over the bunch of clothes scattered around her bed. She rushed from her bedroom with saggy, stained panties, without a shirt, showing her drooping thinning breasts, into the kitchen, where the voices were coming from. She spotted her oldest daughter Fire standing with the refrigerator door open, drinking from an orange juice container.

"Damn, Ma"—Fire almost choked on the orange juice at the sight of her topless mother—"Go put some clothes on, woman. Don't nobody want to see that."

As soon as anyone saw Fire they automatically knew she was named that because of the red mane of hair that she so proudly kept up. Tonight it was braided up in a spiked Mohawk. Fire's absent father was a red-headed white man. The only white man Adrianne had ever had sexual relations with.

Since age sixteen, Fire had sprouted a body amazing enough to make a grown man risk catching a case. Now twenty-one, with her light skin and fiery-red hair, she was like a topnotch video vixen, always receiving an offer.

"*You* need to put some damn clothes on," Adrianne replied, making no attempt to cover her bare breast. "Where's my fuckin' money?"

The girls were dressed scantily, as they usually were when they worked the clubs, and they both had the bodies for it. Marcy was just as stacked as Fire and pretty, except she was a shade darker than Fire. Marcy's father was a slain drug dealer, who Marcy never had the privilege of meeting. But according to Adrianne, Marcy looked exactly like Frederick (her father). Neither one of them resembled their mother in the slightest bit.

"If we did put some clothes on, we'd all be broke and hungry," Fire said candidly.

"Uh-huh. She's not talking about you, Mom." Marcy frowned. "You really need to cover that up."

Adrianne went straight at it, cracking on Marcy. "C'mon, please cut the small talk and give your momma some money, baby."

"Don't give her shit, Marcy. I just gave her fifty dollars."

"Listen, Fire, I went to get my stuff last night and some muthafucka stiffed me," Adrianne explained.

"Yeah, I bet. Now you're trying to stiff Marcy."

"Here, Momma; don't get stiffed for that, 'cause you'll be ass out this time." Marcy hated to see her mother was in that condition and would do anything to get her back on track. "Take this thirty dollars. That's all I can afford to give you tonight. Bills are due."

"She's already ass out, and I wish she'd cover it up." Fire chuckled. Her and Marcy both laughed on their way into the bedroom they'd been sharing since they came to Miami.

Before the joke could hit Adrianne, she scrambled into her bedroom to gather up her clothes from the floor. She dressed faster than a fireman preparing for a fire alarm blaze and was out the door with lightning speed as if she slid down a pole, the entire time, her jones screaming, *Hurry up, bitch!*

The Warning . . .

The life of the neighborhood was just coming awake. The garbage men jumped off and on of their big noisy green trucks, as groups of kids headed to school and several honest citizens headed to work. The morning breeze, as faint as it was, felt good on Adrianne's skin. It was something she only noticed when she wasn't high. Withdrawal was worse than torture. Her monkey had become a full-grown ape, a silver-back gorilla, heartless, merciless, relentless, which made her race to tame the feeling.

Adrianne trekked to the south side to purchase her small white bags of relief. *How do you spell relief?* *H-E-R-O-I-N.* Adrianne laughed at her little joke, sniffling a gob of snot dribbling from her nose. She was sick, and it wasn't from the change of weather. She knew she'd only feel better when she reached the dope man to put that grey snow in her life. When Adrianne reached her destination, she skipped like a happy child up to the house, a small one-level three-bedroom home with a large front yard known to many as the get-high gallery. The front porch was cluttered with junk.

A woman named Stacey answered Adrianne's knock on the door. They'd been friends a little over three years. When Stacey answered the door, she appeared paranoid. Although this was Stacey's home, she wasn't in control of the daily happenings. The shooting gallery was run by a group of hustlers. The hustlers only came by to drop off product and to pick up money. So although they dictated the rules of the gallery, their presence was rare. Adrianne had never actually seen them, but she knew about them from word of mouth. And she'd heard enough to not want to run into them.

"Why the fuck are you knocking on my door like the damn police?" Stacey asked, wide-eyed, looking over Adrianne's shoulder into the street for any signs of cops.

"I don't know how the police knock on doors, but I do know you look like you lost your mind, bitch." Adrianne pushed her way in.

"What you need?"

"I need three bags." Adrianne pulled the money from her pocket. "And I wanna stay to shoot my shit."

"Hurry up, girl." Stacey pulled her into the house, closing and locking the door behind her.

The kitchen looked a mess, and there was trash everywhere. On the floor, on the table, in the sink, on the stove. And the place reeked of spoiled food.

Stacey pulled a crumbled paper bag from somewhere down in her pants and removed three small packages of heroin. She handed them to Adrianne in exchange for the money. "A'ight, you have to go now." Stacey pushed Adrianne towards the door.

"What? Uh-uh; I'm trying to shoot my shit."

"Take ya ass home and shoot it."

"Stacey, I been waiting all night to get a bag. I'm not in the mood for this. I paid my money. I wanna go in the back there like I usually do!" Adrianne raised her voice, so she'd get her way. She knew Stacey didn't want to hear her mouth. What she didn't know was why Stacey was acting so nervous.

"Shhh. Be quiet. Come on in the back. But you have to shoot it and get up outta here. Understood?" Stacey walked away before Adrianne could respond.

Adrianne followed Stacey to her bedroom in the back of the house. While passing through the living room, Adrianne noticed a group of young men sitting around passing blunts. They watched her as she passed, becoming the center of attention. She didn't have to give much thought to figuring out who they were. Judging by their ages, late teens and young adults, and their expensive clothes and jewelry, she knew they were the hustlers who provided Stacey with product. This explained Stacy's behavior. Her employers were around.

I'll be damn if I get nervous around these young niggas. They look about the same age as my girls.

On the way to shooting up, she bumped right into a six-six, 330-pound, brown-skinned, baldheaded giant, known to many as Gator. Appearing to be in his late forties, Gator had to be the one calling the shots.

Adrianne had to look straight up towards the ceiling to see his face. "Excuse me."

"Bitch, watch where the fuck you're going."

"Fuck you. I said, 'Excuse me.'"

"This junkie bitch lost her mind," Gator said, feeling very disrespected. He reached for Adrianne's small, skinny frame, intent on doing damage, but Tricky, a much shorter, stocky young man grabbed him, stopping him before he could snap Adrianne in half.

"Chill out, Gator. Hold up a minute," Tricky ordered with a heavy Southern drawl as he came to Adrianne's rescue.

"Thank you, baby," Adrianne said to her hero. "I apologized for running into him. I don't know what was his fuckin' problem."

"Shut the fuck up." Tricky moved past her. "Stacey, who is this bitch?"

"She's all right. She came by to spend some money." Stacy didn't want trouble for Adrianne, but she knew how low-down Gator could be. She knew he wasn't going to stop it there and was hoping big-mouth-ass Adrianne didn't say another word.

"You don't have to vouch for me, Stacey. I don't need to be validated for these little muthafuckas. I'm a grown-ass woman." Adrianne didn't know that her mouth was about to get her ass in hot water.

Suddenly, she found herself surrounded by Gator, Tricky, and the other young men in the living room.

Shit! Adrianne thought to herself. *Maybe I went too far.* "Look, I just came to get high. I don't want any trouble." She tried to stop what she could see was about to happen. The sass in her voice was gone. She opened her hand to show the three bags of heroin she was holding to prove why she was there.

Without warning, Gator snatched the bags of heroin out of her hand roughly.

"Give me my shit back!" Adrianne shouted at Gator. The thought of possibly getting her ass whipped faded when she thought of losing her get-high.

"You ain't getting' nothin' back, you junkie bitch!"

"Well, Stacey, give me my money back," Adrianne demanded.

Tricky answered for her, "Stacey ain't giving you shit either. In fact, Stacey, take your ass in the room. This big-mouth bitch needs to learn a lesson."

Adrianne's heart began to race as she watched Stacey leave her alone with the disrespectful young boys and the one grown man she thought she could talk some sense into. Now, she wanted to be civil towards them.

"Please, I spend good money at this house. I just want my dope back, and I'll go about my business," Adrianne explained, backing her body against the wall. "You look like a smart older businessman, uh, uh, Gator. I don't want to start any trouble. All I wanna do is get high."

"Fuck that! Since you got all that mouth, we're gonna put it to good use." He balled up his fist and moved it back and forth in front of his mouth, insinuating she had to give them blowjobs. "Then, I'll decide if I wanna give the dope back. Now, how bad do you want it, bitch?" Gator shook the three bags in her face, trying his best to tempt her. For a man of his age, he acted very immaturely, as if he needed to make up for missed time.

"You must be crazy. I'm not sucking shit! You can keep that dope. I'm out of here." Adrianne turned toward the front door, but her exit was quickly cut off.

She turned back to address Gator, who she knew was the leader, and was terrified by the large silver gun that he pointed in her face.

"You must've misunderstood me. Bitch, you gon' suck some dicks, or you're gonna suck this gun—which is it? Huh? I think cum will go down your throat better than bullets."

"Yo, that junkie bitch ain't suckin' a muthafuckin' thing on me. Man, look at her. She look like she sick." Tricky backed out the room. "Gator, you and them young niggas can do what you want, but I'm gone."

"Whatever, nigga. Leave then."

Although the young boys were laughing, Adrianne realized how serious Gator was. And the sight of that gun told her she'd do whatever they demanded. *Damn, I should've listened to Stacey.* She stood there watching the eager young boys acting like they'd never been sucked off before.

Gator approached her first, forcing her to her knees. He rubbed himself against her lips until she opened her mouth and took him in.

She closed her eyes and imagined it was Warren she was giving superb head to, but it wasn't working. The more she tried to think otherwise, the more she fought the urge to vomit as he rammed his thickness in and out of her mouth. *This is what you call rape. I'm actually being raped.* Adrianne kept repeating over and over in her head. She was on her knees for so long, her jaws began to ache.

When he was finally about to climax, Gator grabbed her hair and shot a hot load of cum into her throat, causing Adrianne to vomit all over his gator shoes. "You dirty bitch!" Gator shouted angrily as the young boys began to get aroused.

Ta'shawn, one of the young boys, said, "I know you're not gonna let her go. I've been waiting patiently to get my joint blowed."

"Shut up, you dumb lil' nigga. She ain't sucking nothing else after what she did." Gator pushed them out. "Now you really gonna pay. These are five-hundred-dollar gator shoes. Look what you did to my shit. I got something for that ass." He pulled out a condom from his black slacks. "Pull those jeans down."

Stacey peeked through the doorway and tried to get him to stop. "Hey, Gator, you're gonna fuck that junkie bitch?" she asked, trying to sound disgusted.

"Mind your business, Stacey, before you're next. You know how I get down."

Adrianne was shaking. "Please don't do this to me. Would you want this to happen to your mother?"

"Drop your pants, bitch, and bend over."

She did as she was told, but when Gator positioned himself behind her, she felt him pressing his erectness against her virgin asshole and panicked. "Wait a minute, that's the wrong hole."

He ignored her protest and rammed directly in her back door.

She felt the pain explode in her buttocks, as he forced himself on her. She cried out in agony as he sodomized her for several minutes. It seemed like the more she screamed the harder he rammed it in her.

When he was done, he handed Adrianne her three bags of heroin and the bloody, cum-filled condom he'd used. "Here, bitch," Gator told her. "Take all ya shit with you and don't come back."

The young boys pushed her out of the front door, with her pants still to her ankles.

"You're gonna get yours, muthafucka," Adrianne shouted hysterically. "All of you bastards, I'll get all of you on charges."

Adrianne anxiously pulled up her jeans. Even after being sodomized, she still yearned to shoot her dope. Her asshole was aching, her jaw was sore, and she was emotionally distraught from being violated, but her mind was focused on the bags of heroin she was clutching.

Fire and Marcy were in a deep sleep by the time she made it back home. Adrianne locked in, as she normally did when she got high at home. She respected her daughters enough not to let them see her getting high. She sat on the corner of her bed, tied a belt tightly around her arm, and shot the poison into her vein. The dope took no time to take effect, washing away the pain physically and emotionally, temporarily taking her mind away from her latest trauma.

Nine Days Later . . . The Incident

"You see, girls, now that's music," Adrianne told Fire and Marcy as they sat around the small living room painting their nails, listening to the radio. Al Green's "Love and Happiness" was smoothly coming from the speakers, reminding Adrianne of a much happier time. Before heroin was her best friend.

Marcy remarked, "You old people kill me, talkin' 'bout, 'Now that's music,' as if what we bump ain't real music."

Fire agreed. "I know, right. They get all hyped up like that sad-ass music they listen to is the shit."

"That sad-ass music is what got both you girls here. We had that baby-making music back in the good ole days."

"You wanna talk about baby-making music, throw in some H-Town or Silk. That shit y'all listened to, Mom, had y'all tricking back in the day. It wasn't anything but pimp music. We got that real baby-making music," Fire said, slow-grinding her hips.

"Preach, girl, let her know."

Fire continued dancing. "Throw on some Jodeci, Next, or some Mary J. and I'll get that pussy poppin'."

Marcy slapped Fire on her ass. "She don't hear you, sis."

"Young girl, sit down. Y'all need to listen to the Whispers, Isley Brothers, Marvin Gaye, or some Earth, Wind and Fire. Must I go on?"

"You really think that old shit is better than the hot shit that's out now?"

"You know what it is, Marcy. It's all about the memories and experiences behind the music. I was young and in my prime when my music was the shit. It brings back good memories, just like your music will bring back good memories when you're my age."

"Good memories, my ass. You wanna forget all that shit you've been through and I'ma help you. Who wants to reminisce about their sister getting killed? Their daughter's father getting killed? Another father leaving you to be a single parent? Or not talking to your sister for years because of a man? Let's not even talk about the addiction that you don't wanna face. Like I said, I'ma help you. Get your old butt up, and let's dance your worries away." Fire tried to get her up.

"Yeah, Mom, jiggle it." Marcy joined in, shaking her soft, fluffy ass.

"No, I'll sit this one out, girls." Adrianne grinned at her flesh and blood.

Indeed these were her babies, and she loved them to death. That's why she didn't want to tell them about the rape because, if she had, one of them would've caught a charge. Now, she had to make an excuse why she couldn't get up and dance. She was still experiencing sharp pains in her anus, and it sure didn't help much that she didn't go to the hospital to have her injuries treated.

Adrianne's sore backside wasn't the only thing keeping her from joining in the fun. The rest of her body was aching and weak. It was almost three o'clock in the afternoon, and she hadn't received her daily dose of dope. It wasn't that she didn't have money. Fire and Marcy had given her twenty dollars each that morning, and she rushed out to spend it as soon as it hit her hand. She went to every heroin dealer in the neighborhood in hopes of scoring, but everywhere she went they told her to go to Stacey's house.

She didn't want to go back to Stacey's. Her fear of running into Gator was keeping her away from there, but her desire to get high was starting to diminish that fear, as she began to realize the only place to stop her craving was Stacey's. Not even her daughter's entertainment could make her stay put.

Doing her best to fight the urge, Adrianne put on her shoes and took them off repeatedly, until finally making a dash for the door when they were on. Once she was in motion, she became more confident in her decision.

"Where you going, Mom?" Marcy asked, grabbing at her.

"I've gotta go handle something, sweetie. I'll be right back."

"You ain't going nowhere until you shake that thing." Marcy smacked her ass playfully, not realizing how much that light smack hurt her.

Adrianne clenched her teeth, fighting the pain without letting it show. "I'll be right back," she said, pushing past Marcy. "Why don't y'all clean up the house while I'm gone."

"Yeah right. You know Marcy not cleaning a damn thing."

Adrianne rushed out of her house and checked on the forty dollars in her pants pocket as she passed the house across the street. The young boys that hustled weed at that house were always polite and kind to her, most likely because they had a fling with her daughters.

"Hey, Ms. Adrianne. How are you?" Clifford called out. He was Marcy's friend.

"Hey, Cliff. I'm good. How you, baby?"

"Is Marcy home?"

"Yes, she's in there. Be careful, though. She might put a hurtin' on you today," Adrianne stated with an easy smile.

Two years ago, she'd walked in on Cliff and Marcy having sex in her kitchen. She didn't mind that they were having sex because she felt they were mature and responsible. Her girls went from pre-teens to women without a transition period. There wasn't any in-between time to grow. As soon as they became fully developed, Adrianne explained to them the power of having gold between their legs. "Listen now, the best blessing God could've given a woman is this right here." Adrianne patted her prized possession, as her two girls, only ten and twelve watched her.

Marcy, being the youngest and the most unaware, didn't quite understand. "What's the blessing?"

Fire had experienced her first sexual encounter at eleven and was given a crisp hundred-dollar bill by the boy, who was five years older than her, so she explained it to her. "It's when you lay on your back and let a boy get in between your legs and hump back when he's humping you, dummy. You know what 'doin' it' is."

Adrianne laughed on the inside at her daughter's explanation. She wasn't even the least bit upset to learn that her twelve-year-old daughter was having sex. This only made her take them down to the clinic to get them both on birth control pills, so neither of them would get pregnant.

As they got older, they used that advice. Fire never really took a man that seriously because she felt almost all of them were tricks, but Marcy was the one always falling for the game.

After her long walk to the south side, Adrianne found herself standing nervous and indecisive in front of Stacey's house. She was wondering if Gator or the young boys were inside and, if they were, how she'd escape. Her instincts were warning her. *Fuck this! Turn back, Adrianne. Go home and try to sleep this shit off.* But that wasn't enough to make her turn back. She couldn't control her actions.

An older junkie named Murphy opened the door. "May I help you?"

"It's me, Adrianne. Is Stacey home, Murph? Y'all got anything?"

"She's in the back room," Murphy informed her and let her in.

"Thanks, Murph. Ah, any of those niggas up in here?"

"I said she's in the back." Murphy walked into the empty living room area.

Good! They ain't in here. Adrianne exhaled. She looked around timidly as she walked through the filthy house and headed to the back room. She peered into Stacey's bedroom, the final room in the house, and saw her sitting around with three junkie women and one man. Everyone was shooting needles into their arms except Stacey. Stacey wasn't a shooter, she was a snorter.

Adrianne called from the doorway, "Hey, Stacey. Where's that good shit at, girl?"

Stacey looked up from her nod. "Adrianne, is you crazy? What the fuck is you doing here?"

"I need a few bags to take the edge off. I'm sick as a dog," Adrianne told her, meaning she was dope-sick going through withdrawal.

"Gator and Ta'shawn are gonna kill you if they catch you. I know you don't think they're letting you get away with what you did to them."

"What I did to them, Stacey? They got off easy. I didn't even call the police on they asses. Shit, if I recalled correctly, the big donkey-dick nigga raped me in your house, and you let the shit go down. I should get a few free bags for what I went through."

"Bitch, you sent the cops to my house. You almost got me locked up too. I'm not selling you shit. Get the fuck out of my house before I call Gator and Ta'shawn."

"Stacey, I didn't call the cops. I didn't even tell my daughters about what happened to me. I don't know what you're talking about."

Stacey looked into her eyes for a few seconds, trying to feel her out. "After you left that day, about twenty minutes later, the police raided my house. They locked up Gator, Ta'shawn, and the young boys for drugs and guns they had on them."

"Why didn't you get locked up then? You had drugs on you?"

"I jumped out of the window when the cops busted in the front door. A few days later, when Gator and Ta'shawn posted bond, they came over here looking for you. They all think you called the cops on them. They said they're gonna kill you when they catch you."

"What the fuck makes them think that it was me who called the cops? The police have a job to do. I'm sure they been knowing it's drugs up in here."

"Yeah, but you're the one who told them you were going to get them back. How ironic is it that the police ran up in my house right after you left like that? They not gonna believe you didn't call them. You should've never said that shit if you didn't mean it."

Adrianne flashed back to what she'd said as she ran from the house. She did say she'd promise to get them back. She'd just been violated. What did they expect her to say? She was pissed-off, angry and hurt, but she wasn't stupid enough to call the cops on them and have them hunt her down. Yet she knew they'd never believe her.

"Stacey, I swear to God, I didn't call the cops."

"Adrianne, girl, I believe you, but it doesn't matter what I believe. If Gator finds you, you're done," she said, fishing two bags of dope from her pocket. "Here, that'll help your sickness. Keep your money. Hurry up and shoot your shit and get out of here before they find you here. After today you can't come back here anymore. I don't want your death on my hands."

"I owe you big time. I should take mine and go."

"They ain't coming around no time soon today. I'm fully stocked. You can stay. I'll be up front watching the window in case they show up." Stacey rushed out of the room.

Adrianne cooked her dope, filled her syringe, and filled her arm with smack. She laid back and took a deep breath, waiting for her relief to come.

The room suddenly started spinning at seventy-five miles an hour. Adrianne's stomach locked up on her, and her throat constricted. She dry-heaved twice, before retching violently, throwing up everything in her stomach. Her body got warm, and then hot. It wasn't the same as usual. This time her entire body was ablaze with intense heat. She fell to the floor in agony, convulsing violently and uncontrollably. Her jaws locked up on her so hard, she cracked two of her back teeth. She looked up from the floor in a haze. She couldn't hear anything or comprehend anything, only conscious of the pain. Her body didn't move, and she could barely breathe, let alone scream. What she did feel was herself dying a violent death. She watched as the other junkies jumped up in a panic, looking down at her shaking in a puddle of her own vomit. She could read their lips.

"Are you okay?"

"What's wrong with her?"

"It must be the dope. Damn, Stacey! You gotta give me some of that!"

"I think the bitch is overdosing. I think she's gonna die. I'm outta here."

They all fled the bedroom and left Adrianne to die alone. She closed her eyes and cried inwardly. Adrianne wasn't crying for herself—she wasn't afraid of death— she was crying for Fire and Marcy who she was leaving behind. She knew she hadn't been much of a mother to her little girls since she'd started getting high. There was no question that her life affected them, and she was really remorseful for the way she'd raised them.

Adrianne blacked out and came to so many times, she lost track of time. Each time she blacked out, she thought she was slipping off into death. Every time she woke up, intense pain ran through her, ensuring her that she wasn't dead.

When she came to again, the pain still hadn't stopped, but the fear that seemed to die down before immediately came back. This time, she was no longer alone. Stacey was standing over her with Gator and Ta'shawn. At this point, she welcomed death. Anything to end the pain. Her ability to hear was slightly returning, the voices sounding as if they were off in the distance even though they were standing over her.

Stacey stretched forth her hand. "She said she didn't call the cops, but I know she did."

"Here's the money for giving her the special dope for us." Gator handed her two hundred dollars in twenty-dollar bills.

"She shot up a lot of that shit. She should be dead by now. What are you going to do with her?" Stacey asked.

Just then, Ta'shawn signaled two young boys to come into the room. The two young boys who entered were escorting two large vicious-looking pit bulls. "I'm going to feed her to my dogs," Ta'shawn announced.

This jolted Adrianne. She tried her hardest to get up, but her body wasn't moving. She was already in grave pain, and those pit bulls gnawing on her wouldn't help matters any.

Gator bent over and looked into Adrianne's face. "You're gonna love this," he said before stepping aside.

The two young boys released the dogs, which came straight at her. One dog locked its powerful jaws on her thighs, sinking its teeth in her bone. The other dog bit into her arm, jerking its head violently, trying to pull it off.

Adrianne screamed in agony as the dogs played tug-of-war with her frail, paralyzed body. She tried to scream, but nothing came out of her mouth. She felt the flesh, tissue and muscle being torn from her thigh. She felt her arm snap and watched the broken bone tear through her flesh. She saw her own blood squirt across the room, splashing on the floor as Gator, Ta'shawn, and the two young boys enjoyed the human massacre.

Then, she saw a pit bull's mouth descending on her face, after which she couldn't see anything.

Lap Dance, Anyone?

Fire and Marcy were still dancing in their living room after Adrianne left. Only now, they'd changed the music. The sounds of Ne-Yo and Ghostface filled the room: *You don't get a nigga back like that. Naw.*

The girls lit up some more weed, and incense to garner the smell, and continued to shake their voluptuous asses. Fire glanced over her shoulder and noticed they had an audience. She directed Marcy's attention to the window by the front door. On their front porch peering through the window were Cliff, Block, and Vic, the young hustlas from across the street.

Fire walked over and opened the front door. "May I help you?" She pressed her well-shaped lips against the glass, causing her cleavage to pop up from her pink wife-beater. Even with her Chanel scarf tied around her fiery-red hair and a wife-beater with booty shorts with furry pink slippers on, she was still sexy.

"Are there bullets in ya bra or are your nipples glad to see me?" Block joked, causing Cliff and Vic to laugh.

"Nigga, you wish." Fire turned and poked her ass out as she walked backed into the living room.

"Young-ass country boys always talkin' shit!"

"Why we gotta be lames, Marcy?" Cliff grabbed his crotch. "You know you love dirty-dirty."

"Please, ya dirty-dirty ain't enough for this here." Marcy bent over to touch her toes. "Cliff, you all right and all, with your cinnamon-brown ass, but you could use a little work in that department."

Fire stood there laughing at how Marcy was able to easily get Cliff worked up

Cliff didn't let that hurt his pride at all. Him and Marcy didn't have a relationship per se, but they did share each other's bed often enough to become jealous if they dated outside of their friendship.

"Fire, can I get a private dance?" Block wanted her to continue the show and hopefully take it to the bedroom.

Eyeing Block down, Fire sat on his lap to get him more aroused. She was in the mood for a little erotic exercise. "How much you got in your pocket?"

"You know that nigga can't afford you, Fire. He use to fuckin' wit' cheap-ass hoes."

Block tried to motivate Fire with the sight of cash. "Shiitted, I got a wad a money right here for dat ass."

"What else you got? 'Cause I heard you like deep-sea diving too. For the right price, I'll let you taste this."

"Let's get the party started then." Vic removed a plastic bag of weed from his black Sean John jeans and pulled out his .45 from under his black Sean John T-shirt to place it under the couch.

Vic was only sixteen, but at five-eight and 163 pounds

he was molded perfectly. The young girls loved them some "pretty boy" Vic. His paper-brown skin was without blemish. Marcy was mad that he was too young when she first met them. Otherwise, she would've chosen him, instead of his cousin Cliff. Times had changed, though. Vic was almost legal, and Marcy wanted to test him out.

Marcy cut her eyes at Cliff and Vic. "Ain't nobody gettin' no pussy without dollars being exchanged."

"Yeah, whatever." Cliff never had to pay to get pleased by her, and was curious to know why she threw that out there.

Marcy pulled Fire to the side, away from them, and whispered. "I'm tryin'a fuck Vic. Two's company, three's a crowd. Cliff gotta go."

"What? You were just hugged up with Cliff two days ago. Now, you wanna fuck his little cousin. He's still a baby. His dick ain't even matured to size yet, Marcy."

"It don't look like it to me."

"Don't do that to my boy Cliff. You know he's good to you, but on the other hand, if Vic got more cash, do what you gotta."

"Okay, watch me fuck up Cliff's head."

"Get it, girl." Fire smiled. "Cliff must've made you mad," she said, walking back into the living room. Fire knew she was hiding something, because Marcy had a habit of nibbling on her pinky nail when she was lying, and was doing that as she stared into the living room at Cliff.

The room was clouded with smoke as they waited patiently for Fire and Marcy to jumpstart this private session.

Fire grinded her ass on Vic, locking eyes with Block, who was seated directly across from him.

Block licked his lips in desire, as he watched Fire make her ass bounce.

She was demonstrating what Block was in for, using Vic as an example. She stayed on Vic's lap and opened her legs, easing off her shorts, and jumped down into a split, exposing a sample of her fluffy kitten, which was parted by her thong. Fire noticed the look Marcy gave her and backed off of Vic to tease Block some more.

Marcy eased past Cliff and began rubbing on Vic's already throbbing muscle. She was trying to start some trouble and was doing a pretty good job. Vic's hands roamed all over Marcy until his fingers slipped into her hot spot.

Fire watched Cliff's reaction, as Vic eased his fingers in and out of Marcy.

Even Marcy was surprised by Vic's boldness, but she didn't stop him. In fact she lowered herself onto his hand, taking more of his fingers inside of her.

Cliff, who'd been playing it real nonchalant, finally lost his cool and snatched Marcy by her arm off Vic's lap.

"Come on, cuz, stop hatin'. She want me to hit it!" he shouted at Cliff.

Cliff tipped off Vic. "Nigga, sit ya young ass down, before I sit you down." Then he turned to Marcy and said, "We need to talk—now!"

Fire observed Cliff haul Marcy off towards the bedroom, and Marcy went along willingly, grinning the entire time.

This set off a train of events. Block decided to follow

Cliff's lead. He jumped up and pulled Fire away. "Yo, Vic, the party is over for you, boss," he announced. "Me and Cliff got this, young blood. I don't like the way you gawking either. Nigga, you reminding me of ya Uncle Smitty. Don't tell me that shit run in the family."

Vic smirked and went to retrieve his gun from under the couch. "Fuck you, nigga! I'll get at y'all, especially you Marcy. Here, Fire, give Marcy that. She was real wit' her shit. Baby deserves her keep," he said as he left the house. *I'm gonna fuck the shit out of her when I do get the chance.*

Fire went over to collect the three hundred dollars Vic was throwing Marcy's way. When her and Block were alone in the living room, she put back on her booty shorts. "Why are you still here?" she asked. "You said it yourself—party's over." Fire avoided eye contact with Block as she played the innocent-girl role.

"Party's over? You must be mistaken, sexy. The party is just about to get started, the private party between you and I." Block took Fire in his arms and kissed her passionately. All of her provocative dancing, hip-gyrating and ass-clapping had him ready to get up in that.

Fire could clearly tell that Block was pretty worked up when she saw his sweatpants rise up in between his legs. She took this opportunity to fondle his warm vulnerable manhood in her small, delicate hands. Block's thick pipe felt so good in Fire's hands, she removed it from his pants, wanting to feel him in her mouth. She leveled her body, then her mouth, to his crotch and took him in, working it well with her tongue and lips. She bobbed her head back and forth, forcing him deeper into her throat.

After a few minutes of pleasure, Block pulled himself from her mouth and stepped back.

Fire was puzzled. "Damn, baby! You wasn't feeling that?"

"Fo' sho'. Now lay your fine ass back on that couch. I'm about to turn it up in here." Block made his way into the kitchen and returned with a cup of ice. He crouched to his knees, removed her shorts, and spread her juicy thighs. Then he placed some of the crushed ice in his mouth, chilling his tongue and lips, and went to work on Fire's clit.

Fire closed her eyes and cried out in ecstasy as his cold tongue squirmed between her bottom lips.

Block licked and swirled until he felt her body quiver. Once she did, he prepared to climb on top of her, but Fire stopped him.

"I want you to get this pussy from behind," she moaned, turning around and bending over on the couch. She arched her back and spread her legs, giving Block easy access to her wet center.

He entered her gently, pushing every inch deep into her. Then he sped up his pace, gaining speed and momentum with every stroke. He went from making love, to sexing her, to fucking her, to blowing her back out.

Marcy could almost see steam coming from Cliff. She loved the way he looked when he was angry. *He's so fucking cute, even when he's mad.* She gleamed, finally getting his undivided attention, even though he was yanking her to the bedroom and handling her tough.

Only minutes ago, she was getting her freak on with his cousin, while he watched upset. It was true she wanted to fuck Vic. Just not tonight. Tonight, she wanted to get Cliff jealous. As much as Cliff tried to act like he wasn't bothered at first, she knew she'd get to him eventually.

When Cliff saw Vic's fingers slide deep into Marcy's clean-shaved pussy, his carefree attitude fell apart. Now he was dragging her to the bedroom to confront her. Once they were in Marcy's bedroom, Cliff slammed the door shut and leaned against it. He took a few deep breaths to calm himself. "Shaw-tay, what you doin'?" Cliff asked, gritting his teeth in anger.

"What the hell are you talking about, Cliff?"

Cliff raised his voice. "You lettin' my lil' cousin finger-fuck you right in my fuckin' face? You s'posed to be my baby."

"Your baby? You need to slow up sippin' that syrup. Just two days ago, I wasn't ya baby when I caught your monkey ass coming out of your house with that bitch!"

"You act like you don't understand our relationship. We agreed to be together when we're together. It's been clear that we can see other people. Now you wanna start acting brand-new?"

"No, Cliff, *you* agreed to that shit, *I* didn't." Marcy had been waiting for two days for the opportunity to confront him about this. No one knew how she really felt about Cliff, not even Fire. Marcy had fallen for Cliff, disregarding their agreement, yet she still wanted to be able to do her thing without him tripping out on her, but wanted him to be exclusive to her.

"Marcy, you did agree to it. You nodded your head and walked away."

"You know what fucks me up about you, Cliff? You seem to always throw that in my face when it's convenient for you. You gon' miss me when I'm gone."

"Do you, man, just not my cousin, okay? For the cash, I could've been fucked ya sister, but did I?"

"I didn't fuck Vic. I only gave him a lap dance."

"Don't play stupid, Marcy. You know what you were doing."

"Look, I don't like the fact that you're fuckin' other broads, but it's clear that Cliff is gonna be Cliff. I just ask that you don't do that shit in front of me. You live right across the street, so it's obvious that if you bring a ho to your house, I'll know about it, dumb ass!"

"Listen to you. You swing pussy in niggas' faces every day, and I can't bring a honey home. I know what's going down at Golden. Whatever you down there doing, you better be making those niggas strap up." Cliff hated what she did to get money, but every time she threw that power pussy on him, he tolerated it.

"Same goes for you, dirty-dirty," she teased.

Cliff laughed. Then he grabbed Marcy around the waist and picked her up. He wrestled her to the bed, as they fondled each other, play fighting.

Marcy ran her tongue into Cliff's mouth, and the two began to kiss softly. She could feel the bulge in his jeans swelling, as she rubbed her exposed pussy against it. Marcy fed Cliff one of her swollen dark nipples, while she unzipped his pants. She lowered herself on him, swallowing every inch of it, and bounced on him like a wild horse.

The argument they'd just had didn't seem to matter any more. At the moment nothing seemed to matter.

The girls were so caught up in lust that they didn't even notice that their mother hadn't returned for the night.

The Call . . .

Ring-ring!
Bang! Bang! Bang! Vic was beating the door as hard as he could.

Fire awoke with a slight hangover and a sharp pain in her back. When she shook the cobwebs of sleep from her brain, she looked around and realized she'd spent the night in the living room butt-ass naked. Then she noticed the weight of Block's naked leg lying across her naked body and thought, *What is he still doing here? The sex was good, but he gots to go!*

Ring-ring!

Bang! Bang! Bang!

The sound of the telephone ringing and the banging at the door caused her to push Block's leg off of her and sit up. She rushed into the kitchen, searching for the phone, following the ringing noise, and went to see who it was at the door.

Damn! What is wrong wit' muthafuckas all early in the

morning? The damn phone ringing off the hook and someone is knocking harder than a muthafucka at the door.

Ring-ring!

"Hello," Fire answered the phone, still groggy. "Who is it?" she asked the person at the door.

"It's Vic. Let me in. Yo, some foul shit happen. Open the door."

At the same time Vic was talking, so was the woman on the opposite end of the phone.

"It's open, Vic, come in. Let me take this phone call."

"Man, fuck that phone call. You wanna hear this shit."

"Hello, hello."

"Be quiet, Vic," she hollered, trying to listen to what the woman had to say.

"Good morning, ma'am. Is this the residence of a Ms. Adrianne Evans?"

Fire guessed, from the sound of her voice, that she was white. The only white people who called their house were bill collectors. Since she wasn't in the mood to deal with that type of shit, she headed to her mother's room. She wasn't sure if she was home because she hadn't heard her come in. In fact, she knew her mother hadn't come home. If she did, she was awfully quiet about her and Block sprawled out naked on her couch. Fire knew that would've never happened because her mother's mouth was much too big. Adrianne would've said, "Fire, this ain't no damn whorehouse. Take that shit to his house or a motel."

"Hold on a minute, please," Fire told the woman on the phone, while pushing her mother's door open. The room was vacant, and Fire was relieved her mother wasn't there. "Sorry, miss, she's not home. Can I take a message?" Fire asked reluctantly.

"That's what I've been trying to tell you," Vic butted in. "Block, get up, man." He began to shake him. "You got to hear this shit."

Fire tried to tune Vic out until she got off the phone.

"Oh no, ma'am, I know she's not there. Ms. Evans has been admitted into the emergency room some time early this morning. This is Jackson Memorial Hospital. We're searching for her next of kin." the woman told her, shaking the remainder of sleep from Fire.

Fire froze. She began to replay in her mind every word the woman said. *Emergency room? Next of kin? Is this bitch trying to tell me that my mother is dead?* "In the emergency room for what?"

"Yo, niggas did some foul dog-eating shit to your moms, Fire," Vic blurted out.

"Who am I speaking with?" the woman inquired.

Fire turned her head back and forth, trying to listen to the both of them. "This is Ms. Evans's daughter, Fire Evans. Why is my mother in the E.R.? Is she all right?"

"Your mother has been admitted. I can't divulge the nature of her illness over the phone. They're taking her up to the intensive care unit. If you could come by the hospital—"

Fire hung up the phone before the woman could complete her sentence. She dropped the phone and screamed at Vic, "What happened to my mom?"

Block wrapped his arms around her naked body to cover her.

"Old man Murphy said some niggas found her in the

alleyway left for dead. Dirty." Vic shook his head at Block. "Murph said the niggas let the pit bulls get at her 'cause she got niggas cased up."

Fire ran to her bedroom to tell Marcy, but she wasn't there. Her and Cliff had left around one to hit the clubs. *She's not even home!* Fire panicked, tears filling her eyes. She yelled downstairs, "Vic, call Cliff and tell him to meet us at Jackson right away."

"I'll give you a ride down there, but I need to go handle some business after that." Block wasn't about to spend hours and hours in the hospital with her. He had money to make.

"Just get me down there. That's all I need you to do."

"I'll stay with you, Fire, until Cliff comes," Vic offered. From what he was told, he knew she would need support once she got to the hospital.

Fire dashed down the steps. "Come on, I'm ready. Did you get in touch with Cliff and Marcy?"

"Yeah," Vic told her. "They gonna meet us there."

"Let's go then."

Back in the Hospital . . .

Fire pushed down the door handle to the ICU unit and rushed to find out what room Adrianne was in. "Adrianne Evans room, please."

"Are you the young lady that I spoke with this morning?"

"Yes. Is she going to be okay?"

"Doctor Stevens is in with her now," the head unit nurse told them. "She's in there, room 309." The nurse pointed them towards room 309.

Marcy loved her mother so much and couldn't bear the thought of her death. Yet she stomached her mother's heroin abuse. She always knew that she was slowly committing suicide every time she stuck that needle in her arm. Even after feeling like that, she continuously turned a blind eye to her addiction.

Fire was the daughter that always argued and fussed about it, but she'd still give her money. Now, as they charged towards the room, oblivious of their mother's condition, they were determined to put their foot down about her dope habit. If they had to confine her to a bed to get her to leave that dope alone, they would.

When Fire entered Adrianne's room, her heart almost stopped as she gasped at the sight of her. Adrianne was laid in bed with many tubes and machines connected to her. One of her legs and arms was broken and elevated in a sling, and her face was completely bandaged on the right side.

Doctor Stevens and two nurses stood near Adrianne's bed. Dr. Stevens, a tall, balding black man in his late forties, turned to face Marcy and Fire when they entered the room.

"Good morning. Are you relatives of Ms. Evans?" he asked, looking at his clipboard.

"Yes, we're her daughters. I'm Fire, and this is my sister Marcy. Do you know what happened to our mother?"

"Not actually. We do know that Ms. Evans is in critical condition. She's in a partial comatose state, almost vegetated. She can hear, see, and feel everything going on around her, but she's lost control over her bodily functions due to brain damage, so she's unable to communicate. I'm sorry."

Fire burst into tears. "What happened to her?" She held Marcy, who was also crying.

"It appears that she was given heroin mixed with battery acid and some sort of rat poison, which can cause permanent brain damage. We're not sure how many, but judging by the size of the bites and torn flesh, we assume she was attacked by dogs."

"Oh my God!" Marcy cried. "Who the fuck did this?"

"We were hoping you'd have an idea," a nurse answered. "Your mother was discovered in an alley, left for dead, we were told. You may want to give this detective a call. He left this number for you." She handed Fire the business card.

"To hell with the police," Marcy said. "Will my mom get better?"

"She's suffering from a traumatic experience. Hopefully she'll recover. Only time will tell. Does your mother have health insurance?"

"No, Dr. Stevens," Fire quickly answered. "Don't they have a social worker here that can help her apply for Medicaid to cover hospital expenses?"

"Yes. We'll make sure she applies for medical assistance. Don't worry, we're going to make sure she's taken care of. Whoever did this wanted her dead, so you young ladies really need to cooperate with the police."

Fire walked away from the doctor to her mother's bed. Crying, she stood over what was left of Adrianne and held her hand. She wondered, *Who would do something like this?* This was so confusing, so senseless. Adrianne never did anybody dirty, she didn't need to. Granted, she was a heroin addict, but Fire and Marcy always gave her money for her habit. She didn't need to steal from anyone to get drugs. *So who would do some sadistic shit like this to her?* That's what played in Fire's mind.

As she contemplated the answer, she couldn't take her eyes off of her mother. She was initially under the impression that her mother's open eye was staring off blankly, focusing on nothing in particular, but she realized she was wrong. Adrianne was staring directly at her.

The doctor had told Fire that her mother was in a co-matose state, but Fire found herself wondering whether Adrianne could see her.

At that moment, she noticed a tear trickle down from her mother's eye, the one that wasn't covered with bandages. Adrianne was looking at her and crying.

Fire leaned over directly in Adrianne's face. "Ma?"

"Mur-Mur-Murph," Adrianne murmured, her voice trailing off.

"What did you say, Mom?"

Adrianne forced out one last word before she closed her eyes. "Murphy."

"Ma! Ma!" Fire tried waking her. "She just spoke to me. My mother just spoke," she announced.

"Are you sure?"

"I ain't hallucinating or imagining shit," Fire insisted angrily.

"Fire, your mother has been through a hell of an ordeal. I understand your turmoil. We all wish for her recovery, but it's going to take some time."

"So how do you explain what I just heard from her?" Fire asked, her hands on her hips.

"Your mother is currently going through heroin withdrawal. She's being administered methadone, but she's still going to have some symptoms of withdrawal. She could get the shivers, twitching, vomiting, and grunting, but none of her actions should be interpreted as a conscious act. I'm sorry." The doctor walked off to tend to his other patients.

Fire waited until he was out of earshot before telling Marcy, "She talked to me, Marcy. I didn't imagine shit."

"What did she say?"

"She said it was Murphy."

"You mean dope fiend Murphy?"

"That's the only Murphy I ever heard her speak about."

"Then we're going to pay Stacey a little visit," Marcy stated, taking her mother's hand.

Fire nodded and stroked Adrianne's matted hair. "We gon' get 'em, Ma."

Knock, Knock . . . Who's There?

After visiting hours were over, Marcy called Cliff to pick them up from the hospital. The girls were so distraught about what happened to Adrianne, they were silent for most of the ride home.

Cliff broke the silence. "How's Ms. Adrianne doing?"

"Cliff, I really don't wanna talk about it. My mom is in a fucked-up way. All I keep thinking about is old man Murphy knows exactly what happened and I want to get to the bottom of this." Fire retrieved the detective's card from the back pocket of her jeans. "Maybe we should get Detective Ed Mayfield," she said, reading over his business card.

"Fuck the police! They're not gonna move any faster than we would."

"That's what you say, Marcy." Fire placed the card back in her pocket for future reference.

"We need to go see Murphy. You know where he stays, Cliff? As a matter of fact, where is Vic? He's the one Murphy told."

What if Murphy had something to do with it? Fire and Marcy had committed crimes, but never violent crimes. If Murphy had something to do with it, he had to be dealt with.

"Murphy be over dopehead Stacey's house. It ain't hard to find him. First thing I would suggest, though, is for you to go home and change your hooker clothes, Marcy. You looking like last night, and that outfit ain't so nice anymore." Cliff tried to get them to laugh.

Marcy popped him on the back of his head. "Shut up, boy! You the one who told me to put this shit on."

"Is fucked-up, though. You really think Murphy had something to do with it?" Cliff asked, sounding skeptical.

"If he doesn't, he knows something, and we're going to find out. That's why I need your help, Cliff." Marcy stared out the car window.

"Name it, you know you can get whatever you want from me, girl." He winked at her.

Fire was in the back seat of the car with her head rested back, in deep thought.

"I need to borrow one of your hoop rides. One that you haven't driven in a while and that's in somebody else's name," Marcy told him.

Between Cliff and his boys they had over seven cars.

"You got it, but remember what you said, 'In somebody else's name.' Don't get upset when you read the registration, a'ight?"

Marcy cut her eyes at him. "If it's in one of ya bitches name, that's even better."

"A'ight, I hear you."

"I also need to borrow two guns," Marcy added.

Cliff looked at her to see if she was serious. Then he glanced into his rearview mirror at Fire, who now had her head upright. "Marcy, you ain't no damn gangsta! What are you conjuring up in that twisted mind of yours? How about, I get my people and we go handle it for you?"

Fire could tell he didn't feel comfortable giving them guns. She couldn't believe how irrationally Marcy was thinking. "That would make more sense, wouldn't it?"

"Thank you, Cliff, but no thanks. It's only old man Murphy we're talking about. I think we can handle him ourselves."

"Baby, I'm sure someone else is behind this."

"How the fuck are you so sure, Cliff?" Marcy asked suspiciously.

"Yo, don't even bring it to me like that. I'm just saying, the way you said your mom got fucked up, Murphy wasn't the only one behind this."

"Don't even worry about it, nigga. We'll handle whoever is responsible."

Fire rubbed the inside of her eyes, trying to get the sleep out of them. She was exhausted and needed some sleep before she tried to talk Marcy out of trying to be the Thelma and Louise of 2007.

Later that evening, a midnight-black Chevy Lumina with tinted windows was parked two houses down from Stacey's. Inside the Lumina, Marcy and Fire crouched low on the seats, alert and watching the streets for any sign of police. The girls were dressed in all black, their hair tucked up in black Yankee's baseball caps. Using the faint light shining in through the windshield, they loaded their weapons, with latex-gloved hands.

Fire's heart was racing, her mind overwhelmed with thoughts of what could go wrong. *Why did I let this dumb-ass girl talk me into this? Marcy's ass watch too many gangsta movies. What if it goes bad . . . then what?* When it came to a man, Fire knew how to play it, but this shoot-'em-up-bang-bang, she hadn't a clue about.

Nor did Marcy, but from the way she was dictating, she wasn't fazed at all. "You ready, Fire?" A hyped-up Marcy adjusted her baseball cap, pulling it down to cover her eyes. "Just follow my lead."

"I guess." Fire looked at Marcy.

"If Murphy so much as flinches, I'm gonna shoot him," Marcy stated, opening the car door and jumping out.

Fire followed behind her on the dark and somewhat quiet street, not even noticing Gator and Tricky sitting in Gator's dark blue Yukon.

Once on Stacey's porch, Fire ducked low out of sight, while Marcy knocked on the door.

A male voice came from behind the door. "Yeah?"

They thought for sure it was Murphy.

"Y'all got that headnod?" Marcy asked. Headnod was the name of the latest heroin dealers were selling.

The door swung open, and an old dope fiend man stood in the doorway.

Marcy upped the gun in his face. It wasn't Murphy. Even still, she pushed him back into the house and closed the door behind them.

"What's going on?" the man asked.

"Listen, but don't say shit," Marcy whispered, holding the man at gunpoint. "We're not here for you, so don't try to be a hero. Now, where is Murphy or Stacey?"

"Murphy's not here, but Stacey is in the back room," the man informed her, his hands in the air.

"Who's in this bitch?" Marcy inquired as Fire watched in amazement.

His eyes locked on their guns. "Just me and Stacey."

"All right, check this shit out, if you lied about anything—boom!" Marcy pressed the gun to his head. "Lead the way."

Afraid and concerned about how her little sister had transformed, Fire followed behind Marcy. The three of them stopped at every room until they reached Stacey's bedroom. Marcy kicked the man to the floor, and he stumbled and fell onto the dirty mattress on the floor, where Stacey was about to snort another line.

"Watch where you're going, Jake," Stacey shouted. "You almost knocked over my shit!".

"Shut the fuck up, bitch. If you say one more word, you're dead." Marcy shoved the gun in Stacey's face.

Fire asked Stacey, "Where's Adrianne?" to see if she knew anything.

"Don't ask me nothing 'bout that junkie bitch! I don't know where she is."

Instant rage filled Fire as she raised her gun and smacked the shit out of Stacey. "Bitch, do you know who you're talking to?" Fire removed her baseball cap and gave Stacey an ice grill harder than Ice Cube's.

"You're . . . Adrianne's daughter? I don't remember your name, but I'll never forget the face and hair. What do you want with me?" Stacey intended on talking her way out of this.

Marcy kicked her right in the face with her black Air Force One. "Don't play stupid, bitch. You know why we're here."

"I swear, girl," Stacy pleaded, spitting blood out, "I don't know what happened to Adrianne."

"Well, let's see if I can help you remember." Fire handed Marcy her gun then, without warning, she bent low and punched Stacey in the face. *Whap!* She grabbed Stacey by the hair and began swinging her around the filthy bedroom. Fire slammed Stacey's frail body into everything that looked hard enough to cause damage. She rained on Stacey with dozens of punches and kicks, stomping her head into the hardwood floor.

"Okay, okay, all right. I'll tell you whatever you want to know," Stacey said, prompting Fire to stop the brutal assault.

Beads of sweat were trickling down Fire's forehead. "Who did that shit to my mother?" she asked, slightly out of breath.

"It was Murphy. He set her up."

"Set her up for what?"

"For Ta'shawn, this young boy I sell dope for. He gave Adrianne some bad dope then put his dogs on her. It wasn't my fault." Stacey was afraid if she told her it was Gator, she'd end up like Adrianne, left for dead, and decided to give up Ta'shawn instead.

"If it happened in your house, it was your fault!"

"No, it wasn't. I told Adrianne not to come back after Ta'shawn raped her," she lied again on him. "Soon as she left, the cops came and raided my place. Almost two weeks had passed and Adrianne hadn't come around. He thought she was the one who set him up. He said when he caught her, he was gonna kill her. I didn't think she'd come back around, but she did. I shouldn't have let her in. That's how he got her."

"And you stood by and watched? I thought my mother was your friend. Why didn't you help her? You let her get raped and then left her for dead just like that, nigga?"

"I'm a hundred pounds wet. What the hell could I have done?"

"Called the cops, bitch!" Marcy kicked her in her face again.

All the while the frail man in the corner kept his hands over his head to avoid getting beat.

"Where can I find Murphy?"

"He usually comes here every day, but ever since that happened to Adrianne, he's been staying away. I haven't seen him."

"You're fuckin' lying." Marcy suddenly started beating Stacey on the head with the gun, and Stacey was left crawling across the floor, her face and head covered in blood.

"Little man, c'mere." Marcy escorted him out the room and started to question him.

He kept his head down and tried not to peer in Stacey's direction. He was about to get the hell up out of her house, by any means necessary. Even if that meant telling the truth, that Stacey was the one who set Adrianne up.

"Is she lying to us?"

Without speaking, he nodded his head yes.

"Okay. I told you this ain't about you. It's about who did this to my mom. Did Stacey have something to do with this?"

He nodded yes again.

"Is she the one who gave my mom the bad dope?"

He nodded yes again.

"Is she lying on the boy Ta'shawn?"

He nodded no this time.

Marcy breathed out heavily. "Do you know where I can find some of that same dope?"

This time, he moved his fingers, indicating that she should follow him. He took her to the kitchen and pulled out a small bag of the special dope that Stacey had given her from underneath the kitchen sink. "This is what she gave her," he said, speaking up for the first time since Marcy stuck the gun in his face at the door. "I'm really sorry for what they did to Adrianne. She didn't deserve that. Stacey should pay for what they did to her. She's the one who called the cops on Ta'shawn and them so she could steal their dope. This is what they gave her. Here, take this bag. Give her a dose of her own medicine."

"Thank you. My mom didn't deserve that. You can go, but I better not hear you utter one word about this."

"I won't. Thank you for sparing my life."

Marcy stormed her way back to settle the score with Stacey. "Fire, this bitch set Mom up!" Marcy paced around in circles.

"Are you sure?" Fire asked.

"She called the cops on the nigga, so she could escape with his dope. Ta'shawn paid Stacey to set Mom up as payback. This bitch got paid all across the board, and Mom took the fall. Little man just told me."

"Well, why would Mom call out Murphy's name? It doesn't make sense."

"Yes, it does, because Murphy knew the truth. She had us about to do him some harm."

At hearing this new bit of information, Fire's mood really changed. She couldn't believe this lying bitch had her feeling sorry for her. She'd tried to play Fire, just like she'd played Adrianne.

Marcy pulled the small plastic bag and tossed it to Stacey. "Here's your pay for giving us the information on Ta'shawn."

Stacey looked at the bag like it was a poisonous rattlesnake. "No, I'm good."

"It's heroin." Marcy got all up in her face. "You do use heroin, don't you?"

"Y-y-yes, b-but, I'm cool," Stacey replied, inching away from the bag on the floor.

Marcy pointed the gun at her. "Bitch, pick the bag up and handle your business, before I handle my business."

"Please, please don't do this."

Marcy calmly walked up to Stacey and—*POW!*—shot her in the leg at point-blank range. The gun blast echoed through the room like a bomb. Stacey grabbed her leg and screamed out in anguish.

Fire looked around nervously.

"HANDLE-YOUR-BUSINESS!" Marcy yelled, taking aim at Stacey's other leg.

Stacey hurried and grabbed the bag from the floor. She ripped the small package open, poured its contents on the back of her hand, and snorted it up her nostrils. Her eyes rolled back in her head. She grabbed her nose and dropped to the floor at Fire's feet and began shaking, twitching, and convulsing. Then a low growl came from deep in her throat.

Fire and Marcy left her alone to sleep in the bed she'd made for herself.

What You Know About That?

Gator and Tricky observed Jake as he ran out of Stacey's house. Tricky stepped out the Yukon and approached him.

"Who those chicks that went in Stacey's? I know they ain't tryina get high."

"I really don't want to get involved. It's Adrianne's daughters. They want revenge for what Gator and Ta'shawn did to her, not no get-high. Stacey ratted out Ta'shawn too. They think he did it."

"They're posting up like that? A'ight, Jake, get going before they come out." Tricky had to let Gator know what they knew about the incident. He got back in the truck and turned to Gator. "You have a slight problem. Stacey ran her mouth to Adrianne's daughters. They goin' at niggas' heads to find out who did it. What's good is, Stacey told them Ta'shawn did it, and since he got locked up again, they'll run into a dead end."

Gator gripped his chin and stroked his nose. "Let's

keep a close eye on those bitches anyway. In fact, let's get to know them very well."

"Get to know them well? I ain't in that. I didn't have any parts of what you and Ta'shawn did."

"It don't matter. You gon' help regardless, if you want these good prices. When they come out, you follow them, and I'll get with Stacey."

Tricky got out Gator's truck seriously nerved. *This nigga always threatening to cut off the connect when shit don't go his way. Old as he is, he still acting like a young, wild nigga.*

Tricky wasn't like Gator, disguised behind expensive suits made by topnotch designers and expensive gator shoes. He was a stand-up guy that hustled to please his women and take care of home. Gator was all show and tried persistently to keep his image up. He was loud and obnoxious, always trying to be seen and heard. Tricky was just the opposite, laid-back and quiet. The most noise Tricky made was when he was in the bedroom moaning.

Gator waited until Fire and Marcy sped off in the Lumina, and watched as Tricky got inside his car and followed them. When they were out of sight, he went inside of Stacey's and found her unconscious on the floor. Seeing her like that, he left out as quietly as he came in. He called Tricky on the phone. "Tell the young boys to stay away from Stacey's. I think they killed the bitch."

"Done," Tricky responded and started to make the calls.

Excuse Me, Miss

For the next couple of days, Gator and Tricky followed and investigated Fire and Marcy. They tailed them and watched them day in and day out, figuring out the best way to deal with the situation. All they did was visit their mother, talk with the young boys across the street from where they lived, and danced at the Golden Club. They weren't worried about Adrianne talking because Shanice, one of Tricky's girls worked at the hospital keeping them updated on her progress.

"Offer these hoes more money than they getting at the Golden Club to work at Club Desire. It's about money to them. This way we can keep a closer watch. You like fuckin' with dancers, go recruit them," Gator told Tricky.

Desire, was a private gentlemen's club that Tricky and Gator owned. It was also Tricky's favorite hangout. That's how he acquired the nickname Tricky—he'd tricked so much money with the strippers.

"The honey brown one is cute, but the red-head is thick and sexy. I'd fuck her."

Incidentally, they were holding auditions for new dancers at Club Desire, and this was a grand opportunity for Tricky to approach them.

"Do what you need to do to get them, but whatever you do, don't fall for the ho, *Tricky*," Gator said, emphasizing his name.

"Fuck you. I'll get up with you."

"Maybe we should call the cops and let them handle this since Ta'shawn's punk ass is in jail."

Just as Gator and Tricky were investigating, so was Fire and Marcy, and that's the information they came up with—Ta'shawn was in jail.

"You think the cops give a fuck, Fire? Nobody gives a fuck, but us," Marcy said frustrated. "I'm tired of seeing Mom all wired up in a coma, like she's waiting to die."

"Marcy, the nigga is in jail. Let's just stack our money and hope that Mom gets better. Honestly, I can sleep peacefully knowing she's safe in the hospital. Maybe this happening to her was to open her eyes . . . if she comes out of this. Whatever doesn't kill you only makes you stronger. It's made me stronger. What about you?"

"It made me vicious! Fuck being stronger. I hope that nigga die in jail," Marcy voiced as Tricky came within reach of them leaving the Golden Club.

"Can I holla you ladies for a minute?"

They both looked him over. "Who are you?" Fire stepped to him first.

"The owner of Club Desire. Both of you put on a hell of a show. Especially, you red."

"The name is Fire."

Marcy scanned his jewels. "What is it you want, Mr. CEO?"

"I want both of you to dance for me. We're holding auditions over at the club tonight for five slots. We pay our girls very well. Five hundred base fee per night, and you get to keep your tips."

That was more than the Golden Club offered.

Fire looked to Marcy then back to Tricky. "If you've been watching us then you know we can manipulate men better than any other bitches in the city. It's gonna cost you a little more if you want us to leave a stable place where we already have a fan base. Niggas go broke to feel all of this." She ran her hand over her curves and down Marcy's as well. "I'm sure once our fans know we're leaving, they will come to us, which means we're bringing you business. Make that six fifty base fee per night and we still get to keep our tips, and you got a deal."

"Damn, shaw-tay, you tryin'a hit my pockets. Where you from?"

"Brooklyn, baby. We don't play games. We get down for ours. Is it a deal or what?"

"Take down this address and slide through in about an hour."

Marcy grabbed the address. "We'll think about it."

Tricky smiled and walked away knowing they would be there. No dancer would turn down that kind of deal. "I might even have a little extra for you, Fire." He smiled again as he got into his black Mercedes-Benz M-Class sport-utility vehicle.

* * *

Cliff pulled up in front of Golden and tooted his horn. "*Shaw-tay!!*" he called to Fire and Marcy. "Marcy, what . . . you through wit' a nigga? You ain't been answering my calls. Y'all get in. Who was that nigga?"

Since Marcy's stress level had gone up, she'd been keeping her distance from him. "Don't take it personal, baby. I've been trying to handle some business. Did you get your car keys? I left them underneath the seat."

"I got them. I see you doin' you," he said, referring to them holding a conversation with Tricky.

"Nah, actually he was on my sister. Should I even have to explain? Just take me home please. I'm tired and need some rest."

"So you ain't going, Marcy?"

"Nah, you can go and tell me if that nigga is really 'bout what he say. I need to lay my ass down tonight. Cliff, you staying in with me? If you are, let Fire hold your Magnum to go audition for Club Desire."

"A'ight."

Soon as they got home, Fire went to freshen up and put on a real sexy, revealing outfit. She beamed at her beauty in her full-length mirror and thought, *When this nigga see this, he's going to up his price even more.*

Tear the Club Up!!

Fire strutted to the front door of Club Desire, barely dressed in a tight, short Chanel skirt and matching tube top. She was confident that her bombshell body was drawing the attention of every man she passed, jiggling with every step. And it didn't hurt that the nipples on her C cups were poking out like baby pinkies. A sexy dose of murder with a capital *M*, Fire was dressed to kill, and she knew she was killing them.

When she reached the door, there were two of the biggest men in the world standing there.

"Fresh, flavored red meat," one of the jolly black giant twins greeted her. "What's up, shaw-tay?"

Fire smiled seductively. "Hey, big daddy. I'm here for the auditions."

"Baby, I'd give you the job right now if it was up to me. You wouldn't have to audition. How about we go in the back and you show me some gratitude," the bouncer said, holding an enormous bulge in his pants.

"I'd never let you tear my sweet stuff up with all of

that meat you packin', big daddy," Fire politely declined, stroking his ego at the same time.

The guy grinned and handed her a small ticket. "Go on in the back and wait for them to call your number. Good luck, baby."

Fire entered the door, which led backstage. To her surprise, there were so many women waiting to audition, the packed crowd looked like an uncut video audition. The club was exclusively for the ladies to audition. There were women of all shapes and sizes, all colors and creeds. She checked her ticket for the first time and noticed she had number twenty-one.

"Excuse me, what number are they on?" Fire asked an exquisite-looking Dominican girl.

"*Guurrll*, they're only up to number three, and my unlucky ass has number twelve. I'll be up in here all night waiting for this damn audition."

"You? Baby, I got number twenty-one." Marcy held up her ticket.

"Damn, girl! I feel for you. If I didn't have mouths to feed, I'd take my desperate ass home. But I heard these niggas pay good, so I'ma stay my ass in line and try to make it to the top five."

"You ain't lying. I'm staying for the type of cash they dishing out too. Money talks," Fire attested before walking to the stage's curtain.

She looked out into the club, where there were a large group of young guys sitting together watching the woman on stage dancing her heart out for a chance at a job. Seated in the center of the crowd was Tricky.

Fire watched him for a few seconds and thought he looked bored. Since he'd invited her, she wasn't about to wait in the long-ass line, knowing her job was pretty much sealed. She exited the left side of the stage and walked towards the bar.

It only took a few seconds for Tricky to notice her.

She took long, slow, seductive steps, causing her hips to sway sexily, using her ass to communicate with the men. She had Tricky hypnotized, mesmerized, and magnetized by the time she reached the bar, and she knew it. "Put some Henny on ice for me, baby," she ordered.

The bartender fixed her drink, never once taking his eyes off her. He handed her the small glass, touching her hand softly to display his interest.

She took a sip of her drink. "What do I owe you, sweetie?"

"A dance, boo. Just a dance." The bartender licked his lips.

"I got you, daddy. As soon as they call number twenty-one, it's show time for you." Fire smiled and showed him her ticket. She turned around on the bar stool, drink in hand, and noticed Tricky was watching her. She smiled at him, and he waved to acknowledge her. Fire held up two fingers, then one finger. Then she held up her ticket, letting him know she was number twenty-one.

He grinned then he turned back to watch the woman on stage. Girl number three on stage was just finishing up her dance to the cheers and jeers of Tricky's entourage. Tricky himself appeared unimpressed with her and more impressed with LeToya Luckett singing, *Tear the Club Up, Tear the Club Up*, as he nodded his head to the beat.

Fire finished off her drink, and prepared to return

backstage to wait her turn. Then she heard Tricky call out, "Number twenty-one."

You could hear the frustration of the other ladies as they deflated some air loudly.

Fire smiled and walked up on stage with the confidence of a supermodel. She could hear the complaints of the girls backstage. *Hate on bitches*, she thought as she began her performance.

"Keep that same song on. I'ma show these ladies how to get it done." She turned to the line of ladies and set it off like a pro.

After erotically dancing her way out of her clothes, she made love to the pole, flexing her alligator strap-up stilettos. Her flexible pole acrobatics had Tricky and his entourage going crazy.

"Damn, Red! Do dat shit!" she heard one of them say, but couldn't tell if it was Tricky or not.

She stepped off the stage, strolled over to where Tricky was seated and leaped up onto his table, which is when she really got them hard. They were howling louder than the music, showering her with attention. Tricky sat back grinning, nodding his head to the beat of the music.

During the entire performance, Fire never broke eye contact with Tricky for too long. Even when she was upside down with her legs behind her neck.

When she was done, she returned to the stage to collect her discarded clothes to a standing ovation from Tricky, his boys, the bartender, and the two jolly black giant bouncers. She took her clothes backstage and began to dress. Then she got an unexpected visitor.

"Wow!" Tricky exclaimed. "You were even better tonight than other times I seen you dance."

"Excuse me?" Fire asked with attitude in her voice.

"Your name must be *Wow*, 'cause that's what everybody's been calling you."

"I thought a fine-ass brotha like you could come up with a better opening line than that."

"Okay, here's a better opening line—You're hired at eight hundred dollars per night, plus you get to keep your tips."

"I knew I would get hired, but it's nice to hear it," Fire boasted in her best diva disposition.

"What happened to your sister? She scared to make some real money?"

"How'd you know she was my sister?"

"Who doesn't at the Golden Club? Those stilettos sexy as a muthafucka! My old-head nigga Gator would've loved to see those on your beautiful feet. How 'bout we go and discuss what's in your job description over breakfast?"

It was a little after three A.M.

"You mean what I'm required to do or *who* I'm required to do?"

"If you were required to do anybody, it would be me."

"There are some things I won't do for money." Fire stepped closer to him, right in his face. "But then again, there are some things I'd do for free."

"Are we on for breakfast or what?"

"Another time, sweetie." Fire slipped him a card with her cell phone number and made her exit.

"Wow!" he called out behind her.

She just smiled and kept it moving. As she passed the other girls waiting for an audition, they were all staring at her and fuming, except for the Dominican chick that gave her thumbs-up.

Fire mouthed, "Good luck," to her and exited the club. As she walked to the parking lot she thought, *That nigga's dick is probably still hard.*

At the Car Wash

The next afternoon, Fire and her friend Radiance pulled up to the car wash on the south side of Miami. Radiance was the only other female Fire associated with on a personal level, other than her sister. They'd met at the Golden Club the first night and hit it off from there. Radiance was just as bright as Fire, with glowing skin, big, bright, green eyes and long, blonde, curly hair. When those two got together it spelled two words—*Double trouble!*

Fire checked her red Coach watch for the fifth time in the last five minutes.

"They were supposed to call me with an update on my mom. They haven't called yet and I left three messages already." Fire could feel Radiance staring at her. "I know I'm cute, but why are you gawking at me?"

"I'm just wondering why you're hiding your feelings."

"What are you talking about, Radiance?"

"I know you're hurt about your mother, but for some reason you won't talk about it. And Marcy is withdrawing from everyone. All she wanna do is stay up under Cliff now. She don't even wanna make money any more. Maybe y'all need to talk to a professional about this."

"Here we go with some Dr. Phil bullshit. I just mentioned it, didn't I?"

"Stop acting hard all the damn time. You've got a pussy and titties just like me. You're emotional, just like every other woman. It's all right to cry."

"I'll cry for joy when my mom makes it home. Every day I see her in the hospital, I hope she wakes up and we can take her home. What time do you have?"

Radiance sucked her teeth. "Damn,Fire! If you're gonna keep asking me what time it is, why don't you just take my watch, so you'll have two. They'll call."

"You just mad 'cause I won't connect emotionally with you anymore," Fire teased.

Radiance and Fire had an on-again, off-again lesbian affair that Radiance wanted to make exclusive, but Fire loved big wood too much to limit her sexual appetite.

"Connect your lips with my ass, slut," Radiance replied laughing.

"Are you gonna help me wash my car, or are you gonna lust over me all day?"

Radiance had on a pair of blue shorts rolled down to her hips showing off her mid-section and thunder thighs. Before she responded, a motorcade of vehicles with loud music and plenty of bass pulled in the car wash one by one. Each vehicle caught their eyes, a Jaguar S-type, an Acura 3.2, a Chrysler 300M, a BMW 5-series, and a Mercury Marauder, all with shiny paint jobs, tints, and rims.

Radiance watched as the occupants of the vehicles stepped out. "Here comes money," she said.

"They ain't coming to get their cars washed. One of these niggas probably own this spot the way they pulled up in here."

"Look at that big nigga right there." Radiance peered at Gator, who was getting out of his Mercury Marauder.

Gator noticed them as well and threw a few comments their way. "Would you look at this? Stanley Tookie Williams would be proud of you ladies," Gator shouted to them.

Radiance began to water down her car, giving Gator a full view of her back shot. "How so?"

"Bloods and Crips in perfect harmony, looking good together." Gator recognized their red and blue ensembles and noticed one of the females was Adrianne's daughter.

Fire was dressed in all red, and Radiance was dressed in all blue. They chuckled at his awareness of gang colors.

"Yo, Red, how much?" one of the young boys asked.

"Not enough for you," Radiance told him.

"I got enough dick for both y'all to swing on," he shouted, and Gator laughed with him.

Radiance called his bluff. "I tell you what, if any of you niggas can show me more than ten inches, I'll *give* you the pussy. I bet none of you lil'-dick muthafuckas can even pull out eight inches."

"King Kong ain't got shit on me." Gator extended his hands to show them how long his dick was.

"Well, let's see it."

"All right, but get prepared for a date tonight and bring ya lil' friend too." Gator stared at Fire.

"Put ya dick where ya mouth is," Radiance yelled.

Without hesitation, Gator pulled out a thick, swollen dick about eleven and a half inches long, and wagged it at both of them.

Radiance casually walked over nodding her head and grinning.

Gator looked over Radiance lustfully. "What time can I pick you up?"

"She's Fire, and I'm Radiance. We can hook up later. Where should we meet you?"

"Meet us at Jazid's on 13th & Washington Avenue about ten tonight."

"I can't. I'm starting at Club Desire tonight." Fire wasn't trying to be the third party and recipient of his award. She also wanted to test the club out before she officially quit the Golden Club.

"I'm part-owner of the club. Me and my man Tricky run that. Don't even worry about showing up. I'll let Tricky know. In fact, I'll bring him along."

Fire didn't know what to say. *Tricky . . . that's his name, huh.* She'd already given Tricky a rain check, and now she could make good on it.

"Don't let me down, Radiance. I'ma tear that pussy up." Gator sounded like a horny teenager going through puberty.

"We'll see."

Fire's cell rang. It was Marcy. "What's up, sis? Where are you?"

"I'm at the hospital with Mom."

"How's she doing?"

"Not good," Marcy replied, sounding very sorrowful. "We've gotta do something, Fire. I can't stand seeing Mom like this."

Fire was the stronger of the two. It was times like this that reminded her that Marcy was her little sister. She wanted to console her and be that shoulder she needed to cry on.

Marcy had been falling apart in a state of depression ever since she'd found out Ta'shawn was in jail. Him being in jail wasn't satisfaction enough for her. She wanted him dead.

"Everything is gonna be all right, Marcy. Stay at the hospital. I'm on my way."

A Night Out

Later that night at home, Fire examined every inch and curve from head to toe. Her and Radiance helped each other prepare for their dates with Tricky and Gator.

"I can't believe you are going about this like nothing ever happened," Marcy fussed with Fire. "You haven't lost one step, and you damn sure ain't been losing sleep. You really going out on a date with this mutha-fucka you just met?"

"Since when did that matter? The bills still gotta get paid, and it seems you won't be giving up a dime this month. All you do is mope around at home and the club. You ain't even making money when you're at work all depressed. If I get down like you, who's gonna hold it down?"

"She ain't lying," Radiance seconded, applying li-pliner to her lips.

"Shut up, Radiance! Y'all make me sick. I'm going in Mom's room and go to sleep."

"You do that. How do I look, Radiance?"

"Fuckable." Radiance rolled her tongue over her glossed lips.

"I got my sexy on tonight, don't I?"

"And if you really wanna catch his eye, you'd go put those titties in a push-up bra." Radiance arched her back and proudly displayed her perky double D's.

"Some men want nice, round, speedy bags, and some want big, heavy bags," Fire joked. "Let's hit it. We're already late."

Jazid's was snug and comfortable. Not gloomy, but dim and private. Not exquisite, but warm and welcoming. Above all, with the candlelight, soft jazz music, private booths and mellow mood, the place was definitely romantic. Tricky and Gator had private booths waiting.

Fire and Radiance walked in and lit the room up with their presence.

"Wow! C'mere, sexy," Tricky greeted, helping her step up in the dark cherry wood booth, where a bottle of champagne was chilling.

"I told you before, my name is Fire."

Gator whispered something in Radiance's ear, and she started laughing. They were seated right next to them in another booth.

Tricky turned over the champagne glasses and filled each glass. "You know you fired already, don't you, for not showing up to work tonight?"

"Stop playing!"

"I'm serious. Did you confirm with me that you were taking off? For all you know, Gator could've been lying about me, and here you are waiting on a nigga to show up. What kind of business is that?"

"You're right. Had I not known Gator's name when you mentioned him before, I wouldn't have fell for him trying to impress us anyway. Do you know how many men kick that whack-ass I-own-my-own-business line?"

Tricky liked her style.

"So let me ask you, what do you really do for a living?" Fire sipped her glass of champagne, mindful to not drink too much.

"I'm a club owner, a legit club owner. You know that already."

"I mean besides the club, are you a hustler?"

"Are you a cop?"

Fire smiled. "I'm not trying to get into your business. I just don't date hustlers."

"Why not? Mostly all Miami women want a big balla. What makes you different, Brooklyn?" Tricky asked, re-filling his glass.

"Just that—Brooklyn. A real special friend of mine got his brains blown out right in front me behind hustling."

"Niggas in New York be wildin'."

"So do niggas in Miami. Y'all on some other shit down here. Niggas letting animals loose on people, all that crazy shit."

Tricky paused. "Nah, I don't fuck around like that. Let's change the subject."

Fire caught a funny feeling in her stomach and glanced over to Radiance, who was having a blast with Gator.

"Why you get silent? What you thinking about?"

Since Radiance was having such a good time, Fire decided she wanted to let her hair down too. "I'm thinking of whether or not you can dance."

"They say if you can dance you can fuck." Tricky smiled. "I already know you can fuck by the way you dance."

"Well, take me to the floor and fuck me. Fuck me real good." Fire got up from the table and walked towards the small dance floor.

On the dance floor, Tricky took Fire in his arms, and the two slow-grinded to the smooth jazz sounds of Kim Waters.

Fire pressed her softness against his body, making circular motions, wiggling like a snake. She was arousing a sexual force in Tricky that had him so excited, she was sure his boxers was soiled with pre-cum. His breathing was heavy in her ear as she rested her full lips on his neck.

"Fire," Tricky whispered.

Fire groaned as if she had a dick all up in her. "What's up, daddy?"

"I really meant that you're fired. Fuck dancing at the club. You can make more money fuckin' with a nigga like me. I'll take care of you."

"I can still make money at the club."

"No, you can't. I don't like sharing my goods."

"I love your confidence."

"I love your soft ass," he said, palming her ass cheeks with both hands.

"And my ass loves your strong touch."

"I've got a few more things your ass is gonna love."

Tricky stuck his tongue in her ear. "They don't call me Tricky for nothing."

Radiance tapped Fire on her shoulder. "Me and big daddy are about to leave. You cool?"

"She's in good hands with me," Tricky told her.

Gator wrapped his huge arms around Radiance's waist. "Tricky, I'm gon' tear this pussy up!"

After leaving Jazid's, Fire and Tricky rode in silence for a while. Fire was wondering where they were headed; Tricky hadn't told her anything yet. Before they'd left the club, he received a call on his cell phone. He talked in a low tone and hung up quickly, so Fire didn't catch any of the conversation. And Tricky didn't offer any information.

"Where are we going now?"

"I've got some business to handle first. Then we're going to one of my cribs . . . if you don't mind."

"Actually, I do mind. I don't go home with men after our first date." She watched him from the corner of her eye as he scowled in disappointment. "But I do go to hotels."

Tricky smiled and showed her a hotel room key. "Avalon on Ocean Drive, honeymoon suite."

"You are too damn confident," she said, rubbing his right leg as he drove.

Seconds later they pulled onto a dark street. Tricky pulled up to a double-parked Buick. Engine running and the lights off, the Buick was facing the opposite direction, which put the driver face to face with Tricky.

"What's up, family?" Tricky asked one of his young boys.

"Same shit, baby. I got a call from *T*. He said send him some flicks and hit him off lovely 'cause he might be down for a minute. He said Gator ain't even hollered at him yet, and he said if he don't soon, the man gon' secretly find out about what he did to that fiend."

"A'ight." Tricky didn't make eye contact with him at all. He felt it was Gator's job to take care of wild-ass Ta'shawn that he groomed. *I told him not to do that shit. If he's going down, that's on him.*

"Only niggas I know taking care of another man in jail is one that out there getting money with him," Fire commented as they pulled off.

"On some real shit, Fire, I get money how I get it. But I guarantee you I won't be getting locked up, or getting my brains blown out."

In the privacy of their hotel suite, Tricky and Fire went right at each other as if they'd known each other for years. Everything that needed to be said had already been said.

After undressing each other, Tricky laid Fire on the king-size bed and teased her with his tongue. Getting in between her legs, he pressed himself deep into her, stroking his way inside of her.

Tricky's not so bad after all, Fire thought. *He better break me off proper, though.*

Eightball, Anyone?

After Radiance and Gator left Jazid's, they stopped at Eightball, a pool hall that all the hoods frequented, so he could show Radiance off.

Radiance told him, "This shit looks like a block party."

"How long have you lived in Miami?"

"I was born and raised here. I just don't frequent little hole-in-the-wall places like this, and a man of your caliber shouldn't either. You don't even fit in with your black silk shirt lined with all Gator skin, black silk slacks and sandy-brown gator shoes with black soles on. Not to mention, you're about twenty years older than the oldest person up in there."

"We don't have to go in." He pinched her on her thigh. "Just get out and flex a little bit."

"Hell no, and if I was you, I wouldn't get out either because your chances of getting this pussy is dwindling. You actin' like a young boy that never had a real woman before."

The truth was, when Gator was younger, females did-n't seek his big sloppy ass out. His first shot of pussy was when he was nineteen, and it was his first cousin that he took it from. He did fourteen years in jail for raping her, which explained why he behaved so much like a ju-venile. He'd lost time.

While in jail, his flab turned to muscle, and he mus-cled his way in the game, becoming a beast getting money. That still didn't stop him from forcing himself on females.

"This shit turns you off, huh?"

"Indeed. I'm too grown-up for this kiddie crowd."

"It's only two things that really turns me off like that."

"What's that, Gator?"

"I hate junkie bitches and bitches that play mind games with the pussy."

Radiance frowned a bit and eased her back against the passenger's seat. "Where to now?"

"I'm taking you to my spot."

Gator's phone began ringing constantly, frustrating the hell out of him. He looked at the familiar number. "Yeah, ma?" he answered with every bit of aggravation. "Okay, Cissy, I'll stop past there. I'll be glad when your two-week stay is up. You're driving me crazy. It's room 161, right? All right, I'll be there."

Before taking Radiance to "his spot," Gator made a quick stop to drop something off to his mom at South Beach Plaza on Collins Avenue. He'd temporarily housed her there until the renovations on her house were com-pleted. Until then, he had to succumb to her wants, since he was the one that decided she needed the work done. At the age of 65, she was content with the conditions of her home, but he wasn't.

Radiance kept her silence but particularly watched each movement Gator made. Judging by the rubber-banded wad of money that he pulled out, he was taking his mother some cash.

"Bitches! They always want something."

Radiance frowned as she listened to Gator display his lack of respect for women, even his own mother. She wondered if he felt that way about his own mother, then he really didn't give a damn about any other females.

"Stay put," he said as they pulled up to the bungalows. "I'll be right back."

He came back out in less than five minutes and proceeded to take her to his spot.

Radiance hardly thought his spot would be in his office at Club Desire. They bypassed all the action and happenings to the stairwell to his office.

She sat in the nicely decorated executive office on the third floor on the mahogany-leather-pillowed couch. "I hope you don't think you're fuckin' me in here?"

Gator removed his black slacks, ignoring her comment. "Spread them legs. You don't even have to take your skirt off, just ease it up some."

"Big daddy, it ain't that easy. This pussy cost—No dollas, no hollas, got that?"

"Cost? Bitch, please." He stroked his penis to full erection. "You gon' honor your bet. Now open ya fuckin' legs!"

"I don't take dick, only tongue, and to eat this sweet pussy it cost five hundred."

"I ain't payin' for a damn thing, and I sure ain't eatin' no ho's nasty pussy."

Radiance searched around the room for any sharp or blunt objects in case she needed to use it as a weapon. The way Gator was coming at her, he wasn't taking no for an answer. He was about to take what he wanted.

She slowly lifted up from the couch. "You really believed I would give you some pussy for showing me ya dick? What grown-ass man would believe that?"

Gator looked off in a trance, like he was actually thinking about the answer, but didn't say anything.

"Exactly. None!!"

Gator moved over to the door and reached for the remote control on his desk to turn on the music.

"Didn't I just tell you I hate when hoes play mind games with the pussy? I meant that. I don't care what you try to do. You ain't leaving until I stick every inch of this dick in you, just like I did ya girl's mom. That junkie bitch deserved it, calling the cops on me. She'll never see daylight again, and neither will you after I'm through."

Radiance gasped. She knew she was in trouble. *I should've never left with this crazy-ass nigga,* she thought, bracing her body to get victimized.

Gator moved as fast as a cheetah, grabbing her by her neck and slamming her back against the wall. The business license nailed to the wall fell, and the glass shattered on her neck. Every inch of Radiance's frame rattled as her back collided with the wall. Gator held her in place with a vise-like grip around her sleek neck.

Unable to feel the floor beneath her feet, she realized he was holding her elevated above the floor by her neck, hanging her. She struggled for a gulp of fresh air and to free herself from his strong hand, slapping and scratching his face.

Gator only loosened his grip when he chose to, which was a fraction of a second before she blacked out.

Talk to Me

Two days had passed since Fire had talked with Radiance, which was unusual. She hadn't been to Golden, and she wasn't at home.

"Marcy, I think something's up with Radiance. I haven't heard from her."

Marcy curled up with a light blanket on the couch with Adrianne's pillow. "She probably went out of town with some ho-ass nigga. You know she's good for that."

"Mmm-hmm." Fire nodded. "She didn't even call me on the dick report. You know she don't like to get stuck. She's a licky-licky gal."

"Call ya new date. Didn't his man take her out?"

"I'ma do that. What time are you going to see Mom?"

"Cliff is coming to get me in a few hours."

"Good, get yaself together and put on something nice. I know he's tired of seeing you scarfed up in pajamas pants."

"No, he's not. As long as he can get the 'nana,' he doesn't care what I wear."

"I'm stopping by the hospital now before I handle my business. I need to catch up with Tricky to find out if Gator seen my girl."

"Kiss Mom for me," Marcy said and gripped the covers tighter around her body.

Inside Desire in Gator's office in the closet, Radiance sat bound and gagged. Gator had finally informed Tricky what he'd done to her.

"What the fuck did you have to rape the bitch for? You keep taking pussy from hoes. You like it, don't you?"

Radiance wiggled, trying to make enough noise, praying someone would come to her rescue.

"What's that noise?" Tricky asked, moving closer to the desk in front of the closet.

Unfazed, Gator kindly walked over to the closet and opened the door. "It's the ho."

Tricky pounded on the desk. "You's a sick-ass nigga. Kidnapping, rape."

"Attempted murder, all that. Ho should've never played me."

Radiance mumbled, "Help me!" and stared at Tricky helplessly.

"I'll do her like I did Jackie when I found out she was a man after I stuck my dick in his ass—Douse her with lighter fluid and light her up. Jackie Blaze, nigga!" Gator laughed loudly.

Tricky gritted his teeth. "Stop making me a conspirator to your crimes, running your fuckin' mouth, nigga. I'm not gonna let you take me down 'cause of your sickness!"

Gator laughed even louder. "Chill out, partna. The shit was funny."

Tricky peered at him. *This nigga is disturbed.* "The shit won't be funny when she's on the witness stand testifying against you for murder. What else have you blurted out?"

Radiance was throwing her body trying her best to get up. "Help me! Help me!" she kept mumbling.

Gator slammed the door in her face. "Fuck her!"

"You don't do shit like that to people for the fun of it, Gator, man."

"Before you judge me, be mindful that she deserved what she got."

"That's bullshit. You got animalistic tendencies. You need to check that."

"Only thing canine about me is my doggy style. And all the bitches love it."

"Man, these women have children. What if someone did that to your mother?"

"I feel you. But it ain't my mother, so fuck 'em! Adrianne deserved it the most. The junkie bitch tried to put me away again." Gator blew smoke from a cigar he'd lit.

"Real men don't hold grudges. They don't act like ho-niggas. They charge it to the game."

"No, you got it wrong, ho-niggas take bitches clothes shopping, like your trickin' ass. Real men take what they want."

"Real niggas take care of business. The bouncers been having a problem with one of your young boys— Handle that. He's downstairs."

Gator hesitantly stepped to the door. "A'ight. Don't let the ho get away."

"Do I ever?"

Once Gator left, Tricky rushed over to the closet and pulled Radiance up, ripping the duct tape from her mouth. She went to speak, but Tricky covered her mouth with his hands.

"Don't say anything!" He rushed to the desk and retrieved the scissors to cut the tape off of her arms and legs.

Gator had a long trench coat in his closet that Tricky threw to her. "Put this on and hurry." He peeked out the door, knowing he only had a few minutes before Gator came up the steps pissed because he'd lied.

With her arm interlocked with his, he guided Radiance to the fire escape. "Take my keys. My car is in the back parking lot. Get out of here. The closest station is on 9th Street. Just make sure when you go to the cops, my name is clear. I didn't have shit to do with what he's done."

Tears easily fell from Radiance's face, stripped of its glow. She leaned forward and hugged him. "Thank you, Tricky."

"Go now!"

Tricky went back into Gator's office and removed his hidden stash. He knew before the night was out, the police would be raiding Desire, and he wanted to get all that he could before Gator came back and they came.

He felt his cell phone vibrate and answered it as he was leaving.

"Tricky, Adrianne Evans came out of her coma. One of her daughters is here. You want me to call Gator?"

"Hell no! Contact the police for security. Do it now and don't call him."

Shanice puckered her brow. She wasn't about to play savior to save a stripper's mother, so she went against what her man advised her and called Gator.

Tricky made it outside of the club, just as Fire was pulling up with Block. She pushed the button to the power window on her side. "I've been trying to get in contact with you," she said. "I haven't seen Radiance since the night we went out."

Tricky looked from side to side, contemplating if he should tell her in front of her male friend. "Can I get a ride? I really need to talk to you alone." He opened up the door without Block agreeing.

Block intently eyed him down in the back seat of his car. "Don't let me stop you."

Gator went back upstairs to an empty room and began darting his head in and out of the other rooms. From the window in the hallway, he could see Tricky talking with Fire. He dashed down the stairwell emerging from the doors. "TRICKY! TRICKY!"

Tricky slammed the door shut when he heard his name. "Pull off, pull off," he said.

"Tricky, what is going on?" Fire watched a delirious Gator chase behind them with his big ass.

"You gon' have to put some pressure on the gas pedal, bro. Gator's gonna follow us and we can't let him catch us."

"Nigga, what you on?" Block applied more force to pedal, dipping in and out of traffic.

"Fire, I need to tell you this. First, believe me when I say I didn't have shit to do with what went down."

"What, Tricky?" Butterflies began to dance around in her stomach.

"Gator beat and raped Radiance. She was locked in his office closet since the night we went out to Jazid's."

"Oh shit! Where is she now?" Block slammed on the brakes, finding it ironic that Tricky was ratting his man out like that, and speeded up when Tricky began talking.

"I gave her the keys to my car and told her to go to the station on 9th Street."

Fire was taken aback. "Is she hurt really bad?"

Tricky didn't want to tell how battered and bruised she was, much preferring to get everything off his chest. "That's not all, Fire. Shaw-tay, you know I'm feelin' you."

Block glanced over at Fire. Not too long ago he was diggin' her out on the couch.

"It's gon' hurt me to tell you this, but not as much as you gonna suffer—Gator is responsible for putting your mom in the hospital also."

The car came to a screeching halt.

Fire began yelling to the top of her lungs. "Muthafucka, you knew this all along? You had me around this nigga and he left my mother for dead! Block, you got ya piece on you. He's a dead nigga to me!"

"I swear I ain't want you to get hurt, Fire. You're a thorough chick. I even had my girl put security on your mom's door tonight when she called and told me she was out of her coma."

Happiness and anger fought Fire's emotion. She wanted to smile, yet tears and rage stopped her. She placed her head on the dashboard and started beating on it with her fist. "Niggas ain't shit!"

Block had his hand on the trigger. "I'm waiting for the word. Fuck this nigga. He probably had a hand in it too."

"You right, Block. Fuck him! Tricky, get the fuck out the car. Count it as a blessing that you saved my girl 'cause if the only information you had to give me was of my mother—Boom! Nigga, you'd be history like that muthafucka Gator is gonna be. Muthafucka"—She formed a gun shape with her index finger and thumb—"just like that!"

"Ho-ass nigga, get the fuck out." Block didn't even wait until the car door shut to pull out. "Did you fuck dude?"

Fire pulled her chin to her chest, feeling like she'd slept with the enemy.

Block's cell vibrated against the flesh on his hip. He flipped his cell phone open and answered it, "Who dis?"

"Block, it's Radiance. I tried calling Fire, but she's not answering her cell. Is she with you?"

He handed his cell over to Fire. "Here. It's Radiance. Turn your cell phone on too."

"Hey, boo. I just heard what happened to you. I'm so sorry. Where are you?"

"They're transporting me to a hospital so I can get examined. Fire, that nigga raped me and fucked up my face!" she said, her voiced trembling. "They took pictures of me naked. Do you know how humiliating that was in front of all these police officers? Gator cut my face with a razor blade and poured alcohol in my open wounds."

"He's dead, Radiance, believe me!" Fire felt so responsible for dragging her into all of this.

"You don't understand. It burned so bad! I'm fucked-up for life." She began bawling out of control. "If you want to really get him, I've figured out a way."

"You name it, baby."

"You know the saying, You kill my dog, and I'ma skin—"

"Your muthafuckin' cat," Fire said, finishing her statement. "Hell yeah!"

"Well, Gator's mom is staying at the South Beach Plaza Bungalows on Collins Avenue, room 161. It's time to skin the cat, Fire."

"You're right! He said fuck you and my mom, so fuck his! Don't worry, I got it from here." Fire handed back Block the phone. "Block, I need you to find me a nigga that like to take pussy."

Block was motionless. He'd already heard the gist of the conversation. "I don't fuck with niggas that get down like that. What type shit is that to ask, Fire?"

"That nigga raped my mom and my girl. He has to pay. I got information where his mother is staying. I want the nigga to feel the same pain I feel every day when I go visit my mother."

"Damn, baby, that's a tough order to fill."

"Will you fuckin' do it, or will I have to find the next nigga that is willing? Either way, it's going down!"

"I don't know what you expect me to tell you. I told you already, I don't fuck with niggas like that."

"Get the fuck outta here. Every crew got one, if not two niggas, that like to take pussy. Now, who is it in yours? I need your help, Block. Don't do me like this!" Fire was losing every bit of rationality as she plotted. "Who can we get?"

"You are fuckin' crazy, girl!" He turned his head from side to side. "Damn, girl! I don't know why I'm gonna do this shit." He scrolled down his list of contacts and hit *V* for Vic, Cliff's younger cousin. "Vic, put me on the phone with ya Uncle Smitty. I got a job for him."

Vengeance Is Mine!

Vic and Smitty pulled up to the South Beach Bunga-lows, going straight toward the back to bungalow 161, their hats pulled down to meet their eyes. They passed the colorful seasonal décor of flowers arranged around the walkway.

"Nephew, it's up to you. You can stay in the room, or you can wait in the car while I do this."

Vic contemplated if he wanted to watch as his uncle took advantage of this woman, an elderly woman at that. "If I don't come, who's gonna take the pictures?"

Smitty smiled. Vic was becoming a man of his own kind.

They made it down the corridor and stood in front of the bungalow. To their luck the door was already cracked. On the television T. Garvin was cooking up a hell of a meal for his audience.

"Can I help you? I didn't call for help."

"Sure you did."

Smitty immediately locked the door behind them

and did what he was getting paid to do as Vic took pictures of the event.

After they left her sprawled out over the bed, Smitty got on the phone to contact Block. "The job is done, nigga, and I got proof. I need to meet you to get that dough. Where are you?"

"We're at the hospital. Meet us in the front in about twenty minutes." Block placed his cell phone back on his hip and embraced Fire. "I told you I'd come through for you. It's done."

The wicked grin on Fire's face acknowledged that she was somewhat satisfied.

"Now, let's go visit your mom."

Gator left tire marks on each corner he turned, trying to catch up with them. He ran every red light that warranted him to stop. They had gotten away, and so had Radiance. Gator didn't know what direction to head in. He parked the car three blocks from the hospital.

Tricky let her go. I'ma kill 'im when I see him! I won't ever see daylight if I get locked up. Tricky gonna have to die tonight for freeing that ho. I can't go to the hospital. I know she's contacted the police by now. Adrianne's gonna talk. I might as well go all out and kill everybody.

Tricky tried to yell down a taxi to get him safely out the area. This was the first time he'd been without a vehicle since he got his license at sixteen. Now he felt like a sucker for trying to be a Good Samaritan, allowing Radiance to take his car, a car that he needed desperately at this time.

On pure instinct, without the faintest bit of thought, Gator went for his gun when he saw Tricky walking down the street.

But Tricky was much too fast for him. He immediately noticed Gator and dodged around Gator's truck.

Clutching his gun, Gator pulled the trigger, and a bullet whizzed past Tricky's head. You could hear the loud clap from the pressure of the gun.

Then in one swift motion, Tricky released five consecutive shots, lifting Gator off his feet and landing him on the cement faster than a roller coaster.

Gator felt an explosion of pain as he hit the ground, followed by a brief spell of numbness. After which, his entire body began to ache all over, as he faced Tricky standing over him. "You were always a little jealous-ass nigga."

"Eat a dick!"

Tricky could've easily ended it for him, but that was much too easy. Even though he knew Fire was through with him, this was his chance for a truce.

He hit Fire's name on his cell.

So Fresh and So Clean

It was a struggle, but Adrianne managed to pull her eyelids open. Marcy and Cliff were right by her side. Cliff was in the extended chair with his neck back, snoring away. Marcy was exercising her fingers on the remote, trying to find a decent show or movie to watch as she relaxed in the chair next to the hospital bed.

Adrianne heard a bone in her neck crack as she turned to face Marcy. "*Oouuch!*"

Marcy snapped around and screamed, "Mom, Mom, you woke up!" waking Cliff up.

Meanwhile, Murphy led Stacey through the hospital's maze of corridors to the intensive care unit, where they stopped at Adrianne's room. "You better be glad I found you," he told her, "or else you'd be six feet under by now. Since you're well, you really need to see how Adrianne's doing."

"I don't know if this is a good idea, Murphy?" Stacey pondered after she'd done Adrianne so dirty.

"You owe it to her, Stacey. If God wanted her dead, she'd already be gone. At least pay your respects."

"Her daughters tried to kill me. What if they're with her?"

"Life is a gamble, and this is one risk of many you'll have to take."

Fire paced her disorderly abode in deep concentration, twirling her fiery red curls. She relied on controlling any situation she found herself in, and it was tormenting her to feel herself losing control. Even though she felt somewhat satisfied, she still had to explain to Marcy what truly transpired. The instant relief she felt still didn't erase the pain.

"I gotta see my mom first and then Radiance. You ready?"

"Of course, shaw-tay."

Fire couldn't wait to hear the sound of her mother's raspy voice. The anticipation of seeing her with her eyes open gnawed at her nerves. *Here we go,* she said relieved until she met Stacey and old man Murphy gaining enough courage to go inside her mother's room. *Where is the fuckin' security that Tricky said was out here?* Fire thought. *Lying-ass bastard!* "Where the fuck you think you going?"

Stacey stared at her in wide-eyed condemnation. "To apologize to your mother."

"Stay the fuck away from her, she don't wanna see you. I'll tell you what, take this card." Fire dug into the side pocket of her pocketbook where she placed the detective's card. "Call him. He has a warrant out for your arrest, and if he doesn't, you better hope he does. 'Cause you ain't gon' make it out of this hospital alive! Bitch, you better not open you mouth about me or my sister."

"C'mon, Fire, we'll deal with her later." Murphy put Stacey's wheels in reverse, and they moseyed back to where they came from.

"It's about time, dammit. I thought you gave up on your mom."

Fire shuffled around and lit up brightly when she heard Adrianne come to life. "Not on my life." Fire went over to give her an affectionate hug.

"I'll tell you what, my body isn't tired any more. I'm caught up on all the sleep I was deprived of when I was running the streets."

"I hope you learned your lesson this time," Marcy told her.

For about five more minutes they were able to talk openly with Adrianne, until Dr. Stevens and Detective Mayfield swarmed the room.

"Give us at minimum thirty minutes and you can re-join her," Dr. Stevens informed them.

Detective Mayfield stepped out of the room. "Fire, can I talk to you?"

Fire halted briefly. "Sure."

"Radiance wanted me to tell you she's okay. We took her to another hospital for a full examination. It's standard practice when a woman has been raped. She said she'd call you when she can. Question—did you know that Gator raped your mother too?"

It was standard bullshit talk to lure her to express herself freely. Knowing that she'd already talked to Radiance, she toyed with him just the same. "She never told us, but I had my way of finding out."

"Mmm . . . I wonder why she didn't tell you. Could it be because she knew you were going to seek revenge?"

"Me? I don't think so. That ain't even me," she said, leaving him standing there as calmly as he approached her.

She caught back up with Block, Marcy, and Cliff.

Marcy asked her, "What did the detective say?"

Fire still hadn't put her on to the trust, but it was time to. She took Marcy to the lounge area and discreetly explained to her everything that happened and what she'd done.

"Fire, I know you're hurt, but damn, you had his mother raped? I don't know if I would've gone that far. I woulda done something to him, but his mother didn't have shit to do with it."

"Did Mom? Did Radiance? You fuckin' right, I had it done, and I don't feel shit behind it. Fuck that nigga. We're gonna make sure he gets a hold of the pictures. That nigga gonna hurt the same way we hurt, sister."

"Yeah, but what"—Marcy glanced up at Block.

"Yeah, but what, my ass! What's done is done!" Fire felt her phone ringing. "Hold on, Marcy. Hello?"

It was Tricky on the other end.

"We'll be there in less than five minutes. It must be my lucky fuckin' day! Block, Cliff, come on, Tricky got that rapist cornered!"

Soon as they stepped outside Vic and Smitty were pulling up.

"Just in time, follow us," Block stated, going to get the car.

Time's Up

Block and Cliff watched as Fire and Marcy cautiously exited the car, looking up and down the street. Judging by their facial expressions and body language, anyone could tell they came to put in work.

"Come on, before one of them gets killed." Cliff waved on Vic and Smitty from his vehicle.

"I called you because, like I told you, I didn't have nothing to do this. Here's his gun. Do you wanna finish him off?" Tricky told Fire, but watching as the other men approached.

Gator was still on the ground, trying to pull himself up.

As Smitty got closer he recognized Gator's face. "Gate, man, what you done? What's it been, ten years since I seen you? I ain't too long ago get released. I heard you were out here wrecking shit."

Smitty had no idea that the woman he'd just raped was Gator's mother. They did time together in prison,

played on the same chess team, and even at chow together sometimes. They'd even discussed the women
that they'd raped, sharing the same views of them—
whores and bitches.

"Yeah, I'm on some same ole, same ole—get a bitch,
dick a bitch, ya know. I'm glad you're here. Man, help
me get outta here from these lil' punk muthafuckas."

"Wish I could, but I can't. I'm on some, make some
money and then fuck a bitch. I think this bitch you
might wanna see. It's ya momma." Smitty handed him
the photos.

Fire watched to receive the ultimate satisfaction. Instead, all she heard was loud laughter coming from
Gator. "Nigga, that ain't my mama, if that's what you
thought."

Puzzled, Smitty looked toward Vic and Block. *Then
who was it?* he thought to himself.

Just moments before they'd gone to South Beach
Plaza Bungalows, Cissy had spilled a tropical drink on
her bed and called for housekeeping to come strip the
bed. When the older dark-skinned Dominican woman
showed up in the standard blue khaki and white top to
change the sheets, Cissy decided to take a walk. Luckily
for her, she wasn't there, but sadly, the employee was,
and she was the one who got raped.

"Count it as a blessing. Don't worry, though," Fire
grumbled. "You'll never see her again. Block, let me get
that burner."

"You ain't got the heart, bitch," Gator said boldly.

Fire fought with herself. Every ounce of her soul told
her to shoot this nigga, but she couldn't bring herself to

do it. *All I have to do is flex one finger and he's gone. Boom! That's it.* Yet her finger wouldn't move. Her heart was pounding, her hand shaking, but she couldn't do it.

Marcy stepped up. "But, nigga, *I* fuckin' do. Give me the gun."

Fire had nervous jitters. "Seriously, Marcy?"

"As the day Mom up and left Brooklyn. Give me that shit!" Marcy snatched Gator's gun from Tricky's hand.

Gator tried to inch his body away. "All you hoes are the same."

"Not really. Some of us aren't afraid to fight back, rapist!" Marcy unmercifully shot him twice in the head. "One time for my mom, and one time for fucking up my peace. Now I can sleep good at night," she ranted hysterically, tears in her eyes.

"That's my kind of girl—shoot first, ask questions last. We out!" Cliff tussled Marcy to wipe her prints off the gun, and Vic and Smitty jetted from the scene.

Fire thought about Detective Mayfield's question. *No, it's not in me, but I didn't say it wasn't in my sister.* Fire nodded to Tricky and mouthed, "Thank you."

Cliff, Block, Marcy, and Fire rode in silence, engulfed in their own private thoughts. The shock and trauma of what had transpired was just beginning to settle, and reality was kicking in. They were scared, yet none of them would admit that except Fire. She could see the fear in their faces, which were like mirrors, reflecting her own fear.

On the Road Again

Radiance sprawled across Fire's bed and watched the two sisters pack piles of clothes in their suitcases. "Do you really have to move back?" she asked.

"Honey, I've had enough of Miami. I thought New York was the city that never sleeps. Shit, Miami is the city that literally keeps the heat. And up under ya ass too."

"I'll have to come visit some day."

"You know you ain't leaving Miami."

"And you know this! Besides, my girl is here with me. Isn't that right, Ms. Adrianne? We the number one stunnas in our rape support group."

"Indeed, we are. Who you think Fire and Marcy got it from? A little weight gain did me justice. I might find me a new man now."

Adrianne had been home from the hospital for three months successfully recovered. Her humor, as with Fire and Marcy, was great relief. It turned out that talking about her rape rather than keeping it to herself helped not only her but also others.

Fire studied Marcy as she gathered the last little bit of her things. She was concerned about her little sister. They hadn't talked about the shooting yet, and Fire wondered what kind of effect it had on Marcy. It must've been different for Marcy killing a man. She appeared unfettered, but Fire knew Marcy deeper than just the surface.

"It'll be good to get back to New York for a while, huh?" Fire stated, making small talk with Marcy.

"Yeah, hit up the old hood and see what boys grew up to be cute." Marcy smiled.

"I wonder what Africa's been up to," Fire said, referring to their cousin who they hadn't seen since they were little girls.

"Who knows? Let's get up with her when we get there. I heard cousin Zulu is hood rich. I can't wait to get up with that nigga."

Fire placed her hand on Marcy's shoulder and looked into her eyes. "Marcy, I know you're feeling fucked-up right now," she said openly in front of Radiance and Adrianne, "but you're not a killer. It only shows that you have heart. I understand if you don't want to talk about it, but try not to hold that shit in. It will fuck you up for life."

Marcy seemed as if she was going to brush off what Fire told her when Fire released her shoulder, preparing to get back to packing their stuff, but Marcy seized her arm. "Oh my God, Fire, I was so so scared. I was so angry when I did it, but now all I keep thinking is that I'm going to jail for life."

Marcy broke down crying, and Adrianne, Radiance, and Fire surrounded her, hugging her firmly.

"It's okay, Marcy."

"I can't believe I killed a man."

Adrianne wiped the tears from her younger daughter's face. "All right, Marcy, it's time to shake that shit off. What's done is done. You can't change that, but you can change your environment. Y'all have to leave from here. I'll be okay. I love this city. It's 'til death do us part." Adrianne held her right hand over her heart. "I'll be okay. Don't worry about me."

"I love you, Mom," Marcy said. "I know I don't tell you that often, but I really do." She used her palms to dry her eyes.

"Baby girl, you don't need to tell me. I know the both of you do."

"You think Tricky will come after you?"

"Hell no. He's harmless. I haven't seen him around anyway. He probably moved until the storm calms down."

All of them walked outside, and Fire and Marcy began placing their suitcases in Cliff's car.

"Mom, you need to stop being so stubborn and come back to New York with us." Fire opened Cliff's car door.

"You'd rather have me stubborn than a heroin addict."

"You ain't never lied about that! A'ight, Mom, first sign of trouble, we'll tie your ass up and force you to move back with us."

"Straight kidnap you," Marcy chimed in.

Adrianne hadn't smiled this much in years. "Promise me you will."

Cliff came up from behind and bear-hugged Marcy. "You're really leaving me. What am I gonna do without you?"

"Same thing you been doing, running ya women. Just ya main woman will be gone. I'm gon' miss you, Cliff. I guess now you can really play house with ya girl and ya two kids."

Cliff backed up off of her. "How'd you know?"

"Let's just say, I did some investigating the day you let me borrow your car. Take care of yourself Cliff. Oh, and when young Vic turn eighteen call me so I can break him into manhood."

"Get outta here, girl!"

"Fire, you ain't gon' say bye to Block?"

"For what? You know my motto—If they ain't passing dough, what the fuck you need 'em fo'?"

"Y'all know he took over Stacey's house, right. He gettin' all the money coming in there."

"Yeah, and he's gonna get all that time when they run up in there again." Adrianne winked.

SNAKE TO SNITCH

By
Mark Anthony

Chapter One

Mt. Vernon, New York—
Summer 2006
Don Pooh

My niggas, pull triggas, stack figures, whoa, whoa, whoa. Snitch niggas, broke niggas, not my niggas, no, no, no. In the club we sippin' Dom P., sittin' lovely, oh whoa, whoa. Sexy ladies goin' crazy 'cause the beats like whoa, whoa, whoa.

Those were the lyrics to one of the many Lil' Kim songs that the DJ repeatedly kept blasting through the speakers inside of Sue's Rendezvous strip club. The strip club was jam-packed with people. Usually on a Tuesday night, the most popular night for Sue's, the place would be packed wall-to-wall with just niggas, but on this particular Tuesday night, I would say that there was an equal amount of bitches and niggas.

No doubt, the reason the strip club was so packed was because Lil' Kim had just finished her month on house arrest and chose to spend her first weeknight of freedom celebrating with other celebrities at the world-famous New York strip club.

And just like her lyrics said, she was "sittin' lovely, sippin' on Dom P." Lil' Kim had to have had an entourage of about thirty people, and I figured that most of them were there to protect the half-million dollars of diamond-encrusted jewelry that she wore. She sat in the VIP area, having the time of her life, with other celebrities like Jermaine Dupri, Busta Rhymes, Zab Judah, Ed Lover, Buffie the Body, and Angie Martinez, to name a few.

But besides Lil' Kim and her celebrity friends, the other reason that the club was so packed was because it was the night of the highly anticipated strip contest between the best black female New York strippers against Atlanta's best. The Atlanta strippers had flown in for this special occasion to show their skills and to make money.

"Latisha, they killing us!" Lexi screamed into my ear over the loud music as she stood in her clear, slip-on sandals with a six-inch stiletto heel, and her all-white, slingshot, thong bikini. "They getting our money! That's our money they getting!"

"Fuck them bitches! Wait until we get on!" I hollered back over the music as I watched the Atlanta strippers do their thing. And, yeah, I had to give it up to the girls from ATL. They were straight-up freaks, and they had all of the guys and the girls in a frenzy as they shook their asses, made their booties clap, and worked the poles.

"Yo, I'll be right back!" I screamed to Lexi. I quickly walked off in my red, fishnet stockings, red thong, and high heels, and made my way to the dressing room in the back.

"It's on and poppin' tonight!" I screamed to the

other New York dancers who were in the dressing room as I opened my locker, knelt down, and retrieved my lighter and my primo. I quickly sparked the cocaine-laced blunt and inhaled it like my life depended on it.

"Jermaine Dupri got twenty thousand dollars in singles, y'all!" one of the dancers shouted to the rest of us as she applied baby oil to her body.

Latisha, hurry up and smoke this shit and get back out there and get that money! I screamed to myself. I took some more tokes on the primo, and within five minutes or so, I could feel myself getting nice.

"Latisha, let me hit that?" a stripper named Spirit asked me from across the room.

I inhaled on the primo and then looked over at Spirit. I motioned with my index finger for her to come over to me. As Spirit reached me, I exhaled. I was really starting to feel good.

"You want some of this?" I asked.

Spirit smiled and nodded her head.

"Open your mouth," I instructed her. I pulled real hard on the primo and held the smoke in my mouth. I pulled Spirit close to me, put my mouth right in front of her lips, and blew the smoke into her mouth. Spirit was a weedhead like me, and she instantly inhaled all of the smoke that I blew into her mouth.

"That's that shit right there!" Spirit yelled after exhaling the smoke.

I looked at Spirit and knew that I was now officially high. I knew that because her sexiness started to turn me on, and I usually get horny whenever I smoke. But I had to stay focused because I knew that there was a lot of money to get that night. Besides the tips and the money that I was planning on making from lap dances and from private dances, I was planning on winning the five-thousand-dollar grand prize for the top performing dancer. Yeah, there was no way that I was gonna let one of the girls from Atlanta come into my own backyard and take money out of my hands. No way in the world!

Just as I finished the primo and was going in my bag for another one, I could hear the DJ on the microphone calling for all of the New York dancers to make their way to the stage.

I wasn't as high as I wanted to be, so I took the other primo with me and made my way back into the main part of the club. I don't know how, but in a matter of like ten minutes—in just the time that I had spent in the dressing room—the club seemed as if it had become even more packed.

"Come on!" Lexi screamed to me over the music. "Let's show these bitches how we do!" she said as we made our way to the bar, past the bartenders, and onto the stage that was in the center of the club.

Lexi was much taller and much thicker than I was. Everybody called her Baby Beyoncé because she had the same complexion as Beyoncé, a big ass and big legs like Beyoncé, and a long, flowing, blond weave like Beyoncé. As for me, I was much smaller and more petite. If I had to compare myself to someone that was famous, I would say that I looked a lot like the porn star Heather Hunter, just with a shorter hairstyle. I'm light-skinned and short—just five feet tall—like Heather Hunter. But I definitely had much more ass than Heather Hunter, and my ass and my perky tits were my two best assets, which I had no shame in using in order to get mines.

As Lexi and I started dancing, the DJ switched up the song and started playing the Mobb Deep song with Lil' Kim. I loved that song, so when I heard it, it was like I lost my mind. I went crazy shaking my ass.

I must have been doing something right because I had a bunch of guys who started throwing money at me, so I continued on with my unrehearsed routine. But I still felt like something was missing, like I just couldn't get into a groove like I wanted to. I stepped off the stage for a moment, walked up to one of the bartenders, and asked her for a light so I could finish smoking the primo.

"Yo, ma, why you stop?" one of the guys in the club asked me. "You was doing your thing up there."

"I gotchu, sweetie," I said. "I'm going back on in a minute. Make sure you show me some love!" I yelled into his ear over the music.

"No doubt!" The cute, dark-skinned guy placed a fifty-dollar bill into my G-string. "Do something special for me, mama."

I retrieved the fifty-dollar bill from my waist and placed it in the small bag that I carried around to collect my money. Thank you," I said to show my appreciation for the large tip. "I got something special just for you."

That tip motivated me to quickly get back up on stage. And combined with the additional pulls from the primo, I was now feeling that looseness that I needed to feel in order to do my thing.

I started working one of the poles. I held on to the primo and smoked it while I worked the pole. Maybe the spinning on the pole was making me dizzy or something, but I was feeling high as hell all of a sudden. My eyes searched for the guy who had given me the fifty-dollar tip, and when I spotted him, I pointed at him and said, "This one is for you!"

He nodded his head and I continued to dance. I imagined myself being alone in a room with no one, except for me and him. And although it was against club rules to be completely nude, I didn't care, and I was high enough to want to break all of the rules. So without any more delay, I slipped out of my G-string and tossed it to the guy who had given me the fifty dollars.

The guy instantly reached into his pocket, as did a bunch of other guys, and they began balling up their money and throwing it at me. So I laid down on my back, spread my legs open, and started playing with my pussy and tapping on my clit.

"Right here! Throw that money right here and see if y'all can hit this!" I shouted to the guys. I then turned and looked at Lexi.

She was grinning from ear to ear and shaking her head, mouthing the words, "You crazy!"

Before I could blink, it was like the majority of the guys in the club were at my end of the stage and they were all throwing money at me.

The DJ then switched up the song and put on the Doo Doo Brown song. "Uh-oh, ATL, I think Latisha is about to give y'all a run for your money!" the DJ shouted into the mic. "Latisha, you gonna make that ass clap or what?" the DJ asked.

I then stood up, looked at the DJ, and gave the sign as if I was cutting my throat. I did that so that he could know that I wasn't gonna bite off of what the ATL girls had been doing. I was gonna do shit my own way, my Harlem-New York way. I looked at the DJ again, and then pointed at myself, and although he couldn't hear me, I yelled for him to watch what I was about to do.

Most of the eyes in the club were now on me, so I knew I had to do my thing. I danced for a little while longer as I thought about what I should do. Then it just hit me.

"Latisha, smoke that primo with your pussy and you will straight shut this place down!" I said to myself.

And instantly, without hesitation, I laid back down on the floor and placed the unlit end of the primo inside my pussy. I pulled my stomach muscles tight and contracted the muscles in my pussy. I held it for about ten seconds, relaxed my muscles, then pushed out, and a big cloud of smoke emanated from my pussy.

"Ohhhh!" The guys in the crowd went crazy, and they all started throwing money at me. The reaction was so crazy that most of the guys that were watching all of the other dancers left those dancers alone and ran over to where I was dancing.

"Yo, do that shit again! Do that again!" they pleaded.

I quickly honored their request and I used my pussy to take another puff on the primo.

"Yo, JD, I think you need to see this!" The DJ shouted for Jermaine Dupri. "They ain't doing this down in Atlanta, kid!"

Before long Jermaine Dupri had been ushered to the front of the crowd, and I did the pussy-puffing trick for him.

He smiled and nodded his head, and then he started just peeling off hundreds of one-dollar bills at me. He was doing it so fast that it looked as if he was peeling potatoes or something. The entire building was now going crazy, and I never felt better in my life. The rush that I was feeling was bananas.

At that point the DJ then switched up the music and started playing the remix version of the Ghostface song with Kanye West.

Somebody handed Jermaine Dupri a cordless microphone, and he started talking, saying that he had something for me. Then he asked the DJ to lower the music. When the music was lowered, he placed the microphone next to the butt of one of the ATL strippers, and she began jumping up and down. Her ass was clapping louder than anything I'd ever heard in my life.

Just that quick, the crowd turned on me and was now supporting the ATL stripper with the big ass.

"Whatchu gone do, Latisha? She calling you out!" the DJ yelled into the mic as he egged on a battle between me and the ATL stripper. He turned the music back up.

I turned to the bartender. "Yo, let me get a Heineken! Hurry up!" I shouted.

The bartender then placed a Heineken in my hand, and I danced around with it. I guzzled just about all of it in one shot, but I made sure to leave just a little bit in the bottle.

I held up the bottle, pointed to the DJ, and yelled for him to watch me as I pointed at the Heineken bottle and then pointed at myself. I was now high as a fucking kite.

"Don't hurt 'em now, Latisha. Five-O is right outside. Be easy!" the DJ joked.

I smiled, and then without hesitation I stuck the tip

of the Heineken bottle up my pussy and started walking around with the bottle hanging from my pussy.

It was past two o'clock in the morning, so most of the people in the club at that point were good and drunk. No one was shy about joyously voicing their pleasure with what I had just done.

But I wasn't finished. I lay down on my back and hoisted my legs and my ass up into the air. I gripped my ass cheeks with my hands and used my elbows to help balance myself as I let the rest of what was left in the beer bottle drain out and into my pussy.

Then I placed my ass back onto the floor, removed the beer bottle from inside of me, and I spread my legs wide open. Without warning, I forcefully shot all of the beer from out of me and onto the crowd.

"It's over! It's over! She shut it down! Lock the doors and everybody go home! Latisha has officially shut the place down!" the DJ shouted into the microphone.

As the crowd continued to buzz and go crazy and throw money at me, the DJ switched up the music and put back on that Lil' Kim song, "My Niggas."

My niggas, pull triggas, stack figures, whoa, whoa, whoa. Snitch niggas, broke niggas, not my niggas, no, no, no. In the club we sippin' Dom P., sittin' lovely, oh whoa, whoa. Sexy ladies goin' crazy 'cause the beats like whoa, whoa, whoa.

As the music blasted, people milled about, and as order was being restored to the club, Lexi came up to me. "Yo, Latisha, you are wild, girl! How the hell did you come up with that shit?"

Lexi was my roommate, I shared just about everything with her, and I trusted her and looked at her almost like a sister.

I smiled. "The cocaine and the weed made me do it. Yo, help me pick up all of this money! I'll hit you off when we get back to the crib!" I yelled to her over the music.

"Yo, ma, can I talk to you for a minute?" a tall, light-skinned guy asked me as he reached over the railing of the bar.

"Let me go to the back! I'll be right back," I said to the guy.

"How much for a private dance?" he asked as I quickly walked off.

"Twenty dollars a song!" I shouted as I smiled and looked over my shoulder at him. "But I'll be right back."

It took me forever to make it back to the dressing room because of all the male attention I was receiving. Telephone numbers and business cards were being handed to me, and everyone wanted to know if I was done for the night.

"Nah, I'll be right back," I said as I finally made it back to the dressing room, which was pretty empty at the time.

As I quickly rummaged through my stuff looking for a new outfit to change into, I could still hear the music blasting and the DJ still biggin' me up. There was no doubt in my mind that I was gonna walk away at the end of the night with the five-thousand-dollar grand prize.

But even though I was confident that I would win the grand prize, I knew that I had to quickly get back out there, get my hustle on, and get as much of that dough as I could get. I easily had to have made a little over a thousand dollars from just that short amount of time that I was on stage, but I couldn't rest because there was a whole lot more money to get.

I quickly washed down my pussy, threw some water on my face, chest, and arms, and then dried off with a towel. I sprayed Gucci perfume all over my body, applied some baby oil to my skin, and put on a brand-new outfit. A slingshot, G-string bikini similar to Lexi's, only, it was a different color.

When I emerged from the well-lit locker room and entered the dimly lit main floor of the elegant-looking strip club, there was a throng of guys waiting for me. But for some reason, the tall, light-skinned guy that had spoken to me before stood out to me and immediately got my attention. Maybe it was because he was about six-foot four, I don't know, but I spoke to him first.

"See, I kept my promise. I told you I would be back," I said to him. "So you still want that private dance?" I asked to the disappointment of the other guys that were waiting for me.

"No doubt," he replied.

I took him by the hand and led him to the VIP private dance area as I told the other guys that I would be back in a few.

I confirmed with the guy just before we entered the private area. "So it's twenty dollars a song, okay."

He reached into his pocket and pulled out a wad of money. There appeared to be nothing but hundreds in the bankroll. "I gotchu, ma," the guy replied and smiled at me.

The money that he flashed instantly brought a smile to my face.

"He's with me," I told the bouncer that was standing guard at the entrance to the private area. The bouncer quickly removed the rope and let us into the dimly lit room.

"So what's your name?"

"Don Pooh!" he replied over the loud music.

I nodded my head. "Would you mind if I took off my shoes? My feet are killing me."

Don Pooh didn't mind, so I quickly took off my stilettos and stood in my bare feet.

"I didn't realize you was so small," he said.

"Don't let my size fool you," I replied, and then I instructed Don to sit down on the pew-like, carpeted bench that was flush against the wall.

"Spread your legs and get comfortable," I said as I turned my back to him and began dancing real seductively for him.

"Yo, that routine that you did with the weed and the Heineken, that was crazy!" Don remarked in my ear.

I turned my head, smiled at him, and continued to grind on him. I knew he was liking what I was doing because I could feel his dick getting hard through his jeans. As I bent over, touched my ankles, and shook my ass in Don's face, I felt him put some money into my G-string. I reached my hand back, retrieved the money, and saw that it was a hundred-dollar bill.

"Thank you."

Don Pooh licked his lips seductively like LL Cool J and nodded at me.

"So, yo, tell me, what else can you hold in there?" Pooh reached between my legs and tapped on my pussy with his right hand.

Immediately I thought he was talking about sexing me, and that he wanted to know how big of a dick I could handle. Like most of the dancers in the club, I wasn't against fucking the patrons after I got off work, but they had to pay me lovely. There was no way I was gonna fuck niggas for free.

"It depends!" I shouted over the music and directly into Don's ear. I turned around and faced him.

"On what?"

I rubbed my fingers together with my thumb. "It depends on the dough! You feel me?"

Don nodded his head, and I continued on with my routine.

The DJ had to have switched up the music about six times by now, so in my head I knew that I was up to one hundred and twenty from this trip to the private area with Don Pooh.

Don Pooh then stood up, and with me not having on my heels, he had to bend down to talk to me so that I could hear him. "Yo, I ain't gonna hold you all night. But, listen, I'ma give you my number, and I want you to call me on some real shit. I wanna propose something to you where you can get like two *G*'s a week! Real talk!" Don shouted over the loud music.

I just looked at him, but I didn't say anything. I was used to guys telling me things like that. I would be rich if I had a hundred dollars for every time a guy asked me to perform in a porno movie.

"Yo, this is real talk!" Don reiterated to me. He probably could tell that I wasn't really taking him seriously.

I looked at him and then nodded my head.

Pooh handed me his number, along with two hundred dollars. "You gonna call me, right?" he asked.

I had to truthfully admit that I was probably gonna call him since he was talking about dough. Plus, he looked good as hell, so that was also gonna be an incentive for me to call him. "Definitely," I replied.

Don Pooh and I then parted ways, and I made my way back out to the main part of the strip club. Little did I know just how that meeting with Don Pooh would change the course of the rest of my summer, and impact my life in general.

Chapter Two

Harlem, New York
Latisha Lovely

Lexi and I shared a first-floor, two-bedroom apartment in a brownstone building located in a nice part of Harlem known as Striver's Row.

We didn't make it home to Striver's Row until about five-thirty in the morning. And when we did get home, we counted our money and ate the McDonald's breakfast that we had gotten at the twenty-four-hour McDonald's.

I had won the five-thousand-dollar grand prize, and I also now had the dubious distinction of being the top black stripper in New York and Atlanta! I gave Lexi fifteen hundred of the five thousand that I won, and yet I still had a little over sixty-five hundred that I had made from that very lucrative night.

"Yo, I wish every night was like this!" I told Lexi. "I can't believe that I made over three *G*'s on top of the money that I won."

Lexi had managed to make about fifteen hundred dollars from the club, and combined with the fifteen hundred that I had given her, she had about three *G*'s to feel good about.

We both knew that in the stripping business it was usually feast or famine. Like we could be making good money at a club on a regular basis and then come to work the next day and see that the club has been seized and shut down by the sheriff or the city marshal or some shit. Or we could hit dry spells where niggas wouldn't really be tipping, and we would only make like four or five hundred for the week.

So whenever there were good times where we made a shitload of money, we knew we had to treasure it because it could be a minute before we got any more real money.

When we finished eating our food, Lexi went to her room and came back with some cocaine. She loved to snort cocaine, and I liked to smoke it with my weed.

"Damn, girl, you ain't tired?!" I asked as I watched her snort a line of coke.

Lexi was only nineteen years old, and although I was only a year older than her, it seemed to me like she was too young to be doing the amount of drugs that she did.

"Nah, I'm good! Bitch, you know I can't ever go to sleep right away after we come back from the club," Lexi explained to me.

"Gotdamn, you a bad fuckin' influence!" I walked over to my bag, got a twenty sack of weed, and started rolling a blunt. "Got me smoking weed at six-a-damn-clock in the muthafuckin' morning!"

Lexi and I both laughed, and we continued to get

high. I turned on the radio and the television. Oprah Winfrey was on the Oxygen channel with a rerun of one of her earlier shows.

"Yo, she need to put us on that show!"

I looked at Lexi and inhaled my weed. "What the hell would we discuss on Oprah?"

"Yo, come on now, Latisha. Oprah don't never have anybody real on that show. She need to have some bitches like us on her show. Real bitches! Girls from da hood! You feel me?"

"Word, and now that I'm one of the top strippers in the country, we could show chicks how to really get money!" I said.

The weed was starting to kick in, and Lexi and I continued to talk shit.

Lexi thought I needed a new name now that I had newfound ghetto fame. "Latisha is too plain," she reasoned with her cocaine-influenced state of mind. "You need a name like Latisha Lovely or some shit like that."

"Yo, I actually like that!" I said.

We both laughed as I joked that Lexi and myself always came up with the best shit when we were high.

"Matter of fact, I'm getting that name tattooed on my ass cheeks tomorrow!" I blurted out.

Lexi spoke about how much cash Jermaine Dupri had at the club and dreamed about having a big baller like that to just hold her down. "Yo, word is bond! Latisha, if that was my man, I would fuck that nigga morning, noon, and night. I would just fuck him and spend money! That's it!" She laughed as she daydreamed.

That was when I saw Don Pooh's number lying on the counter. I relayed to Lexi how my encounter with Don Pooh went down.

"That nigga just wanna fuck you!" Lexi stated. "Call that nigga right now and if he's really 'bout it, tell him to put his money where his mouth is, and that your girl wants to be down with this getting-money plan."

Lexi was right. If Don Pooh was a real live nigga, then I would instantly be able to tell, but if he was just frontin' and wanted some ass, then I could get him out of my head and know that, if anything, he was just gonna be a one-shot fuck and that would be about it.

So without further delay, I grabbed my cell phone and started dialing his number. I put the phone on speaker so Lexi could hear what was being said.

When the phone rang about three times, I figured it was gonna go to voicemail, but before the next ring, someone picked up. There was a lot of loud music in the background.

"Hello?" I said reaching my head down toward the phone. I sat across from Lexi and the phone was placed on the island kitchen countertop.

"Yo, what up? Who dis?" the male voice on the other end asked as the music was turned down to a normal level.

"This is Latisha," I said into the phone. I was talking as if it were three in the afternoon, forgetting that it was still like six-something in the morning.

"Latisha from Sue's?"

"Yeah."

"Oh shit! What's up, ma?"

"Yo, I got my girl here wit' me right now, my roommate. She dances at Sue's too, and I was telling her what you told me at the club about the two G's a week. So I wanna know what's the deal with that, and can my girl be down?"

Before Don could respond, I blurted out that he was on speakerphone and that Lexi was in the room wit' me.

"Hey," Lexi said into the phone.

"Yo, what's up?" Don Pooh replied. "Listen, this is the thing, I can't really talk about this shit on the phone. I'd rather talk about it in person. And, Latisha, your girl can get with it, but on the real for real, don't talk to nobody else about getting this money! Just keep that shit quiet," Pooh said in a serious-sounding tone.

"Pooh, all I wanna know is if you just gaming me and trying to get some ass, or if you are serious about this money!" I said into the phone.

"Yo, ma, I'm driving a Rolls-Royce Phantom. I'm about this money. This ain't got shit to do with no pussy. Like I told you in the club, this is real talk."

Lexi looked at me, nodded her head, and gave a look like she approved.

"A'ight. I'm just saying I wanna hear you out, but I wanted to sift through any bullshit," I replied.

"I feel you. Listen, why don't we hook up this afternoon and we can talk. And if you and your girl is wit' it, then we can make this happen. Where do y'all stay at?"

"We on West 139th Street," I replied.

Lexi immediately started mouthing the words no and giving me the cutthroat sign.

"In Harlem?" Pooh asked.

"Pooh, this is Lexi. Why don't we just meet in the city

somewhere later on. Like at The 40/40 Club or something like that?"

"A'ight, I'm cool with that. So like at six-thirty tonight I'll meet y'all at The 40/40 near the bar."

"Okay, we'll be there," I replied before we ended the conversation.

"Yo, don't let that nigga know where we live at!" Lexi yelled at me. "We gotta feel his ass out first."

I nodded my head because I knew she was right. Then I took a drag on my blunt and watched as Lexi did another line of coke.

"So what you think?" I asked Lexi.

"The nigga claims he's driving a Phantom, so if that's true, then he must be getting money."

I looked at her and didn't respond. I was ready to head for the shower and then get in my bed.

"We'll see later tonight what's what," Lexi added.

I walked out of the kitchen and made my way to the shower so that I could get some sleep. While most everyday people were probably just getting up and headed to work or to the train station, I was doing the reverse. My day was just ending, and I couldn't wait for the nighttime to come so that we could link up with Don Pooh and see just what was poppin'.

Chapter Three

Pussy Smuggling

What I'd come to learn from living with Lexi during the past two years was that she was a wild girl and that I could just about expect anything from her. I had also learned that she was loud as hell when it came to sex, and sex was something that she never could seem to get enough of.

Needless to say, I wasn't surprised when the sounds of Lexi's screaming and moaning woke me up out of my sleep. It was a little past four in the afternoon, so I wasn't too annoyed at having been woken up, because the fact was that I needed to get up and get myself together so we could meet up with Don Pooh at six-thirty. I had planned to go straight to Sue's Rendezvous after we met up with Pooh, so I knew that I had to get things cracking.

"Lexi, we gotta get up outta here in like an hour!" I yelled as I made my way past her bedroom and into the bathroom. She didn't respond to me, but I knew she heard me.

"Goddamn! Why didn't I wash this makeup off my face before I went to sleep?" I yelled at myself.

I hated the way I looked after sleeping with makeup on. It just always gave me this real tired and dusty look, not to mention the raccoon eyes that I had. But the thing I hated the most was washing off the makeup. It was a gotdamn pain in the ass, but at the end of the day, the makeup added to my looks, and my looks were helping me to pay the bills, so I had to deal with it.

By about five-thirty or so, I had finished getting myself together. Lexi's jump-off had left the crib, and I was waiting for her to get ready so that we could bounce.

"So, what you think this nigga is into?" Lexi asked me as she started running the shower water.

"I don't know. He probably opening up some new club or some shit, or wants to manage us and he'll have us doing bachelor parties or some shit."

"Nah, I doubt that," Lexi said as she stepped into the shower.

Just then my cell phone started ringing, and I picked it up. "Hello?" I said. I didn't recognize the number.

"Yeah, Latisha, what's up? This is Pooh. I got your number off of my caller ID."

"A'ight, so what's good witchu?"

"Y'all still coming through, right?"

"Yeah, we getting ready now," I said.

"Cool. I'm just saying, I'm coming all the way from Long Island, and I didn't wanna waste my time," Pooh stated.

"Pooh, yo, no disrespect, but don't fucking stress me like this! Word!" I barked into the phone.

"Ma, I'm not stressing you. I'm just saying I don't

wanna waste my time fighting through this traffic and you don't show up!"

"Look, if I wasn't gonna show, I would have called your ass and told you that. You got me running out to The 40/40 Club on some ol', blind, let's-get-money bullshit, and now you stressing me? Nigga, I should be stressing you to find out if this shit is even worth it!" I screamed into the phone as my nerves were getting worked over. If there was one thing I hated, it was some bitch-ass shit, and Pooh was definitely sounding like he was on some bitch-ass bullshit.

The phone was quiet for a moment.

"A'ight, so yo I'll be there in like forty-five minutes," Pooh said.

"And we'll meet you at the bar like we said we would," I replied before ending the call.

Before long, Lexi had made her way out of the bath-room and got herself ready in no time. We smoked a blunt together before heading out the door and jump-ing into Lexi's BMW X5 truck. We soon navigated our way to the West Side Highway and were on our way to Twenty-fifth Street.

When we reached the club, we parked in one of those expensive-ass parking garages and made our way up the block and over to the club. Both Lexi and I were wear-ing some skintight Seven jeans, a tight wife-beater, and high heels. Lexi's wife-beater was white, and mine was black.

"Yo, I swear to God if this nigga is on some bullshit, or if this nigga starts stressing me again, I will straight em-barrass this nigga up in here!" I said to Lexi emphati-cally.

Lexi didn't respond, and the two of us walked into the club and made our way over to the bar. It was just approaching six-thirty, so we were on time.

I looked around the club and didn't see Pooh. "Yo, where the fuck is this nigga at?"

Fortunately, just as I was about to lose it, he came walking up to me and touched me on my waist. "Yo, what's up, y'all?" he asked.

"I was just about to call yo ass and curse you out when I didn't see you," I said to Pooh in a non-threatening manner. For some reason Pooh looked more thugged-out than I remembered him looking when we were in the strip club, but maybe that was because I was high as a kite when I was in the club.

"Pooh, this is my girl, Lexi. Lexi, this is Pooh."

Pooh and Lexi said hello to each other, and we made our way over to the bar.

"Yo, what y'all wanna drink?" Pooh asked.

"Straight Henny," Lexi responded with her ghetto ass.

"Let me get some champagne," I replied.

Without hesitation Pooh ordered a bottle of Hennessy along with a bottle of Moet, and he instructed the bartender to bring bottles to us in the Remy Lounge, which was a private VIP room in the club.

We made our way to the Remy Lounge, where there was a big plasma screen television, pool tables, a huge leather bed, leather couches, and small tables. About ten other people were in the room at the time. All of the people, we would later find out, were cool with Don Pooh.

"I reserved the lounge for us. I figured it would be

better than talking at the bar and having niggas all up in our face," Pooh said.

I was definitely feeling the vibe of the room. I had been to The 40/40 before, but I had never been to this particular room before. The music was bumpin', and it was a good look.

Within minutes our bottles of Mo' and Hennessy had arrived in buckets of ice, and Pooh poured us some drinks. While we drank, Pooh decided to walk us around the room and introduce us to everybody else that was in the room. While I was being introduced to everybody I figured that the time was as good a time as any to christen my new nickname. So with the first two people that Pooh had introduced me to, I made a point to correct him and tell him and the person that I had been introduced to that my name was Lovely.

Pooh caught on quick and for the rest of the night he made no more mention of my government name, Latisha.

After the introductions were over, Pooh, Lexi, and I made it back over to the small table where we had been sitting. We sat in leather chairs and continued to drink our drinks.

As soon as we sat down, Lexi gave me this look that said, "Let's hurry up with this shit."

"A'ight, Pooh, so what's the deal, my dude?" I asked him. I could now feel the Moet kickin' in and my head starting to get nice.

Pooh pulled his seat closer to the table so that he would be closer to us, and then he began to speak. "A'ight, here's the deal. Y'all ever heard of Wyandanch before?"

Lexi and I both shook our heads.

"It's a town out in Long Island. It's one of the livest parts of Long Island, and the thing is, I got the whole town on lock. You feel me?"

Lexi and I both just looked at Pooh. I was sure that, like me, Lexi had no idea where Pooh was going. "Nah, not really," I said. "Pooh, just shoot straight with us. You ain't gotta talk in codes and shit. Just talk!"

Lexi took another swig of her Hennessy and nodded her head in agreement.

"What I'm saying is, in terms of all of the weight that moves through Wyandanch and much of Long Island, it moves through me," Pooh added for clarification.

"Oh, okay. I feel you now." I now knew that Pooh was referring to drugs. "So how do we get paid? What's the deal?"

Lexi pulled her chair closer to the table. It was obvious that Pooh now had her attention.

Pooh reached into his pocket and pulled out two small, orange-tinted bottles that looked like they were used for holding prescription pills. He handed one to me and one to Lexi. "Open it up," he told us.

Lexi and I opened up the small bottles and immediately we both knew that we were looking at cocaine.

"That's coke," Pooh confirmed, "and it's the best shit on Long Island." He paused. "Now if y'all wit' it, this is how y'all can get paid. All you gotta do is take bottles just like these, smuggle that shit into your pussy, right, and then take it into Nassau County Correctional Facility, Suffolk County Correctional Facility, and Rikers Island. Y'all could hit one jail a day. I would tell y'all who to go visit. Y'all would show up like you on a regular prison visit, and while y'all sitting down talking, you would push the bottle out of your pussy and then under the table just hand the bottle off to the person that I would tell y'all to go visit. Now all of the bottles hold two ounces of coke. I would pay y'all two hundred dollars for every ounce, so with two ounces in each bottle that means I would hit y'all off with four hundred dollars for each visit that y'all make!"

Pooh poured himself some more of the Hennessy and looked at us, waiting for our reaction.

I looked at Lexi and nodded for her to speak. The deal sounded good to me, but at the same time, I didn't want to seem too eager.

"Yo, on the real it sounds good, but for only two hundred an ounce"—Lexi shook her head and looked at Pooh—"I don't know."

I could see the tension in Pooh's face.

"Pooh, word is bond, if we get caught with that shit, we looking at some serious jail time, so—"

"But you won't get caught!" Pooh said, cutting me off.

"It's gotta be at least three hundred an ounce, or I ain't fuckin' wit' it," Lexi said in true hustler fashion.

Pooh smiled and looked at both of us. "Y'all know how to get that money! A'ight, look, two fifty an ounce. Y'all would be coming off with five hundred a day!"

I slowly nodded my head to show that I was with it. Lexi smiled at me to show that she was with it, but I still didn't want to seem too eager. Plus, I didn't know Don Pooh from a whole in the wall. I mean, for all I knew, he could be a snitch or some shit, so I knew that the best thing to do was to tell him that I would get back with him.

"Pooh, everything sounds good. I definitely wasn't expecting for you to come at us with this, but it's all good, though." I told him. "I'm like ninety percent wit' it, but just give me like a day or two to think about shit and get back to you on it, a'ight?"

"What you gotta think about?"

It was like me and Lexi had our brains fused together because we were both thinking on the same track.

"What she gotta think about? Pooh, no disrespect, but my girl don't even know you! She gotta think about the shit to see if we should go through with it or not. It ain't like you asking us to deliver money to somebody! You asking us to bring work into a gotdamn jail! Let us think about it and get back to you."

"Pooh, it's Wednesday. Just come through Sue's on Friday night, and I'll let you know what's what," I said as I got up from the table.

"A'ight, that's cool," Pooh stated. "Just keep shit quiet. Friday night I'll come through."

With that, our meeting ended.

Lexi and I had some more to drink, and we mingled and talked with some of Pooh's people, and with one of the bartenders. But we bounced at like seven-thirty so that we could go get something to eat and then head to Sue's. We were hoping on getting there by like nine-thirty or ten.

As we drove back to Harlem, heading for a soul food spot called Amy Ruth's, Lexi and I spoke at length about Don Pooh. Lexi just found it strange that Pooh had randomly picked me for his smuggling-by-pussy operation.

"If I hadn't been high and doing all that freaky shit with my pussy, then the idea probably would have never crossed his mind," I told her.

Lexi and I both still wanted to do our homework, though, so we decided to start calling around and asking anybody and everybody that we knew if they'd ever heard of Don Pooh and if so, what was his history. The last thing that we wanted was to be messing with some rat-ass informant nigga who was trying to set us up to get his ass out of some kind of sling with the police.

"Lovely,"—Lexi looked at me and smiled because she was using the new nickname that she'd branded me with—"if this nigga checks out, then I say we do this shit. But yo, since I was like fourteen I've been fucking wit' real live street cats, and I can tell that this nigga Don Pooh ain't really real!"

"What you mean?"

"The nigga is soft and we can play his ass, I'm telling you. Look, if we do this, he is saying between the two of us we'll have four ounces of cocaine a day and he'll hit us off with five hundred a day. That ain't bad, but all we gotta do is take an ounce of cocaine off the top and keep that shit ourselves, and then just add back some baking powder or laundry detergent or some shit. And if we do that, then we would really come off. We could break down that ounce into grams and sell it for one hundred dollars a gram to the chicks in the club, and off one ounce we could be getting like twenty-eight hundred dollars!!! You feel me?"

"Girl, I think you had too much of that damn Hennessy back at The 40/40," I said. "And that nigga will find out and murk both of us!"

"Lovely, he won't find out! And even if he do, he ain't got it in him to murk shit!"

I turned up the music in Lexi's truck because I wasn't really trying to hear what she was saying.

Lexi reached forward and turned the music down. "Lovely, look at it like this—If we do this shit for the nigga, we can't do the shit for too long. We can't do it for more than like a month because if we do, we would just be pressing our luck. But within a month's time, if we take an ounce a day, we could have a whole kilo! And if we sell that kilo at retail, we would be looking at enough dough to go down to Atlanta or something and buy a townhouse and just chill!"

I looked at Lexi. I knew how headstrong she was, but I also knew how wild and reckless she could be. I decided to trust her anyway. "A'ight, girl, I'll trust you. If we can check around, and if Pooh checks out, then I'm with it. But you better know what the hell you doing, 'cause I ain't trying to get killed."

"Lovely, I gotchu, I gotchu! You know your girl would never steer you wrong." She smiled and turned up the volume on the radio.

Chapter Four

Time 2 Get It Poppin'

By the time Friday had rolled around, Lexi and I had completed our homework on Don Pooh. We had been in touch with some dancers who were from Long Island, and they were able to give us Don Pooh's stats. Basically what came back was that Don Pooh had been running with street niggas ever since he was in his teens. He was never the brutal street-thug type, but everybody respected his mind and his savvy, and everyone knew that he knew how to make money.

All of the people that Pooh ran with since the late eighties and early nineties had either been killed or were locked up doing life sentences. So sort of by default, Pooh had inherited his position and status. He had the respect of the younger generation because he was an OG who had lived through and experienced the glory days of the crack era. He was around at the time when the rapper Rakim, also a Wyandanch native, was at his peak. Don Pooh had seen all and lived through it all, and aside from a one-year state jail sentence, he had managed to make it through the fire practically un-scathed.

The main thing that Lexi and I were relieved to know was that Don Pooh wasn't a snitch-ass informant or any-thing like that. The fact that he did have a rep gave us the confidence to go through with the plan. So when he came to Sue's that Friday night, we basically let him know that everything was a go.

"Pooh, the only thing, though, is we gotta get our dough up front if we gonna do this," Lexi said to him as we sat off in a corner of Sue's.

Without hesitation Pooh reached into his pocket, pulled out a wad of cash, peeled off five one-hundred-dollar bills, and handed them to me. Then he peeled off another five one-hundred-dollar bills and handed them to Lexi. The straight-up look on Pooh's face basi-cally confirmed to me that he was definitely about busi-ness.

Pooh then told us that he was gonna call his man so that he could get us the ounces in the prescription bot-tles.

"It'll take him like about an hour to get here, but we got time," Pooh said, being that it was only two in the morning. "So Monday, Lovely, I want you to go to Nas-sau County Correctional Facility out in East Meadow, Long Island, and, Lexi, I want you to go to Rikers. The way we gonna do it is the two of y'all will never go to the same location on the same day. We gotta keep mixing it up so that nobody will get hip to what we doing," Pooh explained.

Lexi and I both nodded our heads as we listened to Pooh.

"And understand this. There is risk involved in this shit. So what I'm saying is this, if y'all get bagged, just fucking keep your mouth shut. Don't say shit to the cops!" Pooh warned.

"We gotchu," Lexi said as she sipped on her drink. Then she spoke up again as if she wasn't fazed at all about the potential risks. "Pooh, we gonna hold you down. Just do what you gotta do, get us the work, and you already gave us the dough, so we straight there. Call Lovely and give her the names of who you want us to see, what time you want us to go, and we'll knock it out, a'ight?" Lexi took another drink from her glass.

After she finished the drink, she put the glass down, smiled, and told us that she had to get back to the main floor so that she could get her money. "Lovely, you better come on and get this money, girl! Pooh, when your man gets here, just let us know. We ain't leaving until closing time." Lexi grabbed me by my hand and led me back to the bar area of the strip club.

One thing about Lexi, she knew how to get that money. She was a hustler in the realest sense of the word.

Chapter Five

Fast Forward—Late August 2006
Snitch Niggas

We were two and a half weeks into our drug smuggling operation, and things had gone off without a hitch. Lexi and I were getting paid easier and faster than we both could ever remember.

Actually, though, there was one incident that spooked Lexi, which I didn't want to give too much weight to or cause to allow more drama than necessary. Unfortunately, Lexi wasn't trying to hear my point of view.

"Lovely, I'm telling you we are outta this shit from right now. Somebody is snitching us out and we gonna get bagged, I'm telling you! I can feel it!" Lexi stressed to me as we sat in my Cadillac Escalade on 125th Street near the Magic Johnson movie theater.

"We been doing this shit for like two weeks. Everything has been moving along like it ain't nothing, no problems whatsoever. Shit is smooth as hell. Going through the metal detectors was never a problem. Getting frisked was never a problem. But outta nowhere a gotdamn K-9 police dog just pops up? Lovely, that shit wasn't no coincidence. I'm telling you, somebody was trying to set me the fuck up!" Lexi barked.

It had to have been her tenth time recounting the story to me about what had happened to her when she went to make a drop at the Nassau County Correctional Facility. She had gotten spooked because after she made it through the metal detector she noticed that there was a police dog on the other side of the detector that was sniffing people just before they were let into the jail's main visiting area.

Lexi reasoned that the dog had to only be sniffing and checking for drugs, since no one was allowed to bring bags or anything like that into the jail. Therefore, the dog couldn't have been sniffing for bombs. Plus, all of those types of personal items had to be checked into lockers prior to getting to the point of the metal detectors, so what other type of contraband could the dog have been searching for?

Lexi explained to me that when she saw the K-9 her heart dropped to her feet, but she was able to think quickly enough on her feet, telling one of the corrections officers that she had to go back to her locker to check her bag to see if she had lost some money that she couldn't account for.

Needless to say, once Lexi retrieved her bag from her locker, she got the hell up outta dodge with a quickness.

"Lovely, if that fucking dog had sniffed between my legs, I would be locked underneath the damn jail right now!"

Lexi always went with instinct, and her instincts were telling her to leave this whole drug shit alone. We managed to pimp Don Pooh for about a half a kilo of cocaine by stealing an ounce off the top of what he had been giving to us to smuggle for him. She was convinced that it was time to bring our scam to an end, but I wanted to keep a good thing going.

As we pulled out of our parking space and headed toward our crib, Lexi's cell phone rang.

"Fuck! This nigga keep stressing me. Why don't he stop calling me!" Lexi vented. She was referring to Pooh, who she'd been dodging for the past day and a half ever since she got spooked at the jail.

"Lexi, just speak to the nigga!" I yelled at her. "I can't keep telling him I don't know where you at. Plus, it's Tuesday night, so you know he gonna be up in Sue's tonight. You don't need him up in there stressing you."

"A'ight, shit!" Lexi reached into her bag and grabbed her cell phone. "Hello!" she said with a bunch of attitude in her voice.

There was a pause, as the person on the other end of the phone must have been talking.

"Hold up a minute! Calm the fuck down!" Lexi screamed into the phone. "First of all, either you or one of your boys is a fucking snitch because how the fuck out of the clear blue is there a fucking K-9 waiting near the metal detector to sniff between my fucking legs?!"

There was another pause. I could hear the voice on the other end, but the words were not audible. All I knew was that whoever was on the other end of the phone was definitely screaming like he'd lost his mind. I was sure it was Pooh, and I knew that he had to be upset at the fact that Lexi had just up and disappeared on him without contacting him.

"Yeah, whateva, nigga!" Lexi said before hanging up the phone.

"That was Pooh, right?" I asked.

"Yeah, that was him and his bitch ass! He talking about I'm fucking up his money! Nigga, fuck you and your money!" Lexi vented in the car as if she was speaking directly to Pooh.

Before I could say a word, Lexi spoke up and continued venting. "The nigga ain't say nothing about the K-9 drug-sniffing dog. All the he concerned 'bout is his two ounces of cocaine and shit. That's how I know he fronting or something!"

No sooner than she finished speaking did my phone start ringing.

"Latisha!" Pooh screamed into the phone, my new-found nickname suddenly thrown out the window.

"Yeees?" I asked sarcastically with raised eyebrows. In my mind I was like this nigga better calm the fuck down and stop with the yelling. I wanted to tell him to bring it down a notch. But he was pissed off and I could hear it in his voice.

"You with Lexi?"

"No," I lied.

"You know where she at?" he asked, still screaming.

"Nah, I ain't seen her."

"Muthafucka!" Pooh shouted. "Yo, that bitch just hung the fucking phone up on me! And word is bond, Latisha, I ain't got no issues with you, but can't nobody fucking disrespect me like that! Now the thing is, all of a sudden can't nobody find this chic, yet she got two ounces of my shit with her!"

"Pooh, listen, just calm down. She just got scared when—"

Pooh cut me off. "Latisha, don't tell me to calm down! That bitch is playing with my fucking money, and all I know is that you introduced me to her ass, so now this shit is your problem too!"

"Whoa! Whoa! Hol' up!" I said, about to get ghetto on Pooh's ass.

"Nah, fuck that! Latisha, you better find your fucking friend and she better have my shit, or she better have six *G*'s for me! Word to my life, I will fuck somebody up!"

"Yo, I don't know what to tell you. I ain't seen her, so I don't know," I said. My tone was changing just a bit, and my sense was kicking in, telling me that maybe it wasn't the smartest idea to be testing Pooh's gangsta.

"Latisha, find your girl and have my money or have my shit, that's all I'm saying!" Pooh hung up the phone.

All the while Lexi was in the background motioning for me to hang up the phone on him.

"Too late. He just hung up on me," I said to Lexi.

"Yo, now the nigga saying he want six *G*'s or his shit or else somebody is getting fucked up!" I relayed to Lexi.

"Fuck that bitch-ass nigga," Lexi calmly replied as she turned up the volume on the radio and listened to DJ Clue on Power 105.1 FM.

I reclined back a bit in the driver's seat of my truck and maneuvered toward our apartment. This type of drama was not what I wanted or had envisioned. And the last thing I wanted was for Pooh to be up in my face or in Lexi's face at the club. Although there were bouncers and security to keep us safe, I just didn't need the drama.

"Lexi, you know the nigga gonna be up at the club tonight?"

"So, we just tell the bouncers not to let his ass in, or to bounce his ass up outta there, and we just do us and get our money!" She then reached in her bag, got some of Pooh's cocaine, and started snorting some of it.

"Six *G*'s. Yeah, I got that nigga's six *G*'s all right. That shit is right here going up my fucking nose!" Lexi sat back in her seat, turned up the air conditioning, and bopped her head to the Chamillionaire song.

I simply blew air out my lungs. I kept driving and didn't respond.

Chapter Six

Bitch Better Have My Money

By the time Lexi and I weaved our way through the congested Harlem traffic and made it back to our block on 139th Street, Lexi was high as a kite from the cocaine she'd been snorting.

We had to hurry up and get ready so we could get to Sue's. We were already running behind schedule. I was fortunate to find a parking space that was only about five houses away from our house. I quickly parked the truck, and we got out and made our way up the steps to the front door of the immaculate-looking, brownstone building.

As we walked, Lexi started loudly reciting the lyrics to one of Ne-Yo's songs. "She makes the hairs on the back of my neck stand up! Whaaat! That is my shit right there! I love that song!" Then she continued to sing the chorus to the song. "Sexy love, girl, the things you do keep me sprung, keep me running back to you . . ."

Just as I was literally unlocking the front door and Lexi was in the middle of her loud singing, a white 745

BMW came to a screeching halt in front of our house. The front and back passenger doors burst open, and Don Pooh and some other big, black, ugly-looking dude stormed out of the car.

"Latisha! What's the deal?" Pooh yelled as he came running toward us, his man following right behind us.

"Ahh shit!" I said to myself. My heart started pounding. I was desperately trying to hurry up and push open the door. I was jiggling to get my keys out of the hole, but it seemed like they were stuck.

"There go that nigga Pooh!" I said to Lexi, who still had her head up her ass from the coke.

"Latisha!" Pooh screamed. He was now right at the bottom of the steps.

Finally I got my key from out of the lock and pushed the door open. I wanted to quickly close it behind me and lock it. "Come on, Lexi!" I grunted and grabbed her to pull her inside so I could close the door.

"Get off of me!" Lexi shouted back at me as she shook her right shoulder loose of my grip. "I ain't scared of this muthafucka!" Lexi slid out of her high heels and was in her bare feet, ready for war.

I needed this like I needed a hole in my head.

Pooh was now at the top of the steps. He reached to grab Lexi, but she sidestepped him and swung and punched him in his face as if she was a dude.

"Bitch, I will fuck you up!" Pooh screamed. He looked like he was stunned that Lexi had swung on him.

"Lexi, come on!" I urged.

"You owe me fucking money and you swinging at a nigga?" Pooh screamed, "Bitch, where is my shit?" and came at Lexi again.

"Nigga, fuck you!" Lexi pushed Pooh in the chest. She definitely had caught him off guard and off balance because Pooh went hurtling backward into his man, and then the two of them went hurtling down the entire flight of concrete steps.

The sight of Pooh letting out a yell and then him and his man hurtling down the steps was too comical, and it also shocked me. Lexi wasn't exactly a small girl. She was healthy in all the right places, and she had muscle tone to her body, not to mention the fact that she'd been with so many street niggas in the past, niggas who used to beat on her, that she had experience when it came to fighting dudes as if she was a dude. Still, I knew it was definitely time for us to boogie, get our asses inside, and call some niggas over that we knew so they could help us get out of this jam.

I asked myself, *How the fuck did Pooh know where we lived at?* But there was no time to ponder that question.

"Lexi, come on in here! Let's call Mike! Get in here!" I screamed.

Lexi was in pure fight mode and wouldn't listen to me. "You want your shit, nigga?" Lexi screamed at Pooh. "Here, take your shit!" She opened up the prescription bottle that held the cocaine and threw it into the air, causing a big, white, dust cloud to appear. She literally had just thrown thousands of dollars into the wind.

"You gonna try to snitch my ass out and then get gully with it?" Lexi screamed as she stood barefoot at the top of the steps.

"Lexi, get in here!" I wrapped my arms around her

waist and pulled her inside. I was a small girl, so I had to use all of my strength to move her and her blowed ass.

Finally I got her inside of the main foyer area and was able to close and lock the door.

No sooner had I closed the door than Pooh and his man were banging on it like they were going to break it down. I went with Lexi into our apartment and locked the door and immediately called this bouncer named Mike who lived in Harlem. He was like six-foot seven and nothing but jailyard muscle. And he was an expert in karate.

As the phone was ringing, I could still hear Pooh and his man trying to break down the door. "Lexi, you are so fucking crazy!" I said. I couldn't help laughing as I thought back to the sight of Pooh knocking over his man and falling down the steps.

Mike's phone went to voicemail, and I left a message for him to hurry up and call me back. I was thinking about calling this African dude that I used to fuck wit', but before I could say or do anything else, the neighbor from upstairs came out of her apartment and was yelling at Pooh and his man, telling them that she had called the cops and that they had better get their asses from around here before they got locked up.

"And don't come 'round here no mo'!" the eighty-something-year-old lady from Alabama yelled through the door. She must have scared off Pooh and his man, because the banging finally stopped.

As soon as Pooh and his man and whoever else was in the car had driven away, our neighbor came knocking on our door. She was wearing a housecoat, and although it was still early evening, she looked like she was dressed for bed.

I answered it.

"Baby, you okay?" Sister Reynolds asked me.

"Yeah, we both okay," I said to Sister Reynolds, even though Lexi was talking real loudly and ghetto on her cell phone to somebody in the background. "I'm sorry about that. It's just, I mean, you know how guys get way too upset at times?"

"Yes, baby, I know!" Sister Reynolds said with her Southern drawl, sounding all concerned like a plantation worker from the days of slavery. "What's your name again, baby? Is it Latisha?"

"Yes, it's Latisha."

"Look, I knows how these young people are today. And I know it is different from when I was young. And Sister Reynolds definitely don't wants to be in yo' business, but I gets worried aboutcha, you and your roommate. You two come in half-dressed, late at night and early in the morning, all hours of the night, and it just don't look good, and, baby, I don't think it's safe. I mean, I worries aboutcha and I prays to God for ya. Just be careful because you can't be bringing all these different mens in here likes you do and not expect one to be crazy or something. And then I hears ya when you and your man friends are having relations, and, Lord, I likes to die! I mean it sounds like somebody down here getting killed or something," Sister Reynolds said.

I wanted to laugh as loud as I could laugh, but at the same time I wanted to crawl under a rock from embarrassment. I couldn't believe that Sister Reynolds had just pulled our card like that, but I knew enough to be respectful.

Just as I was about to say something else, Sister Reynolds spoke up again. "Yeah, I mean, I knows this ain't none of my business, but sometimes I says to myself, it just don't take all that doggone screaming and hollering! And if it do, then you can't handle it and shouldn't even be having sex."

At that I couldn't help but cover my mouth and laugh. In my head I was like, *Okaaaaay!* I reached and gave Sister Reynolds a hug, and thanked her for her concern and for calling the cops. I assured her that Lexi and I would be okay, and that we would try to watch who we brought around and what times we came in. I also told her that we would do a better job at keeping the noise down when we were having sex. I really wanted to rat out Lexi and tell Sister Reynolds that it was Lexi who was the screamer and not me.

Anyway, I went back into our apartment and calmed Lexi down. I also told her that we probably shouldn't go to Sue's that night, not until we figured out exactly what we were going to do about Pooh.

While we spoke, our doorbell rang and my cell phone also rang. The cops were at the front door, and Pooh was calling me on my cell phone. I simply let the cell phone go to voicemail and decided to go deal with the cops. I definitely didn't want Lexi talking to them because she would have gotten our asses locked up or something.

I was real diplomatic with the cops. I explained to them that my roommate and her boyfriend had gotten into a yelling match, but that he'd left already and everything was okay.

The two young, black cops seemed to care less about why they'd been summoned to our house and more about flirting with me. But there was just way too much drama going on at the time, and I wasn't trying to waste my time fucking with no twenty-five-thousand-dollar-a-year cops.

So I soon made my way back inside. I listened to my voicemail. Pooh was venting about how I lied to him and told him that I didn't know where Lexi was at, but meanwhile I came strolling up the steps and into my apartment with her. He then made it perfectly clear that he thought that the both of us were trying to play him like a bitch and that we both had better watch our backs from here on out.

I played the message for Lexi, who was only concerned about getting to the club that night and making herself some more money. She reminded me that we were still holding a half-kilo of cocaine that we had to get rid of, which was gonna make us all kinds of money.

"Lovely, stop thinking about that nigga! You see how I knocked his clown ass down a flight of fucking steps, right?"

I looked at Lexi while she poured us drinks.

"Here, drink this," she said. "Calm your nerves, and go get ready so that we can go to Sue's. Girl, we got money to get and you the top stripper in the country right now. You know niggas is coming to check for you!"

I had to admit, she did have a point about me being the top stripper and all, so I downed my Hennessy and headed for the bathroom to get ready.

Chapter Seven

In The Words of
Notorious B.I.G. . . .
They be sittin' in your kitchen, waitin'
to start hittin'

The rest of that week flowed smoothly. In fact, more than a week had gone by without Lexi or me hearing a word from Pooh or any of his people. There were no phone calls, no visits, no nothing. I still hated the fact that Pooh knew where we lived, and I realized that the way he had known where we lived was when I had slipped up and accidentally told him the street that I lived on during our first phone conversation.

If there was one thing that I had learned from my years of growing up in the hood, it was that bad boys moved in silence. And since I knew that, I was beginning to feel a bit uneasy about Pooh's sudden disappearance from the radar.

Lexi and I took no chances, though. She already had a small .22 handgun that she kept and often traveled with. I never was the gun-toting type. I was always the switchblade and can-of-mace-carrying type. But something told me that it was probably a good time to start packing some heat, and that was exactly what I did. I purchased a chrome .38 revolver from one of the bouncers at the club. My plan wasn't to carry the .38 around with me everywhere I went, but I knew that I had to protect myself where I rested. And since Pooh and his people had violated the space that Lexi and I shared, I knew that he was liable to do it again.

In addition to getting my hands on a .38, during the past three days I had taken a page out of Lexi's note-book, bringing home or inviting over different guys that I knew. The guys were jump-offs that I knew would lead to nothing but booty calls, but at the same time I felt safer just having a dude in the crib with me just in case Pooh decided to show up.

One night, the third Friday in August to be exact, Lexi and I decided to try out this strip club in New Jer-sey called Uncle Charlie's. We'd heard that it was a spot where we could make some good money, so earlier in the week we made arrangements with the owner to dance there, and when Friday came around we headed there to see what was what.

Uncle Charlie's was a'ight, and we did make some money, but it wasn't the type of money that Lexi and I were used to making on a Friday night. So when Lexi approached me with a quick-money proposition, I guess that I was primed to go along with it.

"Lovely," Lexi said into my ear while I sipped on my drink near the bar.

"What's up, hon?" I replied.

"Yo, you see the dark-skinned dude standing over there near the DJ?"

"The one with the blue Yankee cap on?"

"Yeah, him."

"What about him?" I asked.

"Okay, now look at the dude standing over there near the private dance area, the guy in the white Yankees cap."

"Damn, them niggas look just alike!" I shouted to Lexi over the loud music. "So what about them?"

"They identical twins and, get this, both of them just got drafted into the NFL! Fucking first-round draft picks!" Lexi said it with so much excitement in her voice that you would've thought she was about to cum on herself or something.

"Say word!"

"Word is bond! But, Lovely, here's the thing. I told them that me and you were sisters, right? And we was just talking and kicking it, and they was like twenty-five hundred if me and you would bounce with them right now."

"Twenty-five hundred each?" I asked.

"Nah, we'll split it, but I'm saying it ain't really popping in here like we thought, so we might as well go and get this money."

"So they wanna fuck?" I asked after finishing my drink.

"Nah, they just wanna give us twenty-five hundred for a kiss on the cheek! Lovely, of course they wanna hit!"

I looked at the two guys and then I thought about it. They were cute, the money would be a good thing, and they had something going for themselves in terms of the NFL, so there was a possibility that we could start seeing them on a regular. The liquor was talking to me, and if we brought them back to our crib in Harlem, then they could be the night's booty call and provide us with protection at the same time.

"Lovely, you wit' it or what? That shit would be crazy. I ain't never fucked twins at the same time before! And the niggas look good, and they got money! I know you don't like bringing niggas to the crib that you don't know, but we good. These niggas ain't trying to fuck up no NFL money by doing some stupid shit. We good, Lovely."

"A'ight, I'm wit' it," I said as I smiled.

Lexi was like a spoiled kid that loved to get her way. She instantly got happy when I told her that I was wit' it.

I didn't want things to seem obvious to the other dancers, so I told Lexi that we should just go get dressed separately and then go to the car separately, and that the twins should leave the club before we did and just sit in their car and wait in front of the spot.

"Okay," Lexi said with a big Kool-Aid smile on her face as she ran off in her high heels to seal the deal.

Reggie and Ronnie, the two first-round draft picks, followed us in their black Range Rover, as we left the club and made the forty-five-minute trip back to our apartment in Harlem.

I stopped my car when we reached the front of our house.

Lexi rolled down the window and motioned for the twins to pull up alongside our car. "We live right here," she told them, "so just find any place to park and then walk back. We gonna look for a spot to park too."

"Yo, there is no way to tell the two of them apart. They look just alike! I wonder if their dicks are the same size," I said to Lexi, and we both burst out laughing.

"Lovely, you are too crazy! You know I was wondering the same damn thing!" Lexi said through her laughs.

We both were still feeling nice from the drinks that we had at the club, so I knew that was adding to our crazy sense of humor at the moment.

We found a parking spot that was about two blocks away from the house. It worked out good because the twins also found a spot on the same block.

Lexi unlocked her passenger door and got out of the car after. "Let's go put it on them."

Lexi and I waited for Reggie and Ronnie to finish parking and when they were done, we all made our way up the block and toward the house.

"So what position do y'all play?" I asked.

Reggie replied that he was a cornerback, while Ronnie stated that he was a wide receiver.

"Lovely, kill all of that football talk. You know you don't know shit about fucking football. Yo, y'all are fine as hell and all, but before we go any farther, I think we need to take care of business first."

"Out here?" one of the twins asked.

"Yeah. Pay us the fucking money first, or y'all niggas ain't coming in the crib! I'm just saying, business is business."

"We gotchu, ma." Reggie smiled and pulled out a knot of cash.

It was approaching three-thirty in the morning, and we were just reaching our front door.

"Lexi, we ain't gotta be passing money around out here like that. We can take care of that shit once we get inside."

Lexi was cool as hell, but at times she just didn't know how to roll with shit and set shit up for future use. With her abrasive-ass ghetto mouth she was liable to piss anybody off and rub people the wrong way to the point where they wouldn't want to deal with us anymore. Shit, according to Reggie and Ronnie, they had both just received signing bonuses, which combined to more than five million dollars, so I knew that they weren't stressing paying us no twenty-five hundred-dollar chump change.

"A'ight, but I'm just saying, I hope niggas don't think they fucking for free," Lexi said under her breath as I unlocked the front door and turned on the light in the foyer.

"So, this is where we rest at," I said to Reggie and Ronnie, trying to take their attention off of Lexi's ghetto ass. "Don't make no noise until we get into our apartment," I said in a whisper tone to Reggie and Ronnie. "Our neighbor upstairs has been complaining about the noise,"

"Fuck the neighbors!" Lexi brushed by everybody, her heels click-clacking as loudly as could be on the shiny hardwood floors.

"Lexi, you a wild girl," Reggie said and smiled as I unlocked the door.

Before the door to our apartment was even opened all the way, Lexi started in again about the twenty-five hundred dollars.

I shook my head as I walked across the living room to turn on the light. While I was reaching to turn on the light, I was about to ask Reggie and Ronnie if they wanted something to drink. I mean, I wanted them to feel at home and comfortable because I was no dummy, I was looking at this sex rendezvous as the start of a potentially lucrative relationship if we played our cards right.

"Don't nobody say one muthafuckin' word! Nobody move and nobody gets hurt!" A guy in a ski mask held a gun so close to my head that I could feel the coldness of the steel resting against my temple.

The door that we had just entered slammed shut, and I heard the locks being put on. *What the fuck?* I thought, my heart racing as fast as lightning.

"Yo, it's locked. We good!" another voice said, which I couldn't make out.

I was literally starting to sweat.

Ronnie barked at his brother, "Reggie, I told you these bitches was setting us the fuck up! I told yo' ass!"

The guy who was holding the gun to my head said to Ronnie, "Money, shut the fuck up!" and smacked him upside the head with the butt of the gun, instantly dropping him to the floor.

Since the gun was no longer at my head, I was able to turn and look toward my kitchen. I could see two guys sitting on fucking folding chairs, wearing ski masks.

Ain't this some shit! I was wondering why Lexi was so quiet, but then I turned and saw her in a chokehold by some big, muscular, prison yard-looking dude. "Get the fuck off of my girl!" I yelled and charged the guy that was choking her.

I was immediately stopped dead in my tracks by the same guy who'd earlier put the gun to my head. He grabbed a fistful of my hair, yanked me hard to the ground, and put his gun inside my mouth. He barked, "Bitch, you must wanna fuckin' die on some hero shit!"

In all, not counting Reggie and Ronnie, there were about five guys in my apartment looking to do us some serious harm, and I knew in my heart that it was behind that bullshit with Don Pooh. I wondered if he was in the room at the time, but I couldn't tell because everybody was wearing masks.

From the ground I could see one of the guys walk from the kitchen into my living room, and the bitch had the nerve to be eating a gotdamn sandwich that I know he'd made from my refrigerator.

He walked right up to Lexi and spoke. "This can be hard, or this can be easy. Give me my man's shit, or give us the loot. How you wanna do this?"

The guy holding Lexi loosened his grip so that she could speak. Lexi looked like she was having a hard time swallowing, but in an instant she hacked up some phlegm and spat right into the eyeball of the guy's ski mask. "Fuck you, nigga!" she screamed and kicked the guy right in the balls. He immediately doubled over in pain.

One thing I could say about Lexi was that she knew how to fight, and the girl had heart.

The guy holding the gun to me began yelling and telling his people to stop talking to us and playing games, and to take everybody into the bedroom. "Hurry up. Move!" he barked.

We quickly did what he said as Lexi, Reggie, Ronnie, and I all scurried toward Lexi's bedroom, which had been ransacked. I was wondering if my room had also been ransacked.

"Everybody get the fuck on the ground and lie face down!" one of the guys demanded.

We all did as he instructed, and in my mind I had this awful feeling like we were about to all get murked.

Reggie seemed to have the same thing on his mind as he spoke up, sounding like a straight bitch. "Look, I don't know what's up, but—"

"Yo, money, I said shut the fuck up and lie down on the ground!" one of the guys yelled as he kicked Reggie to the ground.

"We got dough," Ronnie blurted out. "How much y'all need?"

There was silence, and then Ronnie continued. "We just got drafted into the NFL. We can get y'all some dough, if that's what y'all after. Just chill for a minute!"

Aww damn! Why the fuck did he say that? I thought.

One of the other guys immediately began checking Reggie's and Ronnie's pockets.

"Jack-muthafuckin'-pot!" the guy yelled, holding wads of cash in the air. "Yo, are these real?" the guy asked, referring to the jewels that Ronnie and his brother both had on. "Yo, Pooh, come check this shit out!"

So that bitch-ass nigga is up in here.

One guy, who I felt had to be Pooh, came over to where we were lying down on the floor and began examining the iced-out watches and the iced-out chains. He also took hold of the large sums of cash.

Pooh decided to take off the ski mask that he was wearing, perhaps because his cover was blown when his name was revealed. "Y'all are two lucky-ass bitches," Pooh said to me and Lexi. "These two niggas just paid y'all shit in full!"

Pooh had this ugly-ass smirk on his face that I just

wanted to slap right off. "So then bounce up outta here then!" I said in a tone of disgust.

Pooh looked at me and smiled a sinister smile.

"Yo, you gotta love it!" he screamed into the air. "You gotta love it!"

I didn't know what he meant by that, but then he continued. "I ain't never seen nobody with as much balls as you and your girl. First, y'all snake me for my shit. Then y'all try to play me like some chump-ass, clown-ass nigga, and now I'm up in your crib with a gun to your head and y'all still trying to call the shots! 'So then bounce up outta here then,'" Pooh said in a mocking tone.

"This is *my* gotdamn house now," Pooh yelled, "and we ain't leaving until *I* say we leaving."

Pooh then menacingly walked around the bedroom, looking at pictures that had been thrown to the floor, looking through Lexi's clothes, and opening her closets. He was doing a damn good job at being totally disrespectful to our living space. And surprisingly, Lexi managed to keep her mouth shut.

"Yo, tie these bitches up," Pooh said. "We got some fucking to do."

My nervousness had disappeared after Pooh got his money, but when he said those words, the nervousness instantly reappeared.

The remaining four guys quickly gagged Reggie and Ronnie, hogtying their ankles to their wrists and leaving them inside Lexi's room, where one of the masked men stood watch over them with a gun, and Lexi and I were quickly shuffled off into the bathroom.

Pooh laughed. "Y'all tried to fuck me, so now it's my turn to fuck y'all."

I knew exactly what he meant, and I was damn sure gonna do my best to make sure that I at least tried to talk my way out of getting raped. Lexi was still surprisingly quiet.

"Pooh, that is some real bitch-shit," I barked at him. "Raping a bitch? You know niggas on the street and in jail don't respect niggas who gotta take pussy."

"Shut the fuck up!" Pooh then nodded at his henchmen, who immediately came toward us and attempted to gag me and Lexi.

But Lexi and I both were not trying to hear that, so fists and feet were flying everywhere. There was an all-out brawl in our bathroom with me and Lexi fighting off three big-ass goons.

Pooh just stood back watching and barking orders. "Hurry up and stop playing with these bitches!"

Before long the goons, who were way bigger and much stronger than me and Lexi, managed to subdue us. They had our mouths gagged and were literally stripping off our clothes.

"See, I don't rape bitches!" Pooh stated while me and Lexi continued to struggle with the goons. "Bitches give me what I want!"

"Go to hell!" I shouted in vain, since my voice was muffled due to the washcloth that was stuffed inside my mouth and a bandanna tied around it.

Pooh leaned up against the wall, like he was Joe Cool or somebody. "There is a big difference in taking what you want, and bitches giving you what you want!" Then he gave the orders to hogtie me and Lexi.

Lexi and I were butt-ass naked at this point. One of the goons quickly left the room and returned with two extension cords that they used to successfully hogtie my ankles to my wrists, and they did the same to Lexi.

"I like my shit clean. I can't deal with no smelly-ass, sweaty pussy! Nah, hell no," Pooh barked. "Y'all been up in these clubs letting everybody get at y'all and putting Heinekens and weed and all kinds of shit up in your pussies! Y'all gots to clean them bad boys before I slide up in there!" Pooh said rather matter-of-factly. He was definitely amusing his boys, which was evident by their laughter.

Lexi, on the other hand, didn't find anything funny as she was trying her hardest to yell something that was totally inaudible.

Pooh walked over to the shower that was attached to the bathtub and turned on the water. "Put they asses in here," he ordered.

Lexi and I were both quickly scooped up and placed into the bathtub, where the warm water instantly began to splash off of our bodies as it rained down from the showerhead above us.

Before long, the warm water turned to hot, and Lexi and I both began to voice our discomfort, squirming and trying to yell through our gags and bandannas.

Pooh and his boys just looked on and laughed.

The water had gone from warm to hot then to the point of scorching hot. I knew that Pooh purposely had not blended the cold water with the hot.

"Ugggggghhhh!!!!" Lexi and I both screamed and violently yelled.

The hot water was causing so much pain that I thouhgt, even with the gags in our mouths, people could hear us from blocks away. We squirmed to try to avoid the water hitting us, but our feeble attempts to shield ourselves were in vain. We were now getting scalded by the water, which was also starting to steam and fog up the bathroom.

"Ugggggggggggggghhhhhhhh!!!!" I screamed even louder through my bandanna.

At that point I knew how lobsters must feel when they were thrown into a pot of boiling hot water to be cooked alive. The hot water was beyond unbearable, and I was more than ready to declare Pooh the winner of the war that he was waging against me and Lexi. But as Lexi and I were getting boiled alive, Pooh and his boys continued to just laugh.

Then Pooh grabbed the extendable showerhead, stretched it out, and aimed it directly at our asses and our pussies. "Yeah, I gotta make sure I get all up in the cracks and crevices!" he told his man. "You can tell these bitches don't take baths or showers, with the way they reacting to this water," he said laughing.

"UGGGGGGGGGHHHHHHHH!!!!!" I screamed as the scalding hot water made contact with my ass and pussy. By far that was the worst pain imaginable. It was far worse than the pain of the water hitting me on my back, arms, and chest. The only relief was when Pooh aimed the showerhead directly at Lexi instead of me. That gave me about fifteen to thirty seconds of comfort until it was my turn yet again to get scalded.

"We got some fucking to do, fellas!" Pooh unbuckled his pants and pulled them down, exposing his boxers.

Then one of his boys asked if he should put some soap on our bodies.

"Nah, just hose them down one more time."

His boy then took hold of the showerhead and aimed it at me and Lexi, resuming the torture and our screams of pain.

Then out of nowhere I heard the loudest boom. It seemed to come from our living room and sounded like a gun blast. I just knew that more than likely either Reggie or Ronnie had been shot.

"What the fuck was that?" Pooh asked, as him and his boys all ran out of the bathroom to see what had happened. Unfortunately they left the water running, and it continued to scald me and Lexi, who continued to scream.

Then we heard another loud gun blast. All I could do was think the worst, and think how we'd managed to end two NFL careers before they even started.

"Latisha? Baby, is you okay?" I heard Sister Reynolds ask.

"Put the gun down, lady!" Someone else yelled.

"What y'all doing in here? Where is Latisha? Latisha, baby, is you okay?" I heard Sister Reynolds screaming out and asking me.

I tried my hardest to scream back, but my screams of pain were in vain.

"Lady, I said put the gun down!"

"I ain't putting down this gun until the cops get here and straighten out what's going on!" Sister Reynolds yelled back.

I was so happy that she'd decided to play nosy neighbor that day.

"Yo, old bitch is crazy!" Pooh said. "Come on, y'all. She fucked around and called five-O."

Before long I could hear the entire apartment go silent. The water was still running on to me and Lexi, and we were both numb to the pain at this point. Then I looked up and saw Sister Reynolds poke her head into the bathroom. To my complete shock and surprise, she was carrying a long, double-barreled shotgun.

"Oh, Lawd Jesus, help me! Baby, what done gone on here?" Sister Reynolds came over to the bathtub and turned off the water. "I hears all kinds of yelling and carrying on, and I's don't want to be nosy or nothing, 'cause I knows you and your roommate likes your man friends coming over, but I just says something ain't right. What y'all doing in this bathtub tied up like this?"

"Mmmmmmmhhhhhhh," Lexi and I both grunted through our bandannas.

Luckily Sister Reynolds got the hint and immediately began trying to untie the knots to set us free from our hogtied position.

"NYPD!"

"Oh, thank the Lawd!" Sister Reynolds shouted as she got up to go confront the police, who were shouting from my living room and hadn't made their way back to the bathroom or the bedrooms.

The extension cords that had been holding us captive were finally loose enough for me to wiggle my hands free, and I was able to finish loosening the knots completely. I could hear the police walkie-talkies getting closer to the bathroom, and almost as soon as Lexi and I got to our feet and removed the bandannas from our mouths, the cops entered the wet, steamy bathroom.

"Lovely, word to my mother's grave," Lexi yelled with

no regard for the cops standing in the bathroom, "that nigga Pooh getting his ass fucked up tonight. I'm calling Hassan, and if we got to drive out to Long Island or wherever, it don't matter, 'cause I am gonna personally kill that muthafucka!"

"Ma'am, I'm Officer Lacy, and this is my partner. You live here?" the uniformed cop asked. "Can you tell us what happened?"

"Yeah, them stupid muthafuckas ran up in our shit and they gonna get fucked up—That's what happened." Lexi stormed out of the bathroom butt-ass naked, screaming about her skin being burned and asking where the hell was her cell phone.

One of the officers followed her out of the bathroom and into her bedroom, while the other officers stayed and questioned me and Sister Reynolds.

"Yeah, it was five of 'em," Sister Reynolds relayed to the cops. "They were wearing black masks, and they had guns. It looked like they dragged two fellas outta here and they had 'em tied up."

My heart instantly sank, realizing that Pooh and his boys had bounced with Reggie and Ronnie. "Oh my God!" I said as I winced in pain from the third-degree burns that covered my body. I quickly told the officers who the two fellas were that had been tied up.

Apparently he recognized the names of the two promising NFL stars-to-be, and asked me if I was bullshitting him.

"I'm dead-ass!" I said to the white officer, hoping he was hip to the slang.

He told his partner what I'd said, and his partner immediately got on his walkie-talkie, asking for a sergeant to come by. He relayed to his dispatcher that he needed an ambulance and that two top NFL draft picks, Reggie and Ronnie Allen, had possibly been kidnapped, and were also two of the four victims of an apparent home invasion.

While he and his partner were doing their thing, the sun was just starting to come up.

I decided to put on some clothes because I knew that with the cop relaying that Reggie and Ronnie were involved in a robbery and possible kidnapping, it was only just a matter of minutes before the news media and a whole slew of detectives showed up at our crib. I didn't want them looking at my naked body, not unless they were paying me anyway.

"Nah, I ain't going to nobody's fucking hospital!" I heard Lexi screaming. "I need you to get yo' ass over here right now with the heat! Tell Rollie and James and all them niggas you roll wit' to meet you. I want this nigga Pooh dead tonight!" Lexi screamed into her cell phone. "Yeah, the cops is here, but so fucking what? Fuck them!"

Not that it hadn't already been confirmed in my head before, but listening to Lexi screaming into the phone, I knew right then and there that it was gonna be a long-ass day and that the drama was just getting started.

Chapter Eight

The Code of the Streets

Lexi went against the cops' advice and refused to go to Harlem Hospital to get her burns checked out and treated by a doctor, but I decided to go. I was treated there for third-degree burns on my back, arms, legs, feet, and hands.

I could live with the burns to those parts of my body, but the thing that I couldn't deal with was the third-degree burns on my ass! Of all places, I couldn't believe that my ass was burnt! I made money with my ass. And from what the doctor was saying, there was eventually going to be blisters and scarring, so needless to say, I instantly started stressing.

What was wild was that I really couldn't even focus on tending to my burns and getting better because detectives and a swarm of news media was in my face as soon as I was ready to leave the hospital. The media wanted to know if my roommate and I were strippers and if we set up Reggie and Ronnie. The one that really got me and made me laugh through my pain was when one reporter asked me if it was true that my roommate and I were gold-diggers.

I didn't get a chance to answer any of the reporters' questions because two detectives, one white and one black, basically scooped me up and asked me if I would come with them to the precinct to answer some questions. Considering that I wanted Pooh and his people locked the fuck up for what they had done to me, I decided to accompany the detectives back to the precinct to see what was what.

When we first arrived at the precinct, everything was all good. They did their best to make me feel comfortable by offering me something to eat and some coffee to drink.

"Nah, I'm good, but thanks for offering." I wanted to hurry up and get to the questions so that I could get home and figure out what the hell I was gonna do about all of the burns on my body.

"So, Miss . . . uh, I'm sorry, but I never got your last name," the white detective said.

"That's because I never gave it to you. Just call me Latisha. That'll be fine."

The detective nodded his head and then asked me to recount everything that had happened the previous night.

I went right into how Lexi and I had decided to go to a club that night in New Jersey.

The black detective interrupted me with, "What club?!"

I gave him a stank look. "Does it matter? It was just a club."

"Look, Latisha, we are trying to help you, so we need you to be as detailed as possible."

"Uncle Charlie's. The name of the club is Uncle Charlie's," I said, never adding it was a strip club.

"Okay," the detective said. "So explain to me how you go from a club in New Jersey to your apartment in Harlem with two football stars who end up kidnapped in the process."

What the fuck? I remember thinking to myself. The way the detective asked the question just didn't seem to sit right with me. I smiled and then I replied with my own smart-ass remark, "Okay, look, Uncle Charlie's is a strip club. You got a bunch of horny-ass niggas up in a strip club staring at half-naked women all night long. What kind of mood do you think that puts most niggas in? Come on now, it ain't rocket science!"

The black detective, with his foul-ass breath, got all up in my face. "I'm gonna ask you again," he said with a twisted look, "and this time stop with the bullshit and answer me straight up. How do you go from a club in New Jersey to your apartment in Harlem with two football stars who end up kidnapped in the process?"

"Wait, hol' up! First off, if I didn't tell y'all that they were NFL draft picks, y'all wouldn't know that shit! That's the first thing. And for you to be all up in my face barking on me like I set them up or something, I don't appreciate that shit! Why would I set them up and then tell the police who they were? That don't make much sense, now do it? So we can all just cut the bullshit. Y'all aren't concerned about what happened to me and my roommate and protecting us and keeping our asses safe! Hell, nah, y'all got your own fucking agenda! I'm outta here!" I said and then got up from my chair.

There was silence from both detectives. They were

silent because they knew I was right and had pulled their cards.

The white detective ran up to me and gently took hold of my shoulder. "Look, Latisha, we are concerned about what happened to you and your roommate. There is just a certain procedure in how my partner and I investigate. All we're doing is asking you preliminary—"

I cut the detective off right in the middle of what he was saying. "Look, I'm not stupid. If I keep talking to you and your partner, then the next thing I know is that me and my roommate will be locked the fuck up on conspiracy or some other bullshit charge. I'll speak to my girl who is a lawyer, and she'll contact you, a'ight?" I said and kept it moving.

"Latisha. Latisha!" The detective yelled out, but it was no use.

I knew it was time to bounce. I had seen it all too many times before where the cops just twisted shit around and niggas got caught out there on some ol' okey-doke bullshit, facing life in the pen.

I figured that going back to my apartment probably wasn't the best idea. I wanted to head to one of my girl-friends' houses so that I could nurse my burns and figure out what the hell my next move would be. I was really in a lot of pain, and that was my main concern at the time.

Before long my cell phone rang, "What's up, girl?" I said to Lexi.

"Where the hell you been? I been calling you over and over."

"I went to the hospital to get these burns checked out, and then I went over to the police precinct and—"

"What the fuck you go to the precinct for?" Lexi barked. "We don't need the police to handle our business. We got this."

"Lexi, look—"

"Nah, Lovely, stop with that snitch shit! You know the code of the streets. You know we can't be talking to the cops!"

"Lexi, niggas was sitting in our crib eating our food and damn near raped us!"

"Exactly! And that's why Pooh's ass is getting killed. Now what's the name of that town in Long Island where he rests at?"

"Lexi—"

"Lovely, just tell me the name of the town!"

"First of all, Lexi, stop fucking screaming at me! My skin is killing me right now, and I don't need this bullshit, a'ight?"

"Latisha, we getting ready to roll on this nigga and you playing games."

"What are you talking about, Lexi? I ain't playing no games!"

"So give me the name of the town, and we'll handle this!"

"Lexi, I ain't with this. This whole shit is getting crazy."

Lexi chuckled into the phone and then she mocked me. "You ain't with this? Yo, you know what, I'm out. I can't talk to you right now 'cause you straight about to piss me the fuck off!"

"Lexi—" I said into the phone, but unfortunately it was in vain because Lexi had already hung up on me.

I just stood there staring at the phone and shaking

my head. This whole thing had spiraled way out of control, and Lexi was straight instigating it and not using any common sense.

I was real frustrated because, in a way, I felt like Lexi sparked all this drama when she came up with that whole scheme to steal from Pooh. And she was acting real ignorant!

Nah, I couldn't deal with this shit. I had my burns to nurse, and then I had to figure out how in the hell I was gonna support myself considering that my ass—my money-making rump shaker—was gonna be blistered up and unsightly for God knew how long.

Forget the code of the streets, I thought to myself. I had to look out for myself, and I knew just exactly how to do that.

Chapter Nine

Dancing at the Bar to Passing the Bar

Most people have heard of how a lot of strippers dance at night at strip clubs and make money. The strippers often justified what they did by saying that they were in college and that was how they were putting themselves through school. Well, my girl Andrea was living proof that stripping to pay for college definitely worked.

Andrea used to dance right alongside me at Sue's Rendezvous until early in the morning. Only thing, she was using her money to pay for college, and then for law school, while I was blowing mine on cars, clothes, and niggas.

Yeah, Andrea had managed to graduate from Columbia Law School and had gone on to become a successful defense attorney with a major law firm in New York City. But she never forgot where she came from. At least once or twice a month, she would pay a visit to Sue's just to get her drink on and to mingle with everybody.

Which was good, because it afforded me the opportunity to stay in touch with her.

So after Lexi screamed on me and hung up the phone, I immediately knew where my next call was going. I picked up the phone and called Andrea and told her that some crazy shit had went down and that I needed her help.

Fortunately for me, Andrea took the day off. She told me to stay put and that she would come scoop me up from a Harlem McDonald's and take me back to her crib out in Queens.

"Damn, girl, you look like a straight, hot-ass mess!" Andrea said, as soon as I stepped foot inside her truck.

I gingerly sat down in her truck because my ass, back, and arms were throbbing from the pain.

"What's up? Tell me what happened?"

"Look at this shit, Andrea!" I pulled up my shirt and turned so she could see the redness on my back. "My whole shit is fucked up!"

"Girl, what the hell is that?"

"Burns! Third-degree burns," I said as I shook my head. "Fucking with this nigga that I met up in the spot."

Andrea maneuvered her black Yukon Denali onto the Triborough Bridge, and after going through the E-ZPass lane, she gave me this look that said she was confused and needed me to explain. Although Andrea was now a lawyer, she was from the streets and from the same life that I was from, so I knew I could be straight up with her and not have to worry about her tripping.

So as we made the twenty-minute ride to her home in Bayside, Queens, I broke down to her how I'd won the contest between New York strippers and Atlanta strippers. I told her that I had met Pooh that same night, or Don Pooh as he'd introduced himself.

"Yeah, so he was open off my skills, and he came at me with this shit about making some money. So you know how we do up in the club, we hustle, so of course, I'm gonna hear him out."

Andrea nodded her head.

"I told Lexi what was up, and we both went to meet up with him at The 40/40 club. He told us what he needed us to do. It was straightforward—We get the drugs into the jails for him, and he would kick us our dough. It was real simple, and with us smuggling the shit in our pussies, we knew we was good. And we *was* good. So money was flowing good, we doing what we had to do, and me and Lexi both was getting money off this."

At this point we had reached Andrea's house. She parked in her driveway and turned off the ignition. "I'm still listening," she said, urging me to continue.

I opened up my door and took my time getting out. The pain felt like it was increasing.

As we entered Andrea's immaculate living room, I continued. "So, right from the jump, Lexi wanted to steal from Pooh by skimming ounces off the top of what we was moving for him, which was sheisty as hell, but it was all good and I went along with it."

Andrea smiled and shook her head.

I went on to tell her how Lexi got spooked with the drug-sniffing dog and how from that point on she was done with Pooh. I explained how Lexi felt disrespected, and how Pooh came to the crib the first time and Lexi played his ass by pushing him down the steps.

"Get outta here!" Andrea said, spitting out her juice from laughing so hard.

"Andrea, word is bond! And the shit was funny as hell. You shoulda seen this nigga tumbling down the steps and knocking over his man and shit."

Andrea and I kept laughing.

Then I went on to tell her how after that Pooh just sort of disappeared, until him and his boys popped up on us the other night when we came home from the spot in Jersey.

"Damn! And y'all had the two niggas in the crib ready to put it on them?" Andrea knew that meeting two ballers like Reggie and Ronnie was a stripper's dream come true, because if your skills was right and your game was tight, somebody like Reggie or Ronnie could be pimped and milked dry.

"Yeah, I know! But, Andrea, the nigga Pooh and his boys were on some real grimy gangsta shit! They burned us with bath water!"

Andrea got up, walked to the other room for something, and yelled to me. "Latisha, you know that nigga's coming back, right?"

I immediately stood up and walked into the other room where Andrea was.

"Anybody that thinks up some crazy, psychotic shit like that—burning bitches with bathwater—yo, you gonna have problems with that nigga until he kills yo' ass!" Andrea said rather matter-of-factly.

"But he got his money now from the dough he took from Reggie and Ronnie."

"Latisha, listen to me, I defend these crazy bastards every day. I know how they think and how they tick. And these niggas don't tick normal like the average Joe. For a nigga to do some shit like that and to wanna rape y'all too, it ain't got nothing to do with the money. It's about power, straight-up. And I'm telling you, Lexi fucked up when she played that nigga and pushed him down the steps. That nigga ain't gonna stop until one of y'all is dead."

I paused in silence for a moment and to take in everything Andrea had said.

"See, Andrea, that's why I knew I had to speak to you. You know what's what and you know the deal. Lexi out there running wild and talking shit about getting back at the nigga, and I'm like, yo, it's time for us to get up outta that spot before one of us gets killed."

Andrea shook her head and then she replied.

"Okay, the textbook, by-the-rules way of handling this is going to the police to get a restraining order against Pooh, but on the real, that ain't gonna do nothing but get your ass killed. But the thing is this, the cops is already plotting and talking to the district attorney about this whole shit, trust me. And no matter what, if Reggie and Ronnie turn up okay or if they turn up dead, the cops and the district attorney is gonna sensationalize the whole thing because of the celebrity of the two football players, and you and Lexi are gonna get locked up and held as prime suspects."

My heart rate dropped when Andrea told me that, because I hadn't even yet told her that was my suspicion as well, based on what had happened to me when I went down to the police station. "Andrea, I don't need the drama!"

"I feel you. On the real, you got one of two options—Either you kill Pooh before he kills you, or somehow you figure out a way to set his ass up and rat him out so that he gets locked up and goes down for all this shit before you get arrested. Otherwise, if he gets bagged first by the police, then you better believe that he's gonna start snitching and implicating you and Lexi. He'll say that y'all set the whole thing up and that he is your girl or some shit like that to get his ass out of a sling."

I looked at Andrea and nodded my head. She was dead-on. I was so glad that she was not only book-smart, but street-smart as well. I sat back and thought long and hard about what I should do. From the time Lexi hung up the phone on me, I knew what I needed to do, but thankfully for me, Andrea had just made it a whole lot clearer.

"Andrea, I gotchu. I think I know what I'm gonna do, but I just need a day to think about it and sleep on it to make sure."

"Girl, you know, no matter what, I'm gonna look out for you. Just think it over and let me know what you decide, and either way, I'm gonna look out for my girl. You know that."

I was dead tired and sore as hell and hadn't been to sleep in more than a day and a half.

Andrea was gracious enough to let me spend the night with her. Her son was out of town for the summer at his dad's house in Los Angeles, so she basically had the house to herself. She made me something to eat and made sure that I was nice and comfortable, and before I lay down to get some rest, she ran out to the pharmacy and got me all kinds of lotions and potions for my burns.

While Andrea put some ointment on my back, we started reminiscing about some funny times in the past, some of the things that we'd been through together, and some of the things that we'd witnessed other people go through. We also caught up on how certain people were doing and what they were up to. It was a good little catching-up chat, and it definitely helped take my mind off of the whole drama with Pooh.

I knew that my little session with Andrea couldn't wipe out reality. Nah, it was time for me to deal with my reality face to face, even if it meant that I would have to do some grimy shit and be sheisty in the process, 'cause when it all came down to it, I knew I had to look out for me, and I couldn't count on or trust anyone else to do that for me but me. It was about to be on.

Chapter Ten

All Strippers Are Actresses

The next day when I woke up, I was kind of bugging out, trying to figure out just where the heck I was. I looked over at the clock, and it was a little past eight in the morning, so I decided to just lie there and think about shit. I was actually shocked that I was up that early because normally my body wouldn't let me entertain the thought of waking up until at least ten-thirty or eleven o'clock in the morning.

Don't stress it and just do it, I told myself. I didn't want to lie there and think myself out of what I knew I needed to do. I immediately got up out of the bed to retrieve my cell phone. I needed to call Andrea, who had left for work at like seven in the morning.

My cell phone was inside my bag, which was in the living room. On my way to getting my phone, I noticed a note that Andrea left for me.

Hey, girl,

I didn't want to wake you up when I was leaving, since it was so early in the morning, but I just wanted to tell you to

make yourself at home when you're in my crib. Eat whatever
you wanna eat, and drink whatever you wanna drink (even
the liquor . . . wink). Don't worry about straightening any-
thing up. I hired somebody for that. Anyway, if you need me,
just call me on my cell. I probably won't be home until like
seven or eight o'clock tonight, so I'll see you later.

Andrea was so sweet. And what was funny was that I
knew she was joking about the liquor, but as soon as I
finished reading her note, the first place that I headed
was her little mini-bar that she had downstairs in her
finished basement near the Jacuzzi. It was still early in
the morning, but I knew that I needed a drink to help
take the edge off. I didn't want nothing too strong and
crazy, just something to get me feeling nice while I ate
the eggs that I was planning on cooking for myself.

In a matter of seconds I had popped open a bottle of
Merlot. I didn't bother to get a cup for the red wine.
Nah, I took it straight to the head, and in one shot, had
guzzled about one-fourth of the bottle. It was one of the
best drinks that I'd ever had in my life.

My buzz was on, and while I scrambled up my eggs, I
chugged back more of the Merlot to build up some
courage.

Before long, I knew that it was time to make that call
to Andrea. Without hesitation, I dialed her number on
my cell phone, and she picked up right away.

Andrea whispered into the phone. "Hey, what's up?
You all right?"

"Yeah, I'm good. Can you talk?"

"I got a few minutes. What's up?"

"Andrea, I been sitting here thinking. And since last

night, and maybe even before that, it's like, I knew what I had to do, but it was just a matter of would I go through with it and do it."

"Uh-huh," Andrea said, sounding like she was listening real attentively.

"Yo, I know what I know, and I know ain't no rat worse than a snitch-ass bitch. I know that. But it's like I'm stuck right now in the middle of some bullshit, and if I don't do something, I know my ass is gonna end up getting killed, you know what I'm saying?"

"Yeah, girl, I know exactly what you saying. Bottom line is, you gotta do what you gotta do."

"So, listen, I wanna rat this nigga Pooh out for violating me and violating my crib like he did. And I know I could set him up something lovely, but the thing is, it's like even if he's locked up, he's gonna constantly be at war with Lexi. Pooh won't end the war until he gets the satisfaction that he needs by striking back at Lexi on his terms and to his liking."

"Latisha, say no more. I know what you're saying, and I can make this happen. And I can probably get you some dough. How soon you want to do this?"

I went on to tell Andrea that I was ready to make this happen with a quickness.

She went on to tell me that she would make some calls to her contacts at the NYPD and get things in motion, but that she first wanted us to get our strategy down tight so we would come at the authorities in the correct way. "The tighter we come at them with what we got and what we can give them and how it will benefit them, then the better chance that we have that they will hit you off with some cash payments as a paid informant."

"Say word?"

"Word is bond. But the thing is, I'ma look out for you and do this for you, but I get my bread from this firm that I work for. I gotta bring in money to these muthafuckas, or otherwise they'll look at me as invaluable. So what I'm saying is, I can make this happen, but if I do, then me and you gotta split this dough fifty-fifty that I'm hoping you get from the NYPD."

I had no problem with that, especially since I hadn't ever planned on trying to get money by going to the cops. I was just trying to get some peace of mind and end this drama that was affecting my livelihood, and which could have even gotten my ass killed. But I could sense when someone was bullshitting me, and I knew that Andrea was bullshitting me. See, she tried to make it seem like if she split any informant money with me that she would have to hand over her portion of the money to her law firm. I didn't say anything to her, because I didn't care about the money. I knew she was more than likely gonna pocket that money.

Anyway, Andrea went on to tell me that if I went through with this whole informant thing that I was more than likely gonna have to play both sides of the fence with Lexi and Pooh in order to get the necessary incriminating evidence for the cops.

"I hope you got some acting skills because you definitely gonna need 'em," Andrea said and laughed.

"Girl, come on now, you used to dance up in the clubs just like I do, so I know that you know that all strippers are actresses." I said that because it was true.

Every night in the strip clubs I was used to acting in order to sell a fantasy to the guys in the club so that they would keep tipping me and giving me money. And as long as they were willing to pay me, I was slick enough and convincing enough to tell them just about whatever it was that they wanted to hear.

But now, with me planning to rat out Lexi and Pooh, I knew I had to come hard with my acting game. It was game time, and I was ready to get it poppin'.

Chapter Eleven

Don't You Know Bad Girls Move in Silence?

"Lex, boogie! What up, baby girl?" I said to her as I walked up behind her as she stood on the corner of 125th Street and Eighth Avenue.

"Hey, what you doing out here?" she asked me.

She had to be surprised to see me. And it was nothing but pure coincidence that I had bumped into her. I just happened to be heading down Eighth Avenue, going toward our apartment, when I saw her, stopped my truck, and jumped out to kick it with her.

"I was coming by the crib to see you."

Lexi looked at me as if she was trying to figure me out. She grabbed the two shopping bags that she was carrying and told me to walk with her to Popeyes to get something to eat.

"So what's up? You ain't call a bitch," Lexi said as we crossed the busy intersection. "You just straight disappeared on me. I was wondering if you was dead or alive."

"I just had to clear my head," I said as I shook my

head. "I mean, you know, just trying to figure out what the hell I should do."

"Do about what?" Lexi asked with a bit of an attitude after she ordered her three-piece meal.

"Lexi, I can't dance. My back and my ass is still all fucked up. I was trying to figure out how the hell I was gonna get my money. I mean, I went to see a dermatologist and all that."

Lexi sucked her teeth and then went on to explain to me how her and some goons came real close to killing Pooh. "Yeah, we just missed that nigga by like two minutes! We was ready to light his ass up like a Christmas tree!"

I tried to downplay the whole beef with Pooh. "Lexi, to be honest, the only thing that I'm concerned about is getting some money. Word! Matter of fact, that's what I wanted to talk to you about," I said, as I reached over and grabbed a piece of her chicken.

She smiled at me as I pulled on her chicken wing and put it in my mouth. "You so fuckin' ghetto," she said, laughing.

I knew that as long as I kept Lexi laughing and in a jolly mood, she wouldn't suspect my true motive, which was to snake her and set her ass up.

"Nah, but really though," I said, lowering my voice to a whisper, "you still got them thangs, right?"

Lexi gave me a confused look.

"That coke you took from Pooh!" I said in a loud, frustrated-sounding whisper. "You still got it, right?"

"Oh. Yeah, yeah, yeah, of course, I still got that. Why? What's up?"

"Well, I got a buyer for it. These niggas from Detroit,"

I explained. I continued on about how I had to get my money up to pay for these other specialists in dermatology so they could treat my burns and get my skin back to where it needed to be.

Lexi put jelly on her biscuit and bit into it. "They got cash?"

"Lexi, I wouldn't even bring the shit up if they was some clown-ass niggas."

"Twenty-five thousand, if they want it, and I ain't fucking with less than that." Lexi was just about finished eating all of her food and began to sip on her Sprite as she stood up.

"Lexi! Twenty-five *G*'s?" I asked, trying to sound surprised. "You know that's too much."

"Lovely, we gotta get this dough! You just finished crying to me about you need dough, so let's make these cats pay or let them walk and find another connection."

I paused as we both prepared to cross the street.

"I could milk this shit slowly, lace the ounces to stretch that shit out, and make a lot of dough. So if these niggas want me coming up off my shit, well then they gotta come up off their dough!"

I didn't fight her because I knew I had her right where I wanted her. We had parked in separate directions so we were ready to part and go our separate ways. I told Lexi that I would get in touch with the guys from Detroit and then get back to her and let her know what was what.

"You coming by the crib or what?" Lexi yelled out to me.

"Yeah, I'm coming through in a few!" I shouted back.

I went right to my truck and immediately called Andrea and filled her in on my first move. I explained to her that setting up Lexi would be no problem, and that all I had to do now was try to make contact with Pooh and then reel everybody in.

The thing was that reining in Pooh was not gonna be that easy. I knew that calling him wasn't gonna work because he had either changed his number or he was gonna make sure to stay off of his phone.

I figured that the best thing for me to do would be for me to head out to Long Island where Pooh rested at and try to catch him at this spot near Hofstra University that he always hung out at.

See, when Lexi and I had started to check into Pooh's background, we found out that there was this spot in Elmont, Long Island, called Moments, a café and a lounge, and one of Pooh's favorite spots to hang out. Thursday night was their best night. It was wasn't a real ghetto spot or anything like that. In fact, it was somewhat classy, and from the looks of it, appeared to be a really respectable place.

I rolled up in Moments looking really regular. I had a baseball hat on and all of that. But it was all good though, because it helped me to look and remain real incognito.

I went to the bar and ordered some champagne. As I sat at the bar and sipped on my drink, I looked around to see if I could spot out Pooh, but unfortunately Pooh was nowhere to be found. It was only about nine-thirty at night, so I wasn't too concerned because I realized that Pooh probably wouldn't show up until close to like eleven or midnight.

I waited and waited and I tried to maintain and not

get too drunk, just in case Pooh showed up. I wanted to be alert and in my right mind. There was a large-screen television which was showing a Yankees game, and there was also real loud party hip-hop music that was being played in the background as people mingled with one another. Some danced, some played pool, and some sat and ate their Southern or Caribbean food.

After about five drinks I saw Pooh and a small entourage of about two of his boys walk in with him. Instantly my heart rate picked up a bit, so I guzzled down the rest of my drink in order to build up a bit more confidence before approaching him.

Pooh and his two boys surveyed the lounge to see who was in there. After saying what's up to a bunch of people, he started heading for the bar. In fact, Pooh and his boys were literally standing right next to me while I sat at the bar, but they didn't recognize me, probably because of the way I looked.

They ordered their drinks and started talking shit with each other. I decided to give them about two minutes or so to take a few sips of their drink before speaking up and saying anything.

After the two minutes was up, I kept my hand on my drink, turned my face toward Pooh, and spoke up to get his attention.

"Don Pooh, come up in the spot, stand right next to me, and you don't even offer to buy me a drink?" I said real loud over the music, a blank look on my face.

Pooh instantly frowned up his face as if he was trying to get a better look at me and figure out who the hell I was. After about fifteen seconds or so, a sinister smile appeared across his face and he placed a toothpick in his mouth, tapped one of his boys on the shoulder, and whispered something into his boy's ear.

"What the fuck you doing up in here?" Pooh gnarled.

"Pooh, stop with the screw face and the gangsta shit, a'ight? I'm up in here on some love. You didn't even recognize me until I got your attention, and now that I got it, let's just be straight-up with each other."

Pooh just stared at me real suspiciously and didn't say a word to me.

"First of all, Pooh, that was some real grimy-ass shit you pulled at my crib!" I said, trying to come across convincing.

"Bitch, you and your girl are the—"

"Whoa, whoa!" I said, holding up my hand and stepping off of the bar stool so that I could stand while I spoke to Pooh. "Just hear me out, Pooh! I ain't even coming at you about that shit. All I'm saying is that it was grimy!" I shook my head. "But this is the thing. Right from the gate when I met you up in Sue's that night, me and you clicked and I know everything would have been all love if I hadn't brought Lexi into the mix. She's the one that fucked shit up, but the thing is, I'm the one that brought her into what me and you was supposed to get rocking for ourselves. So that's on me, and I admit that."

Pooh and his boys continued to just stare at me until one of his boys tapped him on the arm and then whispered something into his ear.

"So what are you saying? I mean, you and your girl both tried to disrespect me, and that's the beef I got with both of y'all!" Pooh guzzled his drink and quickly ordered another one.

I held both of my hands up into the air as if to say that I surrendered. "You know what, Pooh, I'm guilty as charged. You hundred percent right, and when I'm wrong, I got no problem admitting that. And right now, right in front of your boys, I'll be woman enough to apologize," I said.

Pooh looked at his boy, chuckled, and then he spoke. "Yo, this bitch think this is some ol' high-school beef or some shit."

"Nah, it's not even that," I said. "The thing is this. Pooh, I knew I could find you here tonight and that's why I came all the way out here. See, this is the thing. I ain't fucking with Lexi no more. She just be on that snake shit. And the thing is, I'm like, why should me and you be beefing over what is really her ass and her underhanded shit? Remember, she the one that disrespected you first. But what you don't know is that she was grimy and was snaking you right from jump by skimming off coke from the ounces that you was giving us."

"What the fuck I tell you!" one of Pooh's boys said to Pooh.

I could see the muscle's tensing and tightening in Pooh's face. He ran his hand down his face before asking me how much Lexi had stolen.

I shook my head and told him, "It had to be anywhere from like half of a brick to a whole brick."

Pooh stood stone-faced and quiet for a minute just playing with his pinkie ring.

"Pooh, this is all I'm saying. She still got the shit. I know she do because I know she can't move it without me. So I'm saying this, let me get the shit back to you, and me and you can squash whatever differences that we had. And as for Lexi, whatever you wanna do, that's on you. I ain't seen nothing and I ain't heard nothing, you feel me?" I nervously waited for Pooh's response.

"A half a brick?" Pooh twisted his lips to the side, looking burnt and pissed off.

I nodded my head. "At least."

Pooh drank some more of his drink and then he spoke up.

"Yo, so that's how she got that new white Denali, right?" Pooh asked.

It was news to me because I didn't even know that Lexi had a Denali.

But Pooh never gave me a chance to answer because he spoke up and continued ranting that he knew something was up and that Lexi was driving a BMW truck and a brand-new Denali that she probably bought with money that was his.

"So how am I getting my shit back?" Pooh asked. "And, yo, on the real, I ain't trying to wait no week for this shit! Today is Thursday. I want that shit back by tomorrow night—Saturday the latest!"

I assured Pooh that I had him and that he didn't have to worry. I then got his new cell phone number and told him that I would call him when I was ready to drop the shit off to him.

"Just get me my shit by Saturday, or shit is really gonna get ugly!" Pooh warned.

"Pooh, I wouldn't have come all the way out here if I knew Lexi wasn't holding the shit."

Pooh said, "A'ight." But then he warned me, "Bring the coke by yourself, I don't trust that bitch!"

I thought fast on my feet because I knew that Lexi

would want to be right there by my side on any deal so that she could see firsthand what was what. But I didn't want to tell Pooh that at the time, because I didn't want him to get alarmed. "Okay, cool," I said as I prepared to leave the bar and told Pooh that I would get right back at him.

As soon as I stepped outside of Moments and headed to my truck I blew out some air. *Whewww!*

The first thing I did was call Andrea and tell her everything that had transpired. She told me that she would be on the horn with her NYPD contacts first thing in the morning. But she also told me that Friday was more than likely gonna be too soon and that the NYPD would more than likely want a day to make sure that they was ready to move on Pooh and Lexi like she knew they would want to move on them. Plus, she told me that she would just have to get the DA to sign off on some shit to make sure that my ass was totally protected all the way around and across the board.

"Okay, so cool. Call me as soon as you get everything squared away on your end, and as soon as I hear from you, I'll finalize shit with Lexi and Pooh," I told her.

"Okay, cool," she said before we both hung up the phone.

Ironically, as I turned on the radio in my truck, Yung Joc's song was soon blasting through my speakers. *It's going dowwwn!* The song's chorus appropriately said, because it was definitely getting ready to go down!

Chapter Twelve

Back Seat of My Jeep

After I left Moments, I decided to go back to Harlem to spend the night in my own bed. I felt too like that would be a good way for me to bond with Lexi and finish selling her on the guys from Detroit that wanted to buy the brick of cocaine. I basically took a chance that everything would work out with Andrea, the DA, and the cops, telling Lexi that Saturday was the day that they wanted to pick up the drugs.

As it turned out, I did speak with Lexi and she told me that she was with the sale, but she held to that twenty-five-thousand-dollar price tag. I didn't make a big deal about it because at that point I knew that wasn't no money gonna be changing hands anyway.

Unfortunately, Lexi and I didn't get a chance to really bond, because she had one of her male jump-offs over at the crib. Other than her showing me her new truck and us talking about the truck and how much she liked it, Lexi was more concerned with getting her sex on and poppin' with the new cutie that she had scooped from the club about a month ago.

"A'ight, girl, do your thing. I'll be in my room," I told her as I walked off to my room and prepared to sleep in my bed, which hadn't been slept in since before that day Pooh ran up in our crib and burned us with the shower and bathtub water.

Anyway, the night went by pretty quickly. In fact, I didn't even hear Lexi and her usual screaming climaxes.

Before I knew it Friday was here and it was quickly whizzing by. But it hadn't completely whizzed by before I got the call from Andrea, the call that I had been waiting for. Andrea told me that she wanted me to come by her house when she got off of work. She said she was gonna accompany me to the police precinct so that she could be there with me while the detectives spoke with me and went over the tactical plans of exactly how they were gonna make the arrest and move in on Pooh and Lexi.

It wasn't a rocket-science plan, and it was definitely a plan that could have been worked out and discussed over the phone, but I think that the cops wanted to get a feel for me, and they also wanted to make sure that I was sure that I wanted to do this, since their lives were literally in my hands to some extent.

So the plan that was devised was that Lexi and I would leave our crib and get into either one of Lexi's trucks and head out toward the FDR Drive and then toward the Brooklyn Bridge. The entire time there would be two different, unmarked police cars that would take turns following us, so Lexi wouldn't get suspicious.

As soon as we were to exit from the Brooklyn Bridge, the cops would flash their lights for Lexi to pull over and they would ask for permission to search the car and then find the cocaine. Because Lexi would be the driver, she would be the one to get arrested. Meanwhile, as Lexi was getting hauled off to jail, I would continue on in the truck and head out to Long Island to meet Pooh and go through with the drug deal. As soon as I handed off the drugs to Pooh, the cops would move in and make their arrest.

"Latisha, are you sure that you can completely go all the way through with this?" one cop asked me as we sat in an office. "If you're gonna back out, I would tell you to please back out now and this way you protect everybody, including yourself."

I knew that part of the deal that Andrea had worked out for me with the DA basically said that if I didn't *fully* cooperate that I would be in violation of the terms of the deal and I would in essence be voiding the deal and opening myself up for arrest and prosecution. So there was no way in the world that I wasn't gonna go through with it. "I'm good," I said to the cops. "I'm not backing out."

The cops were on board, Andrea was cool with everything, and we agreed that we would roll out at eleven in the morning.

I was to just go home that night, Friday night, and play everything as normal, and then wake up the next day and head out to Long Island to complete the deal, although Lexi would think that the deal was taking place in Brooklyn.

"Latisha, whatever you do, make sure that Lexi is the

driver. Otherwise, it might really complicate things," one of the cops said to me as a last-minute reminder.

Then they assured me that, beginning at like nine or ten in the morning, they would be watching the house, and not to worry or look over my shoulder, they would be there and would make sure that I was kept safe.

So that was that, and Andrea and I exited the precinct and went our separate ways.

I called Pooh and told him that I would be coming to Long Island the next day to drop off the brick and that I would be coming alone as he suggested and wanted. Now all of the pieces to the puzzle were in place, and it was just a matter of me trying to remain calm and nervously wait things out without showing my nervousness during the next sixteen hours.

But as soon as I made it home to Harlem, Lexi immediately put me through a scare. As soon as I walked through the front door, Lexi came up to me and asked me what time we were supposed to hook up with the guys from Detroit.

I tried to figure out why Lexi wanted to know that as soon as I had walked into the door. I mean, she didn't even let me take my shoes off before she came up to me and asked me that question. And it was totally out of her normal, laid-back, nonchalant character.

"Umh, I think they wanted to meet either in the morning or the early afternoon," I said, trying to sound laid-back on my own. "I can call them now and find out."

"Well, the thing is, I might be heading to Atlantic City tonight to spend the night, and I wanted to see if we could hook up with them tonight."

Ahhh shit! I thought to myself. *Don't panic. Don't panic.* I laughed and then started taking off my shoes. "Okay, I'll call them now and see what's what." I paused and said, "I'm laughing 'cause you gonna mess around and get this money and throw it away at the blackjack table or something!"

Lexi looked at me as if she was trying to read me. "Oh hell, no, you know I don't gamble like that." She walked off and went into the living room. "Just let me know what the deal is."

"And if they can't hook up with us tonight, you can just go on to Atlantic City, and I'll knock this out and hit you with the money when you get back," I said to play things cool for good measure. I could sense in my gut that Lexi's guard was up and I had no idea why, but I was gonna do my best to try to put her at ease by bluffing like she wasn't really an important part of the equation.

She didn't respond, so I just walked off toward my room and contemplated what I should do. Immediately the thought to just bluff the whole thing came across my mind. I thought about just telling her that I had spoken to the guys from Detroit and that they could meet us tonight, Friday night, so everything would work out. But the problem was, if she decided to call me on my bluff, then I would be fucked.

I just chilled in my room for about fifteen minutes and then came back downstairs and told Lexi that I couldn't get in touch with the guys from Detroit. "Yeah, they ain't picking up the phone," I said to Lexi as I made it back into the living room.

Lexi was quiet for a minute.

I broke the silence. "Why don't you just leave in the morning at like ten o'clock? I'll keep calling these cats until I get them and just set everything up for the morning."

Lexi didn't say anything. She just walked over to the little mini-bar and started fixing herself a drink. I could sense that her wheels were spinning a mile a minute as she started asking me a million and one questions about the guys from Detroit. And with each question she asked, I just lied my ass off and came up with something straight off the top of my head.

I wasn't sure if Lexi bought everything that I was saying, and I wasn't sure what had made her radar go up, but I knew that the best thing to do was to get my ass in my room and try my hardest to fall asleep so that I wouldn't say or do anything that would jeopardize the entire operation.

So before walking off to my room for the final time that night, I assured her that everything would be okay and that we would knock out the deal in the morning. I smiled and said to Lexi, "Just think about the cash!".

She nodded her head, took a swig of her drink, and just watched television and didn't respond to me.

By six-thirty the next morning, I was up and wide-awake. Lexi was still asleep because the house was quiet. Usually as soon as she wakes up she turns on the radio. I contemplated what I was about to do. I wouldn't let myself think too long, though, because if I did, then I knew that there would be no way that I would be able to fully go through with snaking Lexi like I was about to do.

To kill time I got up, took a shower, got dressed, and went to the kitchen to start cooking breakfast.

Soon thereafter, Lexi woke up. It was close to like eight o'clock. She walked past me, said good morning, and immediately grabbed hold of her cell phone and went into the bathroom. I could hear that she was talking on the phone.

"Yo, I don't know why I've been so tired lately," Lexi said to me as she reemerged into the kitchen after coming out of the bathroom.

"You want some French toast?" I asked.

"Nah, I'm good," Lexi replied. Then she told me that she had forgotten something in her truck and had to run outside to go get it.

My palms were literally sweaty because I knew that Lexi was smart as hell, and she was probably just going outside to canvass the block to see if anything looked out of order.

It took her like fifteen minutes to come back inside, but I didn't question her about it. I simply lied and told her that I spoke to the guys from Detroit and that we would roll out to meet them at like ten o'clock.

Lexi nodded her head and then went about her business as I ate my food. But thankfully, before long it was time to get things poppin'.

"A'ight, Lexi, let's do this," I said. "You got the burner and the work, right?" I asked.

"It's right over there." Lexi pointed to a blue bag that was used for holding a laptop computer. She scooped up the bag, and then we headed out the door.

"I'm a let you drive because I don't wanna get spooked if I see the cops or something," I said to Lexi. "Plus, I wanna check out your new whip," I added, referring to the brand-new Denali that Lexi was pushing.

For some strange reason, Lexi was coming across extremely quiet, not even looking at me or acknowledging me by nodding her head when I spoke. I knew in my heart that she had to sense that something bad was about to go down. As street-smart as she was, she probably knew that I was about to set her up, and the thing that I respected about her was that she wasn't putting up a fight. It was like she knew she was being led to the electric chair, but she still had balls enough not to complain and just go through with it. Needless to say, that didn't make me feel any better about myself.

As we approached the Denali, I made sure not to look down the block or up the block. I just had to trust that the cops were in place and ready to move in and follow us.

"We gotta go to the FDR Drive and then over the Brooklyn Bridge," I said as I buckled my seatbelt.

Lexi still didn't respond to me.

I was shocked that she had brought the bag with the brick and the gun into the front seat of the car. But then I got hip to what she was doing, as she nonchalantly placed the bag over on my side so that it was resting right near my feet. I wanted to say something about the bag and try to get her to put it in the rear of the truck, but I kept my mouth shut and closed my eyes as we started to pull off and head down the block.

While my eyes were closed, the only thing that I started to think about was how good my life would be once I entered the Witness Protection Program. I smiled as I thought about never having to worry about paying rent or any utilities and all of that burdensome shit. I giggled on the inside as I thought about how it would almost be as good as getting pregnant by an NBA player in the sense that I would be taken care of financially, simply because of my smart actions. I wasn't having nobody's baby, but I had ratted on somebody and that was going to earn me similar benefits because I had played my cards right.

Lexi interrupted my thoughts as she broke the silence. She asked me to reach into the bag and hand her the gun.

While I was reaching for the gun, she explained to me that she wanted to make sure that she was strapped from the moment that we met with the dudes from Detroit.

I retrieved the gun and handed it to her, and she sat it on her lap while she maneuvered down 125th Street. But as we came to the end of 125th Street, instead of going straight and turning right to get onto the FDR Drive, Lexi turned right and was heading toward the Bronx.

"No, Lexi, you gotta get on the FDR Drive!" I shouted to her. I didn't want her to take things off course and confuse the cops that were following us.

"I got this," Lexi shot back. "Don't worry about it!"

"Lexi, you can't get to Brooklyn this way! Once you hit Third Avenue in the Bronx you'll be all out of the way!" I was panicking because I could sense that the cops that were following us were probably gonna pull us over at any second.

"Damn, Lovely, calm down! I just wanna get something to eat real quick."

I decided to just sit back and keep quiet.

I could see Lexi looking in her rearview mirror constantly. Then out of nowhere, she grabbed hold of the gun, gripped it tightly, and pointed it directly at me while she kept driving.

"Latisha, don't move!" she barked at me. "Pop, you was right! Something is up!" Lexi yelled out.

I had no idea who she was talking to. Then I heard a male voice coming from Lexi's third row of seats.

"Pop, this same fucking car was following us since we left the block. He trying to be slick about it, but I know he following me, and cops don't normally drive them kind of whips, so I doubt it's a fucking cop!" Lexi yelled.

My heart was now in my shoes. "Lexi, what's going on? And who is this nigga?" I looked toward the back of the car and saw a black dude climbing over the seats with a gun in his hand.

"Shut the fuck up, Latisha, and tell me what the hell is going on, or I swear to God, I will kill your ass right now!"

We were driving farther and farther down Third Avenue and deeper into the Bronx, which wasn't a good thing.

"What are you talking about, Lexi? And who is this?"

"Who is this!?" Lexi screamed at me. "This is my nigga from the club, and his man knows Don Pooh and his bitch-ass friends. They told him that you was out in Long Island talking all greasy and shit about me! So I'm thinking you trying to cross my ass with Pooh. The same nigga that ran up in our spot and disrespected us."

"Oh my Goddd! Lexi, you are really trippin' right now!" I said, trying to be convincing.

"Muthafucka! That is the fucking cops! They just turned they lights on!" Lexi yelled. "Shit!"

"Where is the brick?" the guy inside the car asked.

"It's up here in the front!" Lexi told him.

"Yo, drive this truck and pass me that brick!" the guy yelled.

Lexi started driving the whip like a madwoman, weaving in and out of traffic, and the cops were following right on her tail in their unmarked car. And in no time there was also a marked police car that started chasing us as well.

"Yo, hurry up and hand me that shit!" the guy yelled at me and pushed me in my head.

I didn't want to hand it to him because I knew that he would probably split the bag of coke, toss it out the window, and let it blow into the air to destroy the evidence.

"Lexi, calm the fuck down and slow down! I don't know this nigga, so I ain't handing him shit!"

"Bitch, give me the fucking bag!" The guy reached over the seat and grabbed the bag from me.

I began tugging on the bag. I wouldn't let it go. Then all of a sudden I heard a loud BANG! The bang sound was followed by a feeling like I had got kicked in the stomach and someone had poured burning acid onto my stomach.

I instantly let go of the bag and doubled over in pain. It took a few seconds for me to realize that Lexi had just shot me.

"Bitch, what the fuck is wrong with you?" Lexi asked as she nervously maneuvered the whip at top speeds down the busy Grand Concourse.

I immediately started coughing, and globs of blood started running out of my mouth.

"Yo, Pop, we gotta toss this bitch and toss that brick

and the guns!" Lexi screamed. But soon after she said that, the Denali got rammed from the back and Lexi lost control of the car, crashing into an apartment building.

The last thing that I remember was the airbags deploying and the guy Pop yelling for Lexi to hurry up and get out of the car.

I was drifting out of consciousness, but I remember looking and seeing Lexi struggling to get her seat belt loose. When she finally did, she opened her door, hopped out the car, and started running.

"NYPD! Freeze!" the officer yelled at Pop and Lexi as they paid him no mind and kept running.

"Is anybody else in the car?" another cop asked me.

I was too weak and out of it to respond to the officer, and it took the officer a few minutes to realize that I had been shot.

"Oh shit!" he said once he realized what had happened. He immediately got on his walkie-talkie and started screaming that he needed an ambulance.

I heard another cop transmitting through his walkie-talkie that they had apprehended both the male and female suspects that had fled on foot.

"We gonna get you an ambulance, hon!" One of the plainclothes cops that I recognized from the precinct said to me as I drifted in and out.

I wondered if I would live to see that ambulance arrive as my life felt like it was about to end right there in the passenger seat of Lexi's Denali. Like death was right around the corner.

I was a snake and a snitch, and in the end, I guess you could say that I got what I deserved.

STAR QUALITY

By

MadameK

PROLOGUE

South Merrick, NY

1996

The young girl lay in her cold basement bedroom with dried tears staining her cheeks and a threadbare blanket covering her frail, shivering form. She was being punished. It seemed she had been punished since the day she was born.

She squeezed Ellie, her pink stuffed elephant, closer to her chest. It only had one eye and its ears were tattered. She thought back to the day her grandmother had given it to her when she turned five. It was the only gift she'd received that year, and her mother's mother had wrapped it with pretty pink and white striped paper. It reminded her of a candy cane. She didn't want to wreck the beautiful wrapping, but childish curiosity fueled her to rip into the box. She carefully folded and placed the wrapping paper at her side before lifting the lid off the box. Gran had passed away that same night in her sleep. Eight years later, as she lay clutching the toy, Ellie served as a reminder of Gran, the only person the girl felt ever cared about her.

Heat flooded her face as she recounted the beating *he'd* doled out earlier, brought on by nothing more than the fact that she existed and served as a constant reminder of how *he* had failed as a husband. *He* wasn't married to her mother; *he* was married to his job.

She reveled at how the black and blue on her arms, torso, and legs provided a stark contrast to the pale tone of the skin *he'd* missed in his tirade. *He* had told her if she told anyone what he was doing, *he* would kill her, and, even in her youth, she decided not to put anything past *him*. In that moment, as she stared through blurry eyes at the dusty ductwork above her head, the girl promised herself that she would make him pay for punishing her for his own blindness. She turned on her side and clutched Ellie tight.

OPENING ACT
Washington, DC

When the lights dimmed after the final number and the crowd roared its appreciation, Star breathed a sigh of relief. She had made it through another night—another show. Her throat was parched from the vocal acrobatics she'd performed, and her legs ached from the rigorous choreography. She didn't want to be bothered by backstage pleasantries or pats on the back. All she wanted to do was get back to New York and break in the new bitch.

***

Newport, KY

"I don't understand why you have to do this." Jessica stood with her lips pursed and her hands on her narrow hips, her wild eyes ablaze.

"I can't believe you're giving me grief about this. If you knew how big this was going to be—"

Bernard was grasping at straws. They'd been going at it for the last hour, starting right after the call came and he started packing.

"It's just that we've never been away from each other this long." She wilted a little and looked down at the beige ceramic tile that covered their kitchen floor.

"I know, babe. It's gonna be tough, but we'll get through it." He pulled her into his chest and smelled her raspberry shampoo. "Hopefully it'll only take a few weeks to get what I need, and then I'll be back home."

He held on to one of her slight, golden shoulders

with one strong ebony hand and stroked her long black hair with the other and said, "This could be so huge for me, babe. This could mean the end of little bullshit jobs and on to the real stuff. I promise it won't be long, and when I get back we can pick up right where we left off." He wrapped his arms around her waist and savored one last moment.

A horn honked from the street.

"I gotta go now." Bernard broke the embrace and held Jessica's gaze. He cracked a slight smile. "You know I love you, right?"

"Yeah, whatever."

Bernard sighed, picked up his duffel bag, and went outside to the black Jaguar with tinted windows that sat running in front of their house.

Jessica ripped off her ring, taking some of the skin on her ring finger with it. She threw her bloody engagement ring across the kitchen, then slid her back down the kitchen island onto the cold tile and cried.

ONE

Park Slope, Brooklyn

"Lick her pussy," Star directed the new girl named Carmella, a lovely Puerto Rican princess with long, wavy hair.

Carmella stood there naked and speechless. She made a noise that sounded like she was trying to form words, but the effort was in vain.

"Did I stutter, bitch?" Star's voice dripped with venom.

The others—two men, a tall, black, and bald man named Aaron and the other a short, Japanese dude they called Jay, and Vivian, a beautiful Italian girl with crystal blue eyes and a smooth olive complexion—remained quiet but looked on as Star broke in the new "bitch."

A dim light appeared in Carmella's eyes, and she quickly made her way over to Vivian, who was seated on an orange chair facing Star's post on the red contemporary sofa on the opposite side of the room. Vivian looked Carmella in the eyes, nodded, and stretched one of her long legs onto the arm of the chair, allowing easier access to the task at hand.

Carmella kneeled in front of Vivian and began softly stroking her through the black, lacy thong that covered her crotch. Vivian's eyes got wide all of a sudden, and Carmella stopped mid-stroke a split second before Star reprimanded her.

"Bitch, did I tell you to rub on her? You don't do a motherfuckin' thing I don't tell you to do. Do you understand me?"

Carmella nodded rapidly, clearly shaken by the outburst.

"I said, do you understand me?"

Carmella managed a weak "Yes."

Star leaned forward. "Yes, what?"

"Yes, Mistress."

"Good. Now do what the fuck I told you to do."

Without hesitation, Carmella resumed her duties, sliding Vivian's thong to the side before licking her from her pussy hole to the top of her clit and back down again. She didn't dare turn around when she heard the moan coming from Star's direction.

"Lick it like you would like to be licked," Star ordered.

After a quick pause while she conjured up her own fantasy, Carmella focused her attention on Vivian's most sensitive spot and flicked her tongue up and down in a rhythmic motion. Vivian's response was genuine pleasure and appreciation as she looked down at the new girl working her the fuck out. She grabbed her breasts and pushed them together as the waves of pleasure continued through her body.

"Aaron, get ready."

Aaron snapped his gaze away from the lady lunch and said, "Yes, Mistress," as he stood from his position on the red satin comforter covering the bed and dropped his black boxer briefs and began stroking his already hard penis. Aaron was quite blessed in the dick department, and that was one of the reasons Star had recruited him after a private strip show he'd been hired to do.

Star examined the feast before her once again while the aching in her lower region intensified. Carmella's little pussy was staring her in the face and talking to her.

I feel so empty. I need a dick inside me. Help me out, Star.

Star's pussy fluttered when she looked at Aaron's dick and said, "Fuck that bitch."

Aaron moved over to where the action was still continuing and positioned himself behind the Latina lovely. Carmella stopped her work on Vivian for a moment to glance back at Aaron. While he considered reaching around to stroke her and get her ready for take-off, he thought better of it when he remembered what Star had done when Carmella had tried to deviate from the explicit instructions she'd been given. Instead, he penetrated her dry tunnel, causing a gasp to escape her lips. As he pumped her, she looked back again, this time with a tear in her eye. He knew he was hurting her, but there was nothing he could do about it. He wasn't going to lose his gig for anyone.

Meanwhile, Jay had been watching Star undress. She pulled her dress around her waist and resumed her spot on the sofa. She was ready. Star licked her fingers and slid her hand down to her wet soft-spot, moving them in and out of her a few times before teasing her clit. Then she rubbed in small circles and grinded against her own hand.

Jay never tired of the sight of her. Although he had been one of her bitches for six months, the view of Star pleasing herself drove him to a near frenzy. She was just so beautiful. So perfect. It'd seem he'd feel a bit left out by this point, but he was content to drink in the view of Star and her beautiful ritual.

Aaron was still fucking Carmella, Carmella was still driving Vivian to the point of no return, and Star was beginning to peak.

"I'm gonna cooooooommmee," Star's words began in a frenzy and ended in a long, low growl as she climaxed.

A roar came from Aaron as he pulled out and shot his seed all over Carmella's back. A wail escaped Vivian's lips and her mouth formed a crimson "O." Carmella remained in the aftermath of it all, stunned, yet somehow satisfied. It was like the ending of a bizarre skin flick.

Star laid in silence with her eyelashes fluttering for a few minutes until her heartbeat slowed down close to its normal pace. "Get the fuck out. All of you."

They scrambled for their belongings and scattered like roaches when the light comes on.

Star removed the comforter from the bed and replaced it with a fresh one from the linen closet. Then she lay down in the bed and cried herself to sleep.

The knock on the door came exactly three hours later. Star slowly opened her eyes and saw a small shard of light penetrating the side of the curtains.

Fuck! Morning already?

"Star, baby, it's me." The voice was distinctly southern and distinctly Peaches Deveraux.

Star pushed the covers off her and scrambled to find a robe. Grabbing one of the soft Nicole Miller ones from the bathroom closet, she cocooned herself in it and moved toward the door.

Peaches was standing on the other side of the door wearing one of her velour sweat suits. The woman had to have at least a hundred of them, and in every color, style, and designer label imaginable. This was a magenta Lady Enyce one, and the color brought out the cool undertones in Peaches's redbone complexion. She had paired it with some fresh white Nikes and a white Yankees cap. Peaches looked nowhere near her nearly fifty years, despite the Newports and E&J that comprised a large percentage of her daily intake.

"Get dressed, Baby-Girl. We goin' to the old neighborhood today. I need my hair touched up, and, lawd, these nails look like I been breaking up sidewalks with 'em."

The thought of going back to her old neighborhood in Newark brought forth an almost instant scowl across Star's face. "I can't go. I have to ummm, work on some lyrics for the new album," she managed. She nodded for confirmation.

Peaches dug in her white Prada bag for her cigarettes and said, "Now, Baby-Girl, you might think you can run from your past, but I'm here to tell you, it will always outrun you and be waiting for you when you round the bend." Peaches lit her Newport, sat on the orange chair, and continued. "It's better if you just face it, Baby-Girl. Show it you not afraid of it and it can't hurt you no more." She took a drag and looked at Star for a response. This had become a monthly ritual: Peaches trying to get Star to return to the place where they had first met, so Star could face her past and clean up her present.

"It can't hurt me no more? Are you serious? Peaches, it hurts me every day!"

"Baby, I know you been through a lot. If I could take it back and erase all the mess you done seen in your young life, I'd do it in a heartbeat." Peaches looked down at the carpet.

Star flopped down onto the bed and lay back, looking at the ceiling.

"Well, how you gonna know unless you face it?" Peaches retrieved a small, silver flask from her purse and unscrewed the cap.

Star leaned up on her elbows and looked at the flask. "And what are *you* facing? I got my numbing mechanisms, and you got yours, so please, don't talk to me about *facing* things. Peaches, you know I love you more than anyone on this planet, but you've got to understand, I can't go back there. Not now. Not ever."

Peaches's plan to get Star to face her demons was blowing up in her face. She took a swig of the brandy and replaced the cap. While putting it back into her handbag, she caught a glimpse of the tiny Ziploc that held a single lock of hair.

My little Misha. Where have you gone, little girl?

Peaches' daughter, Misha, had run away from their apartment in the crime-ridden section of Southeast DC when she was only twelve. Peaches hadn't seen her since, but she'd kept the lock of hair from the child's first haircut close to her ever since Misha's disappearance.

Misha's father was an Italian man named Vince, who Peaches had met when she was twenty-six and still living in Atlanta. Coming from humble beginnings, Peaches was wooed by his extravagant gifts and smooth talk. Soon, she found out she was pregnant. When she told Vince, he fucked her one last time and told her to leave town or he'd kill her and the baby. Peaches hadn't known Vince was married to a mob boss's daughter, who would be none too pleased to learn he had fathered a golden baby.

Misha was constantly running with the thugs and getting into trouble at school. Peaches had even caught her taking nips out of her brandy. It seemed like Misha was always looking for something, but neither she nor Peaches knew what it was.

While Peaches was concerned for her daughter's happiness, her long hours at the security company she worked for didn't permit her to be around as much as she needed to be, and many nights Misha was left alone with her demons, including her intense fear of the dark.

One payday afternoon, when Misha had just turned twelve, Peaches was working the daylight shift and left work around three. She planned to take her daughter shopping at the mall and go for pizza afterward, but when she arrived at the apartment, Misha was nowhere to be found. After waiting a couple hours, thinking Misha was hanging with her friends, Peaches started calling the few friends she knew of. None of the girls had seen Misha in school that day, which wasn't really all that odd since Misha had been caught skipping school in the past.

Over the course of the next five years, Peaches' life embarked on its downward spiral. Three different detectives had taken the case, but each one had come up short. Peaches' hopes dwindled, and her once-a-month drinking habit became an everyday thing.

Peaches moved to the New York City metro six years after Misha disappeared, hoping to start a new life and move on from the pain she'd experienced in DC. Things didn't turn out exactly how she had planned, though, and soon she was selling her body to keep her rent paid. She met a ten-year-old Star one night on a ho stroll in Newark while the child was wandering the streets, looking for johns to bring home to her mother. From that moment on, Peaches became a mother figure in Star's life—much more so than Star's own mother, Shelly. Star seemed to somewhat fill the void that had been left by Misha's absence, and Peaches vowed to protect Star like she was unable to protect her own daughter. To Peaches, protection meant more than just the physical. She wanted to help the girl with her mental issues as well. She saw firsthand how those could wreak even more havoc on a person.

Peaches was snapped back to reality when Star got up from the bed and walked past her to the bathroom. Once she closed the door behind her, she yelled out to Peaches, "Please, Peaches, go without me. I'm just not ready. See if Junior can go with you. You know your man needs your attention more than me."

Peaches gathered herself and wiped away the tears that had run down her cheeks while reminiscing about

Misha. "Okay, baby, okay. You just tell me when you ready. Junior said he wants to spend some 'us' time anyway. I'll see if he can get away and go with me."

"Tell him I said hi."

Star was grateful that, despite the challenges Peaches had faced in her life, she was able to find such a good man. Junior Rollins was a handsome, retired pianist who lived on Long Island and had taken a special liking to Peaches after meeting her at one of the few blues clubs left in the area. He used to play backup for greats like Muddy Waters, Skip James, and Little Walter, and was now enjoying life and playing when he felt like it. And Junior loved him some Peaches. He doted on her, sending her floral arrangements, taking her on getaways, and showing her that there were good men in the world. Junior even served as somewhat of a beacon of light for Star—a glimpse of inspiration. He reminded her that there was good music to be made and real love to be had.

The twenty-three year-old girl sat in Starbucks with her laptop connected to their free wireless connection. She typed in the website she was looking for, and then immediately clicked on the "Tour" tab on the menu.

She saw that Star Marshall was due for a concert in Cincinnati and scrolled through her cell phone's address book until she came to the Latino man's name.

"Jorge, it's me. It looks like your girl will be in town. I want in."

"Yeah, I've already been notified. And what are you going to do for me?"

The woman twisted her lips and wiped the condensation from her plastic cup. "How does fifty-thousand sound?"

"I can work with that. I'll be in touch."

Her inheritance from Gran came in handy. She had left Cherisse over a million dollars, complete with the instructions that neither her mother or father were to have access to one cent.

She opened a new browser window for Travelocity.com to book a hotel and a plane ticket. It was time to put her plan into action. She laughed out loud at the prospect of bringing the man she had once called Daddy to her own flavor of justice.

The other patrons halted their conversations and stared at the beauty sitting alone who loudly slurped the remainder of her Mocha Frappucino and giggled at the same time.

TWO

Cincinnati, OH

"Give the girl some tits," the blonde bitch said to Rafe, the flamboyant stylist two minutes before Star's cue to come onstage.

The blonde bitch, also known as Miranda Kelly, was an image consultant Scape Records had assigned to Star. While Miranda boasted a roster of high-profile clients in the music, film, and television industries, Star wanted to choke the living shit out of her every time she opened her glossy fucking lips.

"Imagine it, Rafe. A superstar R&B diva with no tits! The legs of Naomi, an ass like J-Lo, eyes like Jada, hair like Aaliyah, and skin like Tyra. But no tits? Dammit, Rafe, do something!" Miranda was nearly flustered, but she held it together almost as well as her Spanx held her ass together. There had been speculation that the image consultant had been victim to a botched butt job.

Rafe got busy with the masking tape and pads, twisting, stuffing, and lifting Star's modest B-cups until they looked to be at least full C's.

"There you go, my dahhling," he said to Star as he kissed her forehead and pushed her out at arm's length to admire his handiwork. His dark brown eyes glistened with pride and a small bead of sweat ran down his otherwise flawless olive forehead. He smacked her on the ass. "Get moving, Fancy-girl! The crowd won't wait forever! Get out there and earn out your advance, you sexy thang!" Rafe popped the collar on his expensive black shirt and took off down the backstage corridor.

During all this commotion, Star said nothing. She had learned the hard way that objecting to anything the blonde bitch, or any other consultant, manager, VP, or otherwise, told her would be a waste of air. Growing up on the mean streets of Newark taught her that nothing she had to say mattered. The music industry only confirmed it.

Star took three breaths—as deep as she could take with an entire roll of masking tape cutting off her circulation—and slipped into her lemon yellow stilettos. She made a little fuss of pulling down the tattered yellow and orange skirt that barely covered her ass and said a little prayer that she wouldn't break her ankle while trying to nail her dance steps in the sadistic shoes. She could already hear the low hum of the crowd that awaited their diva, and when the bassist pounded out the opening riffs of "I'm That Girl," the sound magnified into a frantic roar. She hated that fucking song. It was the stupidest, most juvenile, candy-pop shit she'd ever witnessed. Sarah Vaughan would roll over in her grave at the sheer ignorance of it. But it *had* made her last album go double platinum.

When she stepped onto the glass platform that would

raise and then lower her onto the stage, she slipped a little, sending a shock up her calf and butterflies to her stomach. All she could hope was that this was not an omen of things to come.

"What the fuck were you thinking about?" Tom Michaels downed a glass of Hennessey as the realization of what had just taken place hit him. Star Marshall, dancer, singer, diva extraordinaire, had put on a great show until the last song, when she busted her ass during a complicated reggae-inspired routine.

"I'm sorry. I don't know what happened. Maybe there was water on the stage. I just . . ." Star's voice was childlike, scorned, and apologetic all at the same time.

Star visibly jumped when Tom slammed the empty glass onto her dressing table. "Do you know what this means? Don't you know those candy-ass reporters are gonna have a field day with this shit? We wanted you to appear on *Entertainment Tonight*, we wanted bootleg videos of the show to be posted online, we wanted Wendy Williams to talk about you, but not like this. Oh, God, this is worse than Fergie pissing herself. Fuck, it makes Michelle falling off the stage look like nothing!"

There he went again; from Isaac Hayes to Marsha Brady in no time flat. She raised an eyebrow and tuned him out. She fixated her hazel eyes just above Tom's head, giving off the impression that she was listening. She instantly zoned out the moment someone began going on about how disappointed they were in her, how she had let them down, but she was thinking about the bitches and what she was going to make them do tonight. She simply nodded in agreement with whatever Tom was saying while she internally hatched out her plan for the night's activities.

After an hour of Tom's Hennessey-laden tirade, Star was showered, changed, and finally alone in her chauffeured Hummer and on her way to her favorite hotel in Cincinnati. The Rouge Room boasted 100 guest rooms decked out in nothing but red. The velvet curtains that hung from the windows blocked out everything, allowing Star to fantasize that she owned the hotel, the city, and the fucking world. Her power was within those walls, within that room, and she couldn't wait to assume her throne.

She had to enter through the service entrance in the rear of the hotel to avoid fans, but she didn't mind. The moment she stepped out of the limo, onto the damp pavement, and into the freight elevator, she breathed a little easier. The heaviness of others' expectations and letdowns dissolved. She missed Peaches, though. She hadn't accompanied Star this time because she and Junior were attending a soiree in Long Island. Star made a mental note to call her before the real shit went down.

When Star arrived on her floor, a jolt of arousal shot through her clit. The mere thought of socking it to these mothafuckas filled her with anticipation. She ran a flattened hand down the silky grass-green dress covering her skin to her crotch and squeezed. *Pleasure awaits.* Her full bow lips curled into a naughty smile as she inserted her card key. She took a breath when the green light flashed and turned the brass handle.

* * *

"Baby, I know you upset about what happened tonight, but please take it easy on those souls. Jorge vouched for them, and he hasn't steered us wrong yet. I just worry that one of these days we gonna get a bad seed." Peaches' concern for the hookers was of no consequence to Star, but she let the woman have her moment to speak. Star could hear muted voices and soft jazz playing in the background.

"I know, Peach. I will. How's the party?"

"Chile, these folks are so bougie, I think they got they own personal ass-wipers. Remind me to check shit out before I let Junior take me to another one of these things. Now, you know I like to live well, but these folks is over here eating raw fish and little tiny fish eggs. That's just nasty! I shoulda brought me a little somethin' somethin'."

Star chuckled as she pictured Peaches arriving to the party in the sultry white Michael Kors dress Star had purchased for her, with a foil pan of mac and cheese in her arms.

"Okay, now. You be good, and don't give those folks too hard a time." Star was becoming antsy at the prospect of the auditions, which were now just five minutes away.

"You know I love you, Star. You like one of my own. I just worry bout cha. You know I ain't gonna judge nothing you do, but all I ask is to please be careful. Oh, I wish I was there to help you weed out the duds."

"I know, I know. I love you too. I'll call you when I touch ground tomorrow, I promise."

"All right, baby."

Star hung up the phone with mixed emotions. Some-where deep inside, she knew what she was doing was wrong, but that part of her was buried too deeply be-neath the hunger that consumed her. She popped open the bottle of red Alize that was chilling in the ice bucket and placed the call.

"I'm ready. Send them up."

Carmella had become a pain in Star's ass in record time. It took her just one month to make Star lose all interest in her. It seemed she had something to say about everything, and Star was sick of her mouth. The concierge at The Rouge Room had arranged for some auditions, and it was imminent that Carmella's walking papers were about to be signed, sealed, and delivered. Star hated it when there was a quick turnover with the bitches. It was getting harder for her to trust people, and she was slightly unsettled by the thought of bring-ing in more fresh meat.

Star sat on the red velvet couch and sipped her drink while she waited. Five minutes later she had a nice, gen-tle buzz and someone was knocking on the door. She got up from her relaxing position to let them in. When she opened the door, a beautiful dark-skinned man with a Caesar haircut, chiseled features, and a tight body was standing there with three women and another man behind him.

He took her hand. "Hi, I'm Foxx. Jorge from down-stairs sent us."

Star was taken aback for a split second, but quickly pulled her hand away and narrowed her eyes. "Every-body in, and don't say a fucking word unless I ask you."

Foxx looked down before bringing his eyes up to

meet hers. Then, he led the way for the others and Star closed the door behind him. The bitches-to-be stood there clueless while she resumed her spot on the couch.

"You first. Tell me your name and your specialty." She nodded at the curly redhead with the amber eyes wearing a red satin spaghetti strap gown and matching marabou slippers.

The girl held her head high and looked Star in the eyes. "My name's Cherry and my specialty is eating pussy." Cherry licked her juicy red lips, never taking her eyes off Star's.

Star felt a tingle between her legs. Girlfriend was in. "Okay, Cherry. Go take a seat on the bed." She turned to the light-skinned brother with the curly hair. "And you?"

"My name is Derk and my specialty is breaking backs."

"So unoriginal. But you're cute, so you go stand over there and let me think about it." Star pointed to the foyer area. "And you?" Star nodded to the beautiful biracial sister with the white minidress and knee-high boots.

The girl flipped her long, curly hair and said, "My name is Mocha and my specialty is my flexibility." With that, Mocha grabbed a boot and stretched her leg all the way up, revealing a lacy white crotchless thong. Then she turned around and showed Star her assets, running both her hands over her shapely booty. She looked over her shoulder to gauge Star's reaction.

"Okay, Mocha. Go over and join Cherry." Star could feel the wetness forming in her panties. She looked over to the bold Foxx and then changed her mind, nodding at the ebony sister with beautiful black eyes. She was wearing a Kelly green catsuit and a thick, gold necklace that sparkled against her deep, smooth skin.

"My name is Nia, and my specialty is whatever the fuck you want me to do."

That was what Star liked to hear. She looked at Nia and motioned for her to join the other two girls. There was only one bitch-to-be left.

"So, Foxx, I guess I already know your name. You're a bold mothafucka. So, why don't you tell me why you should be a part of all this." Star pursed her lips and allowed her eyes to roam over his body, clad in a white wife-beater and dark, deconstructed jeans.

"I should be a part of this because you need me to be. I should be a part of this because every fantasy lies in me. My specialty is bringing your every desire, every fantasy, every need to life."

His chocolate-brown eyes, which were framed in the longest lashes Star had ever seen on a man who wasn't in drag, bore a hole into her soul, permeating something that had been in place for as long as she could remember. She had to look away, something she never did. Star could win a staring contest against the best of them, but there was something in this man's eyes that scared the shit out of her and excited her beyond belief at the same time.

She looked at Derk, who was still standing in the foyer looking like a big, dumb kid waiting to be picked for kickball at recess. "Okay, I think you'll all do for tonight. Derk, Foxx, please join the other bitches on the bed. I'll make a final decision about who will come with me to New York after I see what you're working with." Star watched them move toward the bed. Her vantage point from the couch allowed full view of the activity.

At first it seemed like the bitches were shy teenagers waiting to be asked to dance, but Star busted the silence. "I didn't choose you to sit there and look stupid." She turned to Cherry, who sat on the edge of the bed next to Mocha, who was tapping her white boot. "Cherry, do your thing, girl, and test out Mocha's flexibility."

That was all the cajoling Cherry needed. While looking Mocha directly in her eyes, she moved from the bed to the floor, directly between the mixed girl's legs. She ran her long fingers up Mocha's leg, beginning from the toe of her boot to the line of her miniskirt and then forcefully pushed her legs open. Mocha gasped at the act, suddenly feeling the moisture gathering on her thong.

Cherry's ass looked to Star like a juicy maraschino, the satin fabric of her dress pulled taut over her backside. "Lift up your dress, Cherry, so I can see that pussy."

Cherry happily obliged, gathering the satin up around her tiny waist. She wasn't wearing any panties, and her shapely bottom and smooth pinkness bared themselves for all to see.

"Continue, Cherry," Star ordered.

Cherry smiled and turned her attention back to Mocha, who was now wetter than wet. Cherry took her index finger and penetrated Mocha's dripping box, eliciting another gasp. Cherry started pumping the finger in and out of her slowly and then inserted a second. When she felt Cherry's breath warming her hot spot,

Mocha grabbed both boots and formed a V with her legs. Cherry slurped and flicked her tongue over her clit, the friction driving Mocha wild.

Derk's eyebrows shot up as he drank in what was transpiring before him. He was used to sex, hell, he was a male prostitute, but this was just too much. He felt his stiffness crowd his boxer briefs and reached his hand down between his legs to adjust his erection.

"Getting aroused, are we?" Star asked him.

"Oh, yes, Mistress. Very much so."

"Do you wanna touch Cherry's pussy?"

"Please, Mistress."

"Access granted."

Derk moved behind Cherry and started to rub her pink panther, pulling moans and labored breathing from the redhead. He started to sway his hips slightly, imagining what it would be like if he were fucking her. As if she was reading his mind, Star asked, "Would you like to fuck her, Derk?"

"Please, Mistress, please."

Star tossed him a condom from the bowl on the end table beside her and commanded, "Do it."

Star enjoyed watching the new recruits prove themselves. In a matter of an hour, they had all been sucked, licked, stuck, and fucked and were lying in various states of undress around the suite. With the exception of Foxx. He had not been granted access to the orgasmic games this evening. Star wanted to put him in his place for being so bold and making her feel weird, so she had denied him attention. He still sat in the same spot on the bed, still fully dressed with his eyes boring a hole in Star.

* * *

The next morning, Star was furiously working out on the elliptical machine in the VIP weight room of the hotel when she felt her Blackberry vibrate against her hip. She pulled her earbuds out of her ears, interrupting the strains of the harmoniously hot En Vogue blaring through her I-pod, and looked down at the display before her heart dropped into her knees.

"Peaches in hospital. Call ASAP. – Jr."

"Junior? What's going on? Is Peaches okay? Dammit, what's happening?"

"Slow down, my dear. The doctors think she had a stroke. I'm here at South Nassau with her now. She's asleep."

"A stroke? What! Oh, my God. Oh, no. Oh, God." Star stepped off the elliptical and dropped to her knees.

"Look, I gotta go. They won't let you use use cell phones inside the hospital. They're still running tests, and I'm waiting to hear from her doctor and don't wanna be outside too long. I'll call you when I know more."

Star crouched on the floor of the empty workout room as the sob storm racked her body. Before that moment, it had never occurred to her that something bad could ever happen to Peaches. Star had millions of adoring fans, but it dawned on her that if Peaches were gone, then she would truly be alone. No one knew who Star really was except Peaches. No one knew what her struggles were except Peaches. No one knew that beyond the façade of the powerful superstar, there was a scared little girl, except Peaches.

A soft touch on her back jolted Star out of her

reverie. She was afraid to look up to see who had caught her in a weak moment, but she certainly wasn't prepared for what she saw when she lifted her head off her knees and looked into those cocoa eyes framed by long lashes.

"Are you okay?"

She regrouped and stood up, brushing his hand from her body. "Yes, I'm fine. Now, please, leave me be."

Foxx didn't look convinced as he narrowed his eyes, trying to judge how much truth was in her words. The woman he saw before him was a far cry from the bitchy puppeteer he'd witnessed the night before. His conscience wouldn't let him adhere to her request immediately. She was clearly rattled.

"You sure? I was just getting ready to lift. I have a minute if you need to talk to someone."

Star said nothing as she hauled ass out of the room toward the stairwell. She was now shaken by both the fact that Peaches was in the hospital and the idea that she had almost accepted help from one of her bitches.

Cherry lay on the bed in her hotel room smiling a wicked smile. She had to hand it to herself; things were going exactly as planned. A text message coming in to her Sidekick snapped her out of her gloating session.

U R IN. BE READY 2 DEPART 4 NYC @ 5PM. CAR WILL B WAITING IN FRONT OF THE HOTEL. RED NAVIGATOR. IF U R LATE, U R OUT.

The wicked smile returned, and the realization that she was closer to bringing him down made her horny. She rose from the bed and headed to the bathroom. After a steamy romp with the shower massage, she cli-

maxed while envisioning the look of pure horror on
the man's face that would appear when her plan came
to fruition.

Bernard was surprised by the contents of the text
message. He was afraid he'd blown his chances with
Star after both his brashness the previous night and
their run-in in the weight room. For a moment, he saw
his plan shattering, but the fact that she'd seen something noteworthy in him built his confidence back up.

"I'm in," he said to the woman on the other end of
the call he had just placed.

"Perfect. Now's the time to get down and dirty. You
know what to do."

"Of course."

He dialed Jessica.

She didn't even say hello. "When are you coming
home?"

He sighed. "I can't say for sure, but it'll be a while.
The assignment's really taking off."

"I'm starting to get tired of this shit. When I agreed
to move in with you, I wasn't planning on living here
alone. I'm starting to think you're trying to play me."

"Jesus, Jessica. You know how much this means to me.
Can't you just be supportive? I'm not doing anything
but my job." He knew if she knew exactly what his job
had entailed the previous night, she'd flip even more.

"I've been supportive for the last four weeks. Now,
I'm getting pissed. "

"There's nothing I can do about that."

Ending the call, he stomped on the throwaway cell
phone and tossed it in the garbage can under the desk.

As he gathered his few belongings into his green roller suitcase, he thought about where things had gone wrong with Jessica. He knew she'd had a lot of heartache in her past with cheaters, liars, and abusers, but their relationship had started out nearly perfect. She seemed to trust him, and displayed confidence in their union. However, since he'd left for the assignment, she'd done a 180.

Jessica stared at the dead phone in her hands with her mouth gaping open. She'd been dismissed. She flipped the covers off and jumped out of bed to find the business card she'd forgotten about until now.

THREE

West Hempstead, NY

1999

Star was at the bar at Club Vee between sets with her band, Rendezvous. She was waiting in line to have her water pitcher refilled with lukewarm water when she turned around and saw one of the biggest, most beautiful men she had ever seen. She must have been staring, because he shifted his weight form his right foot to his left and ran his gargantuan hand over his shiny, bald head.

"You really ripped it up there." His voice startled her with its depth, its bass.

She was used to hearing this kind of praise in between sets, but this seemed different—more important.

"Thanks." She forced her eyes off his face. "I appreciate it."

"My name's Timothy, but folks call me Tiny Tim." He extended his hand and offered a bashful smile.

She eyeballed his hand and then took it in hers. "Star."

He didn't shake the hand she offered, just continued to hold it in his. "Oh, I know your name. Ritchie's my father, and he's been going on and on about you for months." He looked down at their hands and suddenly remembered what he wanted to do. "But it sure is a pleasure to meet you." He drew her hand to his lips and graced it with a sweet, gentle kiss.

If Star's copper complexion allowed it, she would have blushed. Instead, she thanked him and took the stage for the next set. Throughout the next two hours Tiny Tim remained seated with both feet on the ground in the middle of the audience. His eyes only left her when someone approached his table or she ventured backstage. When the last call lights came on, he was still sitting there. When the band started tearing down their equipment, however, he got to work, loading drum cases and amps in their modest band van, winding up cords, and rolling up their mats.

Star went to Ritchie's office to collect the band's fee, and when she came out, all the equipment had been broken down and loaded. All that was left on the stage was Star's empy water pitcher and glass. She looked around for Tim, but he was nowhere to be found. She knew the van was waiting outside for her to leave for Jersey, but she was torn on whether she should go or wait around to see if Tiny Tim reappeared. Her logic won over her emotion, and she put on her black leather jacket and walked out the back door to the van. The combination of the crisp night air and seeing him there awakened her senses. He was standing there talking to

the keyboard player, Paul. When he saw her, he produced a smile that fell somewhere between "see what I
did, ma?" and "I'm shy, but I want you."

And that was where it had began. After that night,
Star and Tiny Tim were nearly inseparable for the better part of a year. The only time they were apart was
when she had a gig that coincided with one of his away
games. Otherwise, they were in the stands to cheer each
other on.

She'd watch him on the football field with mixed
emotions. On one hand, she knew he was the best
damn defensive end she'd ever seen. On the other
hand, however, it scared her to see him hit and be hit,
the sound of helmets clashing echoing through the
stands. She found herself watching him sleep when she
stayed at his apartment. It had never before occurred to
her that she could feel this way about a man. He became the air she breathed, her biggest cheerleader, her
protector, and the object of her youthful desires.

He never pressured her into making love. In fact, it
was Star who pushed the issue. After four months of loving him with every fiber of her being, she wanted to
take their love to the next level, and she let him know it
with a surprise visit to his apartment. She'd just got
done with her usual gig at Club Vee, and he was on his
way back from a game in Philly against Villanova.

Star was sitting on his sofa completely naked, sipping
a glass of Alize. He opened the door and saw her and
dropped his adidas duffel bag where he stood. She
jumped up from her seat and stood there in front of
him, waiting for him to say something. He looked so
dapper in his suit and tie.

When no words came, she turned around to show him her assets and looked at him over her shoulder, giving him a come hither glance. He finally had the presence of mind to close and lock the door behind him and follow her to the bed where they had innocently lain together many a night.

She sat on the edge of his bed, looking up into his deep eyes. He stood in front of her, with his crotch almost eye-level to Star. He quickly removed his clothing and stood before her with his beautiful abs near her face. She rested her head there, and then moved it lower to kiss the place she'd longed to kiss. He was harder than ever.

He looked down at the woman he loved and asked, "Are you sure you want to do this?"

She didn't answer, just grabbed his hand and pulled him down to lie next to her. They lay there on their sides for a while with eyes locked and souls intertwined, him caressing her soft back, her grabbing his strong shoulders.

He rolled her onto her back and kissed her face and neck. When he came to her breasts, she heard a low moan escape his mouth while he suckled her hard nipple. He moved down her stomach, depositing velvet kisses on the way to her sanctuary. She opened her legs and begged him to knock on the door. He obliged, parting her lips and rhythmically tantalizing her spot. She felt the walls of her sanctuary rumble; heard her heart beating faster than it had when she ran her first mile. She clutched either side of her lover's bald head with her thighs and drifted away into ecstasy.

"Baby, make love to me. Please." She kissed her juices

from his lips and pulled his arms until his body hovered over hers.

"I love you, Star." His erection teased her opening, and she spread her legs wider.

"You are my everything," she said as she felt him enter her sanctuary. It was painful, and he was worried about hurting her, but she encouraged him to continue. She grabbed onto his biceps, on each side of her head, and looked into his eyes as he began slowly moving in and out of her. After about ten minutes, Star was over the pain of it, and pulled him down onto her. She could feel the walls welcoming their new inhabitant, and soon, he let out a sigh of release as she felt his warm nectar enter her. Afterward, she lay on his chest, thanking God that he was hers.

Had she known what would have happened just six months after that beautiful night, she might have left it at that and walked away. Or maybe the experience, as painful as it was, had conditioned her for the music business and the utter lack of control she would feel in it.

FOUR

Oceanside, Long Island

Star had to use a private entrance to the hospital to avoid the havoc she knew she'd create if people recognized her. When the shift nurse escorted her into Peaches' room, she felt lightheaded at the sight before her. Peaches looked like a little girl sleeping in the bed; her lustrous complexion was peaked, and she looked to have lost twenty pounds.

Junior was dozing in the fold-out chair next to the bedside, his white linen outfit a wrinkled mess. *Family Feud* hummed from the wall-mounted television, and Star noted that the room was devoid of flowers, cards, or balloons.

"No one else has come to visit her?" Star kept her voice low to avoid disturbing the couple.

"No, just Mr. Rollins. He hasn't left her side since she came in last night." The young, brunette nurse gathered empty cups and other litter from the bed tray and made her way out the door.

"Ohh, Peaches. You know you can't leave me." Star's

voice cracked and she bent down to rest her head on Peaches' bed.

Peaches' voice was gravelly. "Chile, who said anything about leaving? You know it takes more than this to hold a southern gal down."

"Oh, damn! You're awake!" Star hollered so loud Junior jumped clean out of his chair.

"What? Oh! Baby, you're awake!"

"What's all this fuss y'all making? Somebody get me a drink."

Junior and Star looked at each other with wide eyes and burst out laughing.

"My baby's a firecracker." Junior chuckled and ran down the hall to get some water from the nurses' station.

A tear rolled down Star's cheek as she grasped Peaches' hand. "I got scared. I can't do it without you, Peach."

"Baby, I aint goin' nowhere, and you can write that down, take a picture, whateva you need to do to remember that."

Junior came running in with the flimsy plastic cup of water, likely spilling more than was left for Peaches to drink. He held the cup up to her lips and steadied her head with his strong hand. Peaches sipped, but a strange look came across her face when she swallowed the water.

"Now when did I ever mean water when I said I needed a drink?"

Star and Junior stood there, stunned, for a moment before Peaches winked and said, "Ya'll two take me way too seriously."

* * *

As it turned out, Peaches had suffered a mild stroke. The doctor ordered her to quit smoking and prescribed medication for her hypertension and cholesterol. The episode had brought reality crashing down on everyone. Junior proposed to her the day she came home from the hospital and she happily accepted. Star was helping her with her wedding preparations in between appearances and shows. Peaches' demeanor was that of an excited young girl.

Star envied the feeling. Part of her wanted to feel the same kind of love Peaches and Junior shared, but she was afraid that part of her had died. The feeling it left in its wake was one she vowed to never feel again. The aftermath of the way she'd loved Tiny Tim had been far too painful.

FIVE

Midtown Manhattan

The long, black marble table in the conference room of Scape Records in Manhattan was so shiny Star could see her reflection in it. As she and Tom Michaels, her manager of five years, awaited the label execs and miscellaneous staff to join the twelve o'clock meeting, Star stared at her reflection in the smooth stone.

"Where the hell are they? Don't they know we have to be at the Chelsea Studios at 2:30 for taping? Martha Stewart is no punk! You show up late to her and you're liable to get a nonstick skillet sandwich," Tom tapped his tawny fingers on the table like he was practicing his scales on the piano, leaving his fingerprints on the otherwise flawless finish.

Star just shrugged. She knew it was rhetorical, but she felt the need to respond to his daily tirade, if only to shut him the fuck up.

Carson Nadar had called the last-minute meeting. He was the senior executive who had been assigned to Star three years ago when she signed a five-year deal with Scape. Since then he had become the ruler of all things Star, from her songs to her hairstyle. While Tom talked a good game, he was basically Carson's bitch. His percentages depended on Scape's checkbook, and so he bent over and let Carson have his way more often than not.

Star hated these meetings with every cell in her body. Carson had made a habit of pointing out what he considered to be her shortcomings and misgivings in this public forum. Star had a sneaking suspicion that he did this to intentionally humiliate her, but she couldn't prove anything.

Twenty minutes later the staff began trickling in. They filled in the black Aeron chairs surrounding the table while leaving the one at the head of the table empty. Everyone knew it was taken.

When Carson walked into the room, everyone stopped shuffling their papers and cut their chitchat. The tall, lean, tanned, white-haired man with ocean blue eyes sat in the empty chair at the head of the table and got right down to business.

"We were thinking you should have some work done," Carson began. He didn't look up from his notes, but the entire room knew he was speaking to Star.

"Work?" Star and Tom said simultaneously.

"Nothing too outlandish, just some nose work and a breast augmentation. The procedures are so common these days, they're practically as routine as getting your teeth cleaned," Nicole Williams, Carson's chief minion, assured her.

"I see," Star said.

"Oh, and we'll have to do something about that hideous hair and those hoochie-mama nails of yours. I would think Miranda Kelly would know better," Nicole said, running a hand over her chin-length, straight, black hair and looking down at her own French manicure.

Star self-consciously smoothed down her shoulder-length curly bob and moved her hands under the table to ward off any further examination by the rest of the staff.

Tom spoke up, "Of course. Not a problem."

Carson nodded. "Great. So I think we're all on the same page with that. Nicole, call the image consultant and get her on the case immediately. I want the hair and nails completed before the big show in Prospect Park next week. Also, Tom, get Star on Kevin's schedule for a rhinoplasty and breast augmentation consultation. Next order of business?"

Jerry Allred, the marketing associate who was wearing Buddy Holly glasses and all black, began furiously flipping the pages of his bright yellow legal pad and said, "Yes sir. The next order of business would be Star's third album. Now, we came up with a few titles and I wanted to run them by the group."

Star braced herself. Carson nodded from the end of the table and motioned for Jerry to continue.

"All right. I'm just going to read the list and you stop me if there's something that piques your interest. If we agree on a title, we'll give that to the writers and producers and have them write a title track around it.

Ahem. 'Ghetto Booty,' 'You a Cheating Bastard,' 'Push-Up Bra.'" Jerry flipped a few more pages. "Let's see here, 'Bend Me Over,' 'Cherries on Top My . . .'"

Carson cut him off. "I think we should go with 'Push-Up Bra' in light of the breast augmentation. Yes, I think that's the one."

Star gave Tom a look of death, but he pretended not to notice. Instead, he agreed with his sugar daddy. "Carson, I think we have a winner."

Carson looked quite pleased with himself. "Great, then let's get the ball rolling. 'Push-Up Bra' it is!"

Star felt like she was going to throw up, but there was nothing she could really say without having an alternate solution. She knew they wouldn't want to hear her thoughts anyway. She was just the paper doll in the twisted game these children were playing.

They wrapped up the meeting with instructions to have the writers and producers come up with a title track for 'Push-Up Bra.' Star and Tom bolted out of the conference room to make their taping. They had ten minutes to get there and it was at least a 45-minute jaunt.

When they got in the limo Star's driver, Jake, was waiting in downstairs, Star started in on Tom. Moving to the edge of the seat, she screamed, "What the fuck, Tom? 'Push-Up Bra'? What the fuck, what the fuck, what the fuckin' fuck!!" She scooted back, tilted her head back, and released a mournful sigh.

"Oh, come on. It's not so bad. Carson knows this business. He knows what's going to sell."

"Or sell *out*," Star mumbled under her breath.

"Don't think about it right now. Just let it be for a day or so. Right now you need to marinate on Martha."

"Interesting choice of words."

Cherisse sat in the lobby of the place she would now be calling home, her long legs crossed and bobbing to the nearly nonexistent beat of the elevator music that was piped in overhead. She hadn't considered the possibility that it would be so easy to be welcomed into the fold of Star's stable of pros, but her looks and skills in the pleasure department had worked for her yet again. Jorge had informed her that this would be the best way to permeate the thick barrier Star Marshall placed between her private life and the world, and damned if he wasn't on the money.

She never read anything about Star canoodling with this bad boy or girl-fighting with that starlet, so, at first, she wondered if Star would be the right person to help her expose the bastard. However, after dubious research and a little bit of old-fashioned stalking, she knew Star would be perfect. It seemed Star had a bit of business to attend to with the man as well. It couldn't hurt that he was playing paper dolls with Star, just as he had done with her so many years before.

The pole up Martha Stewart's ass wasn't shoved up nearly as far as Star had originally thought. In fact, Martha was quite accommodating and, for the first time in two years, Star had eaten some carbs. She was still high from the sugar rush the host's elaborately decorated cupcakes provided her.

"Don't get used to that treatment. You know that sugar will blow your ass up in no time. You're better off to pretend those cupcakes never existed." Tom inspected his flawless manicure as they headed down 3rd Avenue toward his overpriced condo in Long Island City.

What never made sense to Star was that, while the yuppies and wanna-be ballers were buying up five million dollar condos, the hoes were strolling less than a block away from their fortresses. Although she'd never admit to it, Star sometimes scanned the faces, adorned with fake smiles and tired eyes, looking for someone who resembled her mother. It was pointless—Shelly was dead, killed by a john hopped up on smack who accused her of not sucking his dick hard enough—but that never stopped her. It was as though Shelly was the one person Star was unable to save, and the guilt and ghosts of the past plagued her mind on a regular.

When Jake pulled up in front of Tom's yuppie island, Star breathed a silent sigh of relief. She was tired of his fucking yapping. ". . . and so, if you can get into a size two, you'll have Ciara spending all her time in the gym instead of working on those dance steps. We'll take over the music industry!" Tom gave Star a rushed hug and hurried out of the limo to greet his doorman.

It was times like these that Star wondered about Tom. One minute, he was a hard-ass, and the next, he seemed like a teenaged girl. Star moved toward the front of the vehicle and lowered the partition as Jake pulled off. "Finally! I thought his ass would never shut up!"

Jake held in a giggle.

She leaned into the space and gave him a set of puppy dog eyes. "Can you hook a sistah up, my man?"

"Now, Miss Star, you know I will never hear dee end of it if your Mr. Tom were to find out. He says it's bod for your vocals." Jake's accent reminded Star of Apu on *The Simpsons*. In fact, his real name was Jagjivan, but everybody always mispronounced it, so he told then to call him Jake.

"C'mon, Jaaaaake! Just one! No one has to know! Anyway, isn't it bad for Hindus to smoke?" She fluttered her eyelashes and pouted her mouth.

A look of shame crossed his face, and Star knew he had been broken. "Okay, Miss Star. But only this once." He stopped at a light and reached into the glove box for the pack of Kools and the lighter. When he turned to hand one to Star, she snatched the entire pack, lighter and all.

She took one out, lit it, and took a deep drag while the smoke filled her lungs. Relieved, she exhaled slowly, reluctant to let the first hit end.

"Ooh ooh, you're a tricky one." Jake waved his index finger at her and proceeded through the light.

Before her temptation overtook her, Star threw the pack and lighter onto the seat in front of her. "You the man, Jake." She moved back to the other side of the space and pressed the button to raise the partition back into place.

Star finished her smoke and thought about the upcoming album on the way to location number five. She still couldn't believe the fuckers wanted to call the shit "Push-Up Bra."

"Of all the idiotic . . ." she mumbled to herself as she

exhaled the last drag of her Kool before tossing it out the window.

She reached over to the control panel and turned up the mix CD that was playing. Carmen McRae was talking about getting no kicks from champagne and Star's mind flooded with memories of her mother blasting the jazz divas while her johns came to call to drown out the sound of the debauchery taking place behind the door to her bedroom. In fact, it was these records that taught Star what it was to be a singer. She learned her phrasing from Ella, her emotion from Billie, her sassiness from Dinah, and her sultriness from Carmen. Not to mention Sarah, whom Star felt epitomized all the virtues of a great singer.

So much had changed since Star had first decided her dream was to sing and follow in the footsteps of those divas who paved the way for her and everyone from Aretha to Mariah. Star had always seen herself as a musical purist, and was put off by the commercialized, sexified hoochies who called themselves singers, but were no more than models who could sorta carry a tune. And yet, there she was. She had become everything she hated in those women, yet she felt powerless to change things.

Sarah's voice came through the speakers, singing "Dreamsville." The tear that slid down Star's cheek left a salty drop on her baby blue top, turning the fabric a deep shade of navy.

SIX

Astoria, Queens

Carmella looked crushed by her dismissal. Thankfully, she knew better than to question the Mistress's wishes and quickly left the location. A sense of relief washed over Star when Peaches called to tell her that it had been taken care of.

"Gather the bitches at location number three. I should be there within the next half hour."

Peaches couldn't shake the feeling that something was off when Vivian, Jay, and Aaron arrived with the two new recruits traipsing in behind them. The woman, whom Star had referred to as Cherry, just seemed way too happy to be there. And the new man stood there with his hands in his pockets and his eyes wide open, sinking in the scene before him.

She hadn't been able to do her background check on these two, and while Jorge assured her they were on point, she didn't trust him like she trusted herself. Star had placed her trust in Peaches to make sure that the bitches were good to go, and wouldn't change their minds one day and demand hush money in exchange for keeping quiet about the deeds they were witness to. She didn't want to freak herself out too much, though. After the stroke, she'd made a promise to Junior and Star that she'd be more conscious of her stress levels.

"Okay, ladies and gentlemen. Your mistress will be arriving shortly. In the meantime, please help yourself to drinks and food." Peaches motioned to the kitchen area, where an elaborate spread of liquor, fruits, and finger foods were on display.

Vivian took action first and led the others to the table. While they indulged, Peaches slipped out the door, locking it from the outside. She still didn't trust those newbies.

When Peaches exited the lobby of the building, she caught a glimpse of a female figure hovered over on the sidewalk, crying her eyes out. She had to fight the motherly instincts that kicked in, and walked past Carmella to the red Navigator that was waiting to take her back out to Long Island.

SEVEN

Midtown Manhattan

"Sex. I need you to exude more sex. Let's do another take."

Star was sure that if her blood pressure rose any higher, her head would pop completely off her body. This wasn't how it was supposed to be. She was supposed to enjoy this.

She nodded and then cleared her throat before hearing the futuristic beat replay in her headphones. The white producer, Mickey, was in front of the mixing board, bouncing his head like an idiot on the other side of the glass.

Her voice rang out through her headphones and the monitors that hung on the other side of the glass, directly above Mickey's head. Within three seconds, he stopped the track. Star sighed and commenced to count the peaks and valleys in the egg-crate foam that lined the walls of the vocal booth.

"God damnit, Star! Why can't you take direction? I

need you to exude sex!" Mickey's face turned a deeper shade of red with each word that exited his mouth.

"Sorry. I'll try." She looked down at the floor and wondered just what kind of sex she could exude when she could only get out five words before being so rudely interrupted.

Carson Nadar entered the studio and, after having his ass thoroughly kissed by Mickey, sat on the beige leather couch in the control room and fixed his eyes on Star. Carson's eyes easily pierced through the sound-proof glass. The air in the vocal booth became thick, and it was all she could do to breathe.

"Okay, Star, let's do this!" Mickey re-cued the track and nodded in he direction.

A single bead of sweat ran down her forehead just before the track started again.

Star began to sing the hook. "You ain't seen nothin', baby, till you've seen me. My lady lumps can take you where you need to be. I've got a secret for only you to see. You ain't seen nothin', baby, till you've seen me."

"And cut!" Mickey cut off the track and turned his back to the vocal booth, furiously waving his hands around and moving his mouth, though she couldn't hear anything.

Carson looked at Mickey, nodded, and then cut his eyes to Star, who stood there holding the headphone to her ear and waiting for hell to rain down.

Mickey's ass accidentally hit the intercom button, and his words emanated through the headphones. "I can't work like this! She doesn't take direction, and, truth be told, she isn't all that good. I've had to use the pitch bender on her voice more than once. She always has an attitude like she's the next Mariah or something, and, let's be honest, Miss Marshall doesn't even come close to stacking up."

Star's heart dropped to her stomach as the lies he was telling registered. She threw the headphones on the floor and ran out of the studio to where Jake was waiting. When she knocked on the window to tell him to unlock the door, he rustled the paper he was reading and tossed it to the side before hitting the automatic locks.

As she closed the door and pressed the lock, she saw Mickey running out of the building with Carson calmly following behind.

"Get me the hell out of here, Jake," she said through the open partition.

"You have got to be kidding me, Star. How the hell do you just walk out of a recording session? Do you have any idea what we are paying for that studio? For that fucking asshole, Mickey?"

Tom was on another one of his rampages. Star tried to tune him out, but the spit he was depositing on the table in front on him had her on edge. She wanted to tell him to say it, don't spray it, but she figured the more she interrupted him, the longer he'd go on. The waitress came by and refilled her green tea, giving Tom a chance to catch his breath and refuel his engine. Great.

"I mean, sometimes you act like we get this shit for free. Say something, damn it!"

"Sorry." She shrugged her shoulders and readjusted her Fendi shades.

"Oh, Lord, help me. And Carson was there? Jesus, Star, you picked a fine time to grow a fucking back-bone!"

"Did you ever consider that I don't *like* how my career is going? Or is your head shoved so far up Carson Nadar's ass, you can't see anything but his shit?"

Tom's mouth dropped open.

"Look, I know you've been with me from day one, and I appreciate it, I do. But when did your title change from manager to record exec's bitch?" She stirred some honey into her teacup.

"Wow. This is the first I'm hearing this."

"You said it yourself, Tom. I have no fucking back-bone. But I have to tell you, I'm tired of being jerked around, treated like a puppet. I want to do something that I'm passionate about, and *Push-Up Bra* ain't it!"

The word "puppet" echoed in Star's head. She thought about the hookers, but quickly pushed that thought aside.

"And by the way, I don't want big breasts!"

"Whew, okay. Just at least go to the consultation, and then we can discuss all this other stuff later."

"No."

"Come on, Star. Do it for me?"

"Fuck no."

"Jesus, will you stop thinking about yourself for five minutes and just go to the damn consultation?" Tom pounded the table, making her tea spill over the brim of her cup.

"Okay, damn. But I don't have to like it." She sniffed.

EIGHT

SoHo

"Peach, have Foxx come to location number three."

"By himself?"

"Yeah, just him."

"Baby, you know you shouldn't be getting too attached to any of these people. This is what they do for a living."

"I don't give a fuck right now, Peaches, please just do it. He better be here alone in forty-five minutes."

"I'll send him over, baby. Star, just be careful."

Star hung up the cordless phone and paced the plush, cream-colored carpet. This location was one of her favorites. It reminded her of some shit she'd seen in Oprah's crib. Some Zen type shit. The living room was mostly devoid of color, save the celery green accents. The furniture, walls, and curtains were all cream, and every time she came there she was reminded of a bowl of Breyer's French vanilla ice cream.

Star bathed and changed into a black satin pajama

set. She twisted her hair up into a bun and applied some mascara and watermelon lip-gloss and then spritzed a few pumps of Lemon Sugar perfume on her pulse points. She didn't know why, but she wanted to look and smell nice for Foxx. Normally she could care less about how she presented herself to her concubines.

When the doorbell rang, Star's heart pounded a rapid rhythm, and restless butterflies flew in her tummy. She hated that feeling. That feeling could get a bitch in trouble.

When she flung the door open, Foxx was standing there smelling like the Calvin Klein counter at Macy's and looking more tantalizing than a Cinnabon. He wore a black bandana around his eyes, and his arms were clasped behind his back.

"You called, Mistress?" Star could smell the cinnamon on his breath.

"You can take the blindfold off now. Close the door behind you." She walked away and sat down on the sofa, folding her legs under her bottom.

Foxx squinted as his eyes adjusted to the light. He stuffed the bandana in his pocket and turned to close the door. He walked toward Star, his steps slow and uneasy.

"Have a seat." She used her eyes to gesture to the armchair directly facing her.

Foxx's breathing was uneven as he rested in the chair.

She lowered her eyes. "This isn't like one of those other times. I just wanted to talk."

"I understand. What would you like to talk about?"

"You. Tell me about you. How'd you get into the business of pleasure?" She felt a hint of warmth gather in her cheeks as she smoothed her hand over the black satin.

Foxx let out a light chuckle. "You want the truth, or you want the interesting version?"

She smiled. "The truth is fine."

"Okay, well, I grew up just outside of the Nati. My mother was addicted to coke, and I was the oldest brother, so I had to find a way to feed my little brother and sister. It was more business than pleasure." He rubbed the back of his neck.

"Sorry." She was beginning to regret the request for his appearance. She felt her grip on control sliding out of her hands.

"Hey, it happens. So, what else you wanna know?"

"Do you think I'm crazy?"

"Excuse me?"

"Nothing."

"No, it's okay."

"Forget it."

Star's eyes darted around the room, looking for a resting place anywhere but on him.

"Can I ask you something?" Foxx shifted in the chair.

"Maybe." She continued her eye Olympics.

"Do you ever feel like something's missing from your life?"

"Why would I feel like that? I'm rich, famous, I look good. What else does a woman want?"

" I don't know, a partner in crime maybe? Love?"

"No, I've tried that. It's not for me."

"Why?"

"It takes too much out of you. It's easier to separate the emotion from things."

"Afraid of being hurt?"

"No." That sure was an interesting painting. It was two black figures entwined atop a red-to-yellow background. It made her more uncomfortable. As if that were possible.

"What if I told you I wanted to know you on a deeper level? What if I told you I wanted to show you that it's sometimes worth the risk?"

She ran out of things to look at, so she had to look at him. He looked like he was hanging on her every breath.

She shrugged.

He stood. She tensed. He sat down beside her. She cowered. He touched her face. She closed her eyes. He pulled her into his embrace.

"What are you doing?" Her eyes fluttered open, nearly matching the pace of her heartbeat.

"I'm sorry. I didn't mean to overstep." He scooted back to the other end of the sofa. "Why'd you say love isn't for you?"

"I don't really wanna bring up old ghosts." Her eyes retraced their steps across the room to the painting.

"Sometimes they need to be. Okay, I'll tell you about one of the times I was in love and then you tell me. Deal?"

She wasn't too happy about the way he way coaxing her. She was supposed to have control. "Maybe."

He was getting bolder. He kicked off his shoes and stretched his legs. She raised an eyebrow. She was severely out of practice at this.

"Jamie Baldwin was my first love. I met her on my first day of school at Madiera Heights Middle School when we were playing kick ball and she slammed me in the head with the ball."

Star let a slight grin make its way across her stoic face as she imagined a tween girl pelting him in the head with one of those red kick balls that made the loud noise when it was bounced on concrete. She used to see girls playing 4-Square with those.

"Oh, you think that's funny, huh? I'll have you know I had a red mark on my forehead the rest of the day. Talk about standing out in a crowd. Anyway, after that, there was something about her that I couldn't quit thinking about. Maybe it was her long, pretty hair that she'd wrap up on top her head during P.E., or maybe it was her feistiness; I don't know."

"Maybe it was that she gave you a challenge. You seem like you're a challenge-seeker." Star got up from the couch and made her way over to the mini-bar to get some Sprites. "Go ahead. I'm listening."

"I followed behind that girl for a month before she'd even look twice at me. Then, I got her."

Star handed him a cobalt glass filled with Sprite and ice. "Thanks." He winked. "So, anyway, I plotted for a while, but she finally agreed to be my girl. We were to-gether from sixth grade until eleventh grade. Then she moved on to bigger, better things, namely the star for-ward on the basketball team."

"Ooh, that's rough." Star was only mildly entertained by the story, but she didn't want it to end because that would mean it was her turn to talk.

"Your turn."

Star fidgeted and clinked the ice in her empty glass. "Not much to tell, really."

"I really wanna know."

She sighed and placed the glass on the end table, folded her legs under her bottom, and crossed her arms across her midsection. "His name was Timothy. He was a star football player for Hofstra. I thought he loved me, hell, I thought we would end up getting married." The pain was starting to flood her veins. She took a deep breath.

"What happened?"

She took a breath and quickly said, "He got hurt in a game—his knee. They said he'd never play again, and would probably be in a wheelchair. He got real depressed. There wasn't anything anyone could say. He stopped taking my calls, and then he disappeared. I don't even know if he's alive or dead."

It was the first time she had said those words out loud. She'd thought them nearly every day since Tiny Tim disappeared, but now it seemed so much more real. It was almost as if it'd all been a dream, but now the vividness was unmistakable.

"Wow. Now, correct me if I'm wrong, but how does a person just up and disappear?"

"I've asked myself that question a million times." She sighed. "I think he left because he felt like he was holding me back. I thought he knew that he was what propelled me forward, but I guess he couldn't see it."

"Men are proud. We don't like to appear vulnerable or weak. It's our nature. But I can't understand how he would let someone so special slip away."

She shrugged and got up to refill her glass. "Too late to speculate. It's ancient history."

Foxx came up and stood directly behind her, wrapping his arms around her waist and pulling her into his chest.

"What are you—"

"Shhh. Just listen."

"To what?"

"Your heart."

"This is crazy." She twisted around and was suddenly face to face with a man. She hadn't been this close to a man in so long.

His cinnamon breath whispered, "It's okay to feel sometimes."

"How do you know what I feel?"

He guided her to the couch, where he motioned for her to sit. Then he knelt in front of her on the floor and looked at her like she was the first woman he'd ever seen. He rubbed his hands across the satin covering her thighs and she closed her eyes, transporting herself from the reality of who she was, the hurt she'd experienced. She pretended she was normal; that he was hers and she was his and this was nothing out of the ordinary.

Star felt his hot breath between her legs through the thin material of her pajama bottoms. When the heat got closer, a wave of desire encompassed her, causing her mouth to suck in a gasp of air. When his mouth landed to kiss her there, her desire overtook her. She lifted her butt off the cushion so he could remove her bottoms, which he did slowly. He placed his warm hand over the place he had just kissed and felt her heat transfer to him.

He rubbed her pussy gently, focusing his attention on the most sensitive area. When her heartbeat quickened, he kissed her pink center and began to lick her rhythmically up and down. When her muscles tightened, he backed off, using his finger to part her full labia and penetrate her wetness. He got her worked up again, and this time he didn't stop soon enough. She panted and moaned her satisfaction.

She was stunned. No one had even touched her there since Tim. She hadn't been led to an orgasm created by hands not her own since her first love. Not only that, but she felt something deeper than the animalistic sexuality she felt when she was the emotionless mistress, ordering her puppets to commit her whims to action. She was terrified.

NINE

"**B**ernard, I need an update. How did the one-on-one meeting go?"

He paused, contemplating telling the truth or making something up. "We didn't have it. She changed her mind at the last minute."

"Fuck! You're gonna have to get something useful while you're there instead of just—"

"I'm doing the best I can. Anyway, we already have enough to do what we came to do."

"I want hard evidence: audio, video, pictures. You're going to have to find a way to get it."

"The older woman, Peaches, she always has us searched before we meet with Star. There's no way I can get anything past her."

"Figure it out."

Bernard looked at the phone to make sure she'd really hung up on him. He wondered at that moment if what Star had told him was true; if feeling things got you in trouble. He was supposed to be there collecting evidence that she had some freaky dealings with hookers. *The Cincinnati Exponent* had commissioned him to do just that after an anonymous tip had come into their hotline.

Now he was caught up between wanting to further his career as a reporter and the feelings that Star had stirred in him. He wanted to protect her.

Iris looked through the blinds to see who was ringing the doorbell of her South Merrick home. At first she thought she was hallucinating when she saw Cherisse standing there, but her instinct took over and she flung the door open to see the daughter she had last laid eyes on eight years ago.

"Mother."

"Cherisse? Is that you? Oh, thank God!" Iris pulled Cherisse into a tight embrace.

Cherisse pulled away. "Hey, Mother. How's life treating you?" Cherisse rolled her eyes and stomped past her mother into the foyer of the sprawling home.

"Where have you been? We thought you were dead!"

"Yeah, I guess *he* hoped I was."

Iris looked down at the floor and wiped the tears from her cheeks. "I missed you."

"I'm not here for a mother-daughter picnic. I want some answers from you, and this time I'm not taking no for an answer."

"Come. Sit." Iris gestured toward the sitting room. Cherisse always hated that room. It was so stuffy and uncomfortable with its traditional furnishings and one-of-a-kind Oriental rug. Yet, it fit her mother so perfectly. Clad in a powder pink Chanel suit, Iris looked like part of the décor.

She stood in front of her mother, who was seated on a mauve settee. "I want to know who my father is."

"Cherisse, please, don't bring up old skeletons."

"I want to know. Now."

"Oh, dear." Iris' green eyes dropped to her lap.

"I know you had a soul once, before *he* crushed it. Now tell me who my father is."

Iris sighed and smoothed her dyed hair. "He was a musician. It was a tumultuous time in my life. Carson was always away on business, and I got lonely."

"A musician?"

"It was a silly indiscretion."

"Oh, so that's what I am? A silly indiscretion?"

Iris' mouth moved to form words of protest, but before they could materialize, they were caught in her throat.

"Does he know about me?"

Iris shook her head. "No."

A wave of relief washed over Cherisse. She had hoped in her heart that her real father hadn't known about her and left her there with *him* to suffer. She hoped that if her real father knew she existed, he would come save her from the torture. Now she knew he hadn't had the chance.

"I want a name."

"Cherisse, I—"

"A name, Mother."

Midtown, Manhattan

Star sat in the waiting area outside Carson's office with the CD she had made in her home studio, safely tucked in her black velvet handbag. The nervous energy that coursed through her body exited through her foot, which was tapping faster than seemed humanly possible. She eyeballed Carson's assistant, Tammy, and distracted herself by counting the freckles that dotted the woman's face. She heard a buzz coming from desk.

Unable to sit there any longer, Star jumped to her feet when Tammy took an impromptu trip to the ladies' room.

When Star opened the door, Carson was on the phone. She stood there for a moment.

"We have to keep this relationship under wraps. Do you know what this could cost me? Don't worry, I'll take care of Iris."

Carson's face was distorted in a snarl, and it looked like a tsunami was raging in his ocean blues. Star fidgeted with the hem on her gold lace top.

"No, don't do that!" He slammed the receiver down onto the base and looked up at Star, his snarl relaxing and his storm transforming into tranquility.

"Star, what can I do for you? I was surprised when Tammy said you'd shown up unexpectedly. Is everything all right?"

Her voice was shaky, and she felt like couldn't breathe. "This is hard for me, but, no. Everything isn't all right." She sat down in one of the cushioned maroon leather chairs in front of his huge maple desk.

Carson's brow furrowed. "Well, let's see if we can change that. What is it you wanted to talk to me about?"

"I've been doing a lot of thinking, and I've decided I want to change my image—move toward a more new-soul vibe instead of the pop vibe." The light that was coming through the shades behind Carson made her eyes glow a warm amber. Her heart pounded in her chest.

"I've taken the initiative to write and lay down some scratch tracks." She pulled the CD out of her bag. "I wanted to know what you thought about this." She stretched her arm across the desk, offering the meat to the lion.

He glanced at the CD before refocusing his gaze on her. "While I can appreciate your efforts, you have to understand one thing and one thing only. I own you. I decide what you sing and how you sing it." Carson's icy eyes pierced into Star. His tone seemed so nonchalant, but his eyes told otherwise.

She wasn't surprised by his reaction, but she had hoped it would be different. She knew it wouldn't be easy, but she had to try. "I understand my contractual commitments. I'm just saying that it could be the time to saturate that market. Jill Scott hasn't gotten much airplay lately, and Algebra and Amel still are fairly unknown." She took a deep breath and continued before he could interject. "I can use the fame I already have to bring spins and fans to this type of music." She shifted in the chair and repositioned herself, her mini revealing her smooth legs.

Carson's eyes moved to her exposed flesh. "You aren't catching my drift. It's a no-go."

"Well, then, I want out of my contract."

The storm was back. "How dare you, you ungrateful little bitch?"

The roar reverberated in Star's bones. She stood up and began toward the door, but he was too quick. He grabbed her by the neck and pulled her in so his mouth was to her ear.

"Why would you want to mess with a good thing, you stupid bitch? We're all making money here, and that's what matters. You fuck with my money, and I promise you, you won't live to tell about it."

She mustered the strength to turn around and face him. "Are you threatening me?"

His eyes seemed to glaze over as he grinned a wicked smile and said, "Star, whatever are you referring to? I hope you have a great day." Then he pushed her out of his office into the waiting area where at least ten necks snapped around to see what the commotion was.

"Watch your step, Star! We all know you're a little clumsy." Carson snorted and closed the heavy door.

When the elevator door opened, Star was face to face with a disheveled-looking Tom.

"What are you doing here?" they said in unison.

TEN

When Star thought of plastic surgery, a vivid image of Pamela Anderson in a pink foil bikini flashed before her eyes. The patients in the waiting room at Dr. Kevin Osbourne's plastic surgery practice ranged in looks from Jessica Simpson to Celia Cruz. Star was stunned by their diversity, and the fact that they were all there made her loosen up a little.

"Star Marshall?" an average-looking woman with above average breasts held her clipboard and scanned the waiting room.

Star stood and followed the woman to Dr. Osbourne's office, where she waited for his arrival. She looked around the modern office with sleek design and spotted a collage on the wall that merged photos of various female body parts. It struck her that in a way, the surgeon was like a kid playing with Mr. Potato Head, arranging parts, taking them away, and adding them at will.

She heard two taps on the door followed by the appearance of a handsome man who looked to be in his early thirties. A giggle escaped her mouth as she contemplated whether he was really 60 years old and was a walking advertisement for his own services.

"Miss Marshall, I presume?" He smiled, but there were no signs of laugh lines or crows feet gathering around his eyes.

Star nodded.

"Carson Nadar and I have been friends for years. His people tell me you're in the market for a few enhancements."

"That's what they tell me."

"So, what concerns do you have?"

Star glanced on his massive bookshelf, and what she saw made her heart nearly stop beating. One of her hookers was posed in a photo with Dr. Osbourne, two other women, a young man, and none other than Carson Nadar. She looked away and then back at it again to be sure the young teen was the mid-twenties hooker she thought it was and she wasn't hallucinating.

"Umm, who's that in the picture?" Star nodded toward the photo.

"Oh, that old thing?" He chuckled. "Let's see, Carson, me, our wives, my son Paul, and Carson's daughter, Cherisse. We were on a trip to Canada. Wow, that must have been taken ten years ago. Terrible thing, Cherisse ran away from home when she was about fifteen or sixteen. Now, why a privileged young lady would—"

"Holy fucking shit," she breathed.

The doctor's eyes widened a bit and he cleared his throat. He flipped through a manila folder and produced three brochures. "Here are some pamphlets that will provide a multitude of information about the procedures you're interested in. Take these with you and look them over, and make sure to call the office should you have any further questions."

"Will do." Star stood, zipped her pink leather jacket, and left behind a confused Dr. Osbourne.

Jessica waited in line at the cabstand outside of LaGuardia, furiously tapping her foot. Her carry-on was light, but it was beginning to rub her shoulder, so she placed it on the ground.

She hadn't received any contact from Bernard, since their argument on the phone two weeks earlier. After the first week, she hired a private investigator to see what he was really up to. She wasn't born yesterday; she knew from experience how deceitful and untrustworthy men could be. She had caught her previous fiancée, Malik, with one of his coworkers and ended up contracting chlamydia from the lying bastard. If that wasn't enough, she'd been smacked around and ended up in the hospital at the hands of the guy before Malik.

She was now determined to end her streak of being the last to know. The P.I. named Hal she hired had pulled up some very disturbing information about his whereabouts. However, it wasn't until Hal told her with whom Bernard had been keeping company that she totally snapped. She had drowned herself in solitude in the house without bathing, and nearly without eating, except for a few candy bars left over from Halloween. For days, she lay there thinking about what her next move would be. On the fourteenth day, it hit her. She packed a small bag and headed for the Big Apple.

Jessica pulled out her phone and sent a text to her best friend's brother, Clive, to find out if her friend had informed him of Jessica's firearm needs. He texted back that he had exactly what she was looking for, and Jessica couldn't wait to feel it in her hands.

"Next!" the line attendant yelled, and she jumped in the cab headed for Clive's place in Ozone Park.

ELEVEN

Astoria Location

Star was seated on the red sofa when Cherry arrived. She saw no point in blindfolding the girl at this stage of the game.

"Yes, Mistress? What can I do to serve you this evening?"

"Cut the bullshit, Cherry. By the way is that short for Cherisse by any chance?"

Cherry's amber eyes grew wide, and she folded into the orange chair, and the combination of the chair, her sienna-colored gown, and vibrant red hair reminded Star of autumn leaves.

"Oh, shit. You know?"

Star nodded. "Now, why don't you tell me who put you up to this? Was it your Daddy?"

"Fuck him! He's not really my father. Look, I know this is going to sound crazy, stupid, and generally fucked-up, but I came here because I want your help." She straightened her back, and her demeanor shifted from the girl next door to a tigress. "I want the fucker to go down."

Star's brows shot up, and she leaned forward. "Can you repeat that for me?"

"Just what I said. I want him to go down. I want him finished." Star could see the skin above Cherry's bronze lips turn white from being pressed together so hard.

"What? Why would you want your father to suffer?"

"I told you, he's not my father."

"Wow. This is all a lot for me to take in at once." Star nearly ran to the bar and poured herself a shot of Patron Gold and downed it. "What the hell?" she asked, and poured and slammed another.

"Tell me why you think I, of all people, would be able to help you. Well, besides the fact that you know my sexual habits." Another shot sounded good right about now. She looked at the half empty bottle and wished she had an extra bottle for these types of emergencies.

"You're his biggest deal. You're his superstar. You go down, he goes down."

Star hovered over Cherry. "What the fuck? Now I'm going down too? You got your bitches mixed up, because I may seem like a nice little kitten, but I'm from the streets, damn it, and I *will* kick your ass." Star's face was a twisted mask of fury.

"Be honest with yourself, Mistress Marshall. I've been doing some research, and I want you to ask yourself if this is what you really want."

"Bitch, you better stop speaking in fucking riddles before I snatch you up and show you how we do on Brick Town." Even Star was taken a little aback by her words. She had never really claimed Newark, but damn, if it didn't sound like a good place to be from in the middle of a spat.

Cherry deflated a little. "Look, I just want you to hear

me out. If what I am proposing is of absolutely no interest to you, you can tell me to leave and I won't ever contact you again."

A bead of sweat dripped from Star's forehead and onto her pink cashmere sweater. She looked down at the Patron, but thought better of it and returned to the sofa. "Okay, fine. Go for it."

"I always knew he wasn't my real father. Besides the fact that I looked nothing like him, it was clear to me growing up that he and I shared nothing more than a home and my mother." Cherry looked down at her nails and continued. "I guess I was the classic case of the red-headed stepchild." She laughed. "But after speaking with my mother, the truth about why he hated me so much is a bit more apparent. She fucked around on him when he was just breaking into the music business. Said she met a piano player one night while Carson was away on business. She told me she used to hang out at the jazz and blues clubs in the city when her hubby dearest was M.I.A."

Star didn't know where Cherry was going with this, but something stirred in her when she said jazz and blues. She simply nodded.

"Anyway, my mother and this piano guy had a running thing going for while. I guess they slipped up and she got pregnant. She told me she ended the relationship then and there and never let on to Carson that there was a possibility the baby wasn't his. I guess he was all up in her face for nine months. She said he was actually excited." She grunted. "Anyway, I guess when I came out looking nothing like him and not much like her, he started to get suspicious. Then it occurred to him that the time frames didn't work out. He was away when she would have conceived me. She said he basically beat the truth out of her the night he brought us home from the hospital."

"That's terrible." Star got up to fix them both a drink this time.

"Yeah, well, you haven't heard the rest. So he couldn't tell her to make me disappear since he'd been going on and on to his family and business associates about the baby on the way. So, he had to live with it. He wanted to kick us both out, make us both disappear, but he didn't have the balls. Instead, he took out his anger on me."

Star handed her a small glass of tequila and Rose's lime juice on the rocks. "Thanks." Cherry took a long swallow.

"So anyway, I pretty much grew up being the whipping girl. Literally. He'd kick my ass on a regular basis, but he was strategic about it. He knew better than to send me to school all bruised up. I hate him, but I almost hate my mother more for allowing it to happen. And now I find out that my real father—the piano player doesn't even know I exist. Oh, and get this, he's black."

Star nodded and added, "I think I have something we can use."

Star wasn't all that stunned to learn that Tom was carrying on an affair with none other than Carson Nadar. It'd taken a whole lot of prodding by both Star and Peaches, but Tom had finally folded when Star brought up the strange phone conversation she'd walked in on at Carson's office, followed by running into Tom on the way out.

TWELVE

When Hal called to inform Jessica that Bernard was on the move, she was immediately in a taxi on her way to meet him at his stakeout location at the SoHo Grand. The package from Clive was safely tucked away in her Gucci bag, but she was too consumed by the anger she felt at having been deceived to consider the consequences that went along with having it in her possession.

Her mind drifted to the stacks of bridal magazines that she had burned before coming to New York. The haze that filled the back yard after she ignited the blaze in their barbeque pit reminded her of the smokescreen that Bernard had placed around himself.

She thought he was a good man, but he turned out to be like all the rest. She'd been misguided, mistreated, misinformed, and misled more times than she cared to count, but Bernard was her knight in shining armor who swept into her life to make all the pain a distant memory. However, now she knew the truth; he was a fake, and she was going to show him that his armor wasn't all it was cracked up to be.

She leaned her head against the window and grinned a wicked grin. A slight condensation formed on the window when her breath hit it, and she used the tip of her manicured index finger to draw a smiley face.

SoHo location

The sun had nearly merged with the skyline when Star gazed out the window as she waited for Foxx to arrive. She stood there thinking about all Cherry had revealed to her and Tom's indiscretions and considered the advantages and disadvantages of going forward with the plan to bring down Carson Nadar.

Carson Nadar was a sick, mean bastard, but there was a part of Star that had to appreciate his aggressiveness and power of persuasion. She'd been the voice, the face, the marionette. He had been the puppeteer, and they had both made millions in the process. She wanted out of her contract to be free to follow her heart, but she couldn't help to think that she wouldn't be in a position to do so had it not been for his industry savvy.

She buzzed Foxx up; it appeared the doorman was changing shifts. She ran to the mirror near the door to make sure she didn't look as fucked up as she felt and heard three soft taps. When she opened the door, she forgot her Cherry predicament and drank him in from head to toe. It was odd to see him without his blindfold, but he was so damn fine.

"Good evening, Star."

She smiled. She knew she was getting too familiar

with him, but she didn't care anymore. She just knew she needed him there with her.

He kissed her, then moved back to look at her face. He tended to a stray strand of hair, which he placed behind her ear. She was a little shocked by the gesture, but figured that after their previous night together, anything was possible.

"What's wrong?"

She paused, considering the complications that could arise if she opened herself up even more than she already had. After all, she really didn't know this man from Adam. All she knew was she was catching feelings from a male ho.

"Nothing. Give me a minute." She retreated to the bedroom, closed and locked the door, and dialed Peaches' cell phone.

"Hey, baby."

"Hey, Peach. I need you to do something for me. Do a little digging and see what you come up with on Foxx."

"What's going on? What'd he do? I'll kill the little—"

"Nothing, Peach. It's cool. I just want to know if there's anything I need to be aware of."

"Oh. All right then. I'll get a hold of my sources and see what they can tell us."

"Thanks. Love ya."

"You too, baby."

When she came back into the sitting area, Foxx had dimmed the lights, allowing the orange glow from the window to bask the room in its warmth. He was standing at the stereo, flipping through a book of CDs.

"Aww damn. No you didn't." He held up *X Marks the*

Spot by Ex-Girlfriend. "I thought I was the only one who bought this." He threw his head back and laughed before popping it in the changer.

"Oh, yes I did. Those sistahs can saaang!" She grinned.

"I wonder what ever happened to them?"

"This business can 'chew you up spit you out. It's *cold blooded*,'" she sang to the tune of one of the tracks on the album.

He laughed. "Dag, you taking it deep on the track list."

They sat there singing along, laughing, and sipping on 7 and Seven. As soon as "Cold Blooded," the song Star had been singing earlier, came on, they both jumped at the sound of someone beating on the door.

Star figured it must be Peaches. She was the only one who could get up to the loft without being announced. There had been many days when Star awoke to Peaches sitting on the edge of her bed.

Star went to the door and was instantly knocked out by a blow to the head.

THIRTEEN

There had to be at least three hundred Michael Rollinses living in the tri-state area. Frustrated with her search, Cherry locked her laptop, downed the last of her white chocolate mocha, and got up to get a refill, and maybe one of those espresso brownies. As she returned to her table, she wondered, as she had many times before, what her father's favorite treats were.

She typed in her password and brought up her Google search page. She figured the best way to eliminate some of the names was to cross-reference musicians. She found a white trumpet player, a black drummer, and an Asian xylophonist. Taking a sip of her fresh steaming coffee, she narrowed it down to pianists and dropped the first name. The search yielded two results: Gerald Rollins, a pianist living in Seattle, and Junior Rollins, a pianist living in . . . she nearly choked on a chocolate chunk . . . Oceanside.

"There you are!" she screamed.

The barista eyed her suspiciously and thought about how some people didn't need caffeine after noon.

"You son of a bitch!" Jessica stepped over Star's motionless form on the floor in front of her and lunged at Bernard, pistol in hand and eyes ablaze.

Bernard stood frozen for a moment, still in shock by what was happening. He was able to regain his wits, though, and grabbed Jessica's thin wrist just before she smacked him in the head with the same weapon she'd used on Star.

"What the fuck is wrong with you? Why are you here? Are you out of your mind?" He grabbed the gun and slid it across the room, out of reach.

Jessica dropped to her knees and pitched a natural hissy fit. "You bastard! How could you do this to me? I trusted you. I hate you!" Within moments, her face was a mess of running mascara and snot.

Bernard ignored her and ran over to Star, who was bleeding from a cut on her forehead and groaning.

"See? You leave me for that bitch? She ain't who you think she is."

Bernard stood to face Jessica. His face glowered at her. "And neither are you, you crazy bitch! Now get the fuck out of here before I do something you'll regret!"

"You ain't shit, Bernard Bally. You ain't nothing but a faker. This ain't about no damn story. This ain't about no fucking small time newspaper job." His stance caused her to think better of lunging at him again.

"Do you realize what you've done? Now I said, get the fuck out of here."

His voice reverberated in her head. She'd been dismissed yet again. She decided today would be the last day someone dismissed her. She went over to the gun that was lying underneath the end table and held it to her temple.

At that moment, Peaches appeared in the doorway, saw Star bleeding on the floor, Bernard hovering over her, and Jessica standing across the room with a gun to her head.

"Now just what the hell is going on here?" Peaches stood with her hands on her hips.

Jessica screamed, "Noooo!"

Peaches' world went black.

FOURTEEN

The bitches had always been handsomely paid for their discretion and loyalty to their mistress. So when Star decided it was time to set them free, she wrote them each a check for a million dollars, placed each one in a labeled envelope, and called them to the Brooklyn location.

"Thanks for coming, everyone."

They all looked at her like she'd lost her marbles. This was the first time she had thanked them for anything, and there seemed to be a calm where Star's storm usually raged.

"I want to thank you for your loyalty and service." She went around the room, passing out the envelopes. "You can go now. I hope you all find what you're looking for from life."

Their faces demonstrated confusion, but Star was in no frame of mind to do any explaining. She ushered them to the door and bolted the lock behind them.

She placed a call to Peaches' hospital room to see if she had woken up yet, but Junior told her there was no change. She lay on the bed, staring at the ceiling.

FIFTEEN

Newport, KY

Jessica's death and the whole Star situation had taken a lot out of Bernard. He wondered what there was that he could have done differently. He saw so many things in Jessica, but he never suspected that she was mentally ill. While he was packing her things to be sent to Peaches, he ran across numerous prescription bottles, most of which were nearly empty, but had once held anti-depressants and anti-hallucinogenics. He also discovered a few photos of her when she was young. He noticed that in every photo she was alone.

Jessica had come to New York in a flurry and left in an even bigger one. Jessica turned the gun on Peaches for no apparent reason and shot her in the abdomen before turning the firearm on herself.

And then there was Star. At first he thought there might be a slight chance that she was still unconscious when Jessica had spouted off at the mouth about the newspaper, but he had no such luck. As he and Star paced the waiting room at the hospital, she had looked at him with sad eyes. The thing that hurt him most was that she never questioned him, never gave him a chance to defend himself. Each time he would start to say something, she'd duck out of the room.

He drank now in the darkened living room in the home he'd once shared with Jessica, waiting for something to happen.

Two days later

She saw him sitting at the bar, hovered over a 7 and Seven. When she approached him, she noticed that a certain darkness had washed over him.

He turned his head and saw her standing there like a beacon of light in her cream-colored coat and boots. She was a sight for sore eyes, but he was still hesitant to believe that she was actually standing there and he wasn't just seeing what he wanted to see.

"Are you just going to sit there or are you going to give me a hug, you jerk?" The corners of her mouth curved into a grin and he finally came to.

He stood up and gently took her in his arms and held her tightly. "I thought you hated me. Peaches getting shot, the story, all that; I caused all this havoc. But loving you, the time I spent with you, none of that seemed wrong."

"I've realized that it was really me who caused all of this. I've been so wrapped up in my own pain, I didn't see that I was causing myself even more pain. Losing my mother and my first love was terrible. But I continued that cycle of pain by the things I was doing and the way I was allowing people to treat me. Now I feel like I have to right the wrongs. I want to bring all this to light."

SIXTEEN

Star accompanied Bernard and Cherisse to Peaches' patient room. Peaches was sitting upright in her bed sipping on cranberry juice and Junior was hollering at *The Price Is Right* when the entourage arrived.

"Finally, some new faces! I've been tired of looking at Junior's funky ass day in and day out." She winked.

"Peaches, you already know F . . . Bernard. This is Cherisse, the young lady I told you about."

"Pleasure to meet you, Cherisse." Peaches extended her hand to Cherisse, who took it in her own and gave it a squeeze.

"Junior, turn that shit off. We trying to have a conversation." Peaches refocused on her guests.

Junior turned off the TV and went next door to grab some unused visitor chairs, which he arranged in a semi-circle around Peaches' bed.

"Junior, Cherisse here has some questions for you." Star looked at Cherisse and nodded her encouragement.

Junior shrugged. "Shoot."

"Do you remember a woman by the name of Iris?"

The blood in Junior's yellow complexion drained and his eyes widened. He fidgeted in his chair and then looked at Peaches.

"Oh, for God's sake, answer the girl."

"Yes, I knew an Iris once."

After Junior learned he was a father, the group put their heads together on how to bring light on Carson Nadar's shady existence. Fussing, hollering, and weeping filled the otherwise quiet hallway.

Junior's voice was calm and even. "It seems to me that you already got everything you need to make this happen." He turned his gaze onto Bernard, who nodded his understanding.

GRAND FINALE

"We can take this as slow as you need to." Bernard leaned forward and rubbed Star's shoulder through her thin yellow top.

"It's okay. I'd really rather get through it as quickly as possible."

Bernard Bally's interview with R&B super-diva, Star Marshall, ran in the *New York Times* on April 1st. Many of the readers thought the story of record executive Carson Nadar's homosexual relations, his abusive behavior toward his stepdaughter, Star Marshall's obsession with

prostitutes, her budding relationship with the inter-
viewer, and the fact that Carson Nadar's wife had
cheated on him with a black man were part of the
paper's April Fool's Day special. It was all the same to
Star. Everyone basically got what they wanted in the
end, and whether the public chose to believe it or write
it off as a prank was of no consequence to her.

She was reinventing herself, anyway. She decided to
leave the industry for a while and hit Clarksdale, Mississippi to learn from some of the old blues men who still
frequented the juke joints. Hell, if Morgan Freeman
could get away from the superstar life, she figured she
could too.

Peaches and Junior had already gone down to look
for homes for themselves and Star. Cherisse, a.k.a.
Cherry, would be living with them for a while until she
figured out what to do with her life. Star knew having
Peaches around would be one of the best things that
ever happened to Cherry. She had experienced the
woman's nurturing ways.

Bernard was coming with her to do a story on the
resurgence of backwoods blues, and even more so, to
be with and protect the woman he loved.

Cherisse had filled Iris in about Tom, and Iris filed
for divorce on April 2nd. She didn't want there to be
any confusion about April Fools. Carson Nadar was
promptly fired from his post at Scape records after the
story broke. It seemed both his wives had quit him.

ENCORE
Three weeks later

Tiny Tim sighed and folded the newspaper he'd been reading. He felt responsible for all the shit that had happened to Star. Over the years, he'd listened to her CDs and pored over her photos to fill the void that was left when he'd left her.

He wished he could go back and do things differently; he was such a young fool back then. He felt so useless after getting injured. He'd never been brainy about anything except defensive schemes and special teams configurations. So, he had wallowed in self-pity and daydreamed the years away. Now, he felt like it was too late to try to go back and erase the damage he'd done.

First, he was too embarrassed that he'd been such an ass so many years ago and threw away a love that had more than proven itself. In addition, he could see that Star was finally happy with this reporter guy, this Bernard Bally. He didn't want to inject himself back into her life and cause her any more pain or stress.

He walked out the back door of his rural Mississippi home into the garden and stood where he'd planted a bed of stargazer lilies and inhaled their sweet fragrance.